RAISING
ORION

Raising Orion

Lesley Choyce

thistledown press

Thistledown Press Ltd.
633 Main Street
Saskatoon, Saskatchewan, S7H 0J8
www.thistledownpress.com

Library and Archives Canada Cataloguing in Publication

Choyce, Lesley, 1951-
Raising Orion / Lesley Choyce.

ISBN 978-1-897235-80-5
I. Title.
PS8555.H668R33 2010   C813'.54   C2010-905543-8

Cover artwork: shutterstock.com
Author photograph: Daniel Abriel
Cover and book design by Jackie Forrie
Printed and bound in Canada

Mixed Sources
Cert no. SW-COC-001271
© 1996 FSC
FSC

 Canada Council   Conseil des Arts
for the Arts   du Canada
 SASKATCHEWAN ARTS BOARD
 Canadian   Patrimoine
Heritage   canadien

Thistledown Press gratefully acknowledges the financial assistance of the Canada Council for the Arts, the Saskatchewan Arts Board, and the Government of Canada through the Canada Book Fund for its publishing program.

ACKNOWLEDGMENTS

I would like to thank Julia Swan and Elizabeth Philips for their wise and generous assistance in helping to improve and shape this novel. I would also like to thank the good folks at Thistledown Press who published my first serious novel, *The Second Season of Jonas MacPherson*, in 1989.

CHAPTER ONE

THE COLD SANG SONGS OF BLUE ice long and steady in his ears. The thunder of his own blood tried to drown out the music but the song of cold was not just sound but place. Then the beauty of the isolation, the sad beauty of losing everything, swept over Eric there at his final destination. And he gave himself over to the curious satisfaction of knowing he was about to die near the top of the world.

The colour of the song was the colour of sunlight on glacial ice. Hard, cold, clean. A song of blue. All around him, an orchestra of light until the returning boom of the drum of a man's heartbeat to drown out the song, melting the ice. Next came the tongues of fire. Finally darkness.

Days passed, they would later tell Eric, before he showed any interest in returning to consciousness. An injured mind. Failing memory. So great a labour even to remember how to breathe. A difficult, difficult journey to find the path to awakening when he had no desire to seek it. Why would someone want to be brought back from the blue-white song of ice, from the complete contentment of cold?

When Eric could finally talk, when he could arrange a handful of words into a vocabulary and make his mouth move, make sounds come out, he tried to sing and it made them laugh. The doctor, the nurse. They didn't understand.

But the Inuit man who cleaned the room didn't laugh. He closed the door and broke the rules. He was not supposed to "bother" Eric. But he spoke. He asked one question each time he came into his room. *What is it like to be dead?*

The sound of his words, sound without meaning, drew Eric's dazzled mind to a certain place of focus. Eric did not answer the first time or the second or several times after that, but on the third day, the janitor repeated his question. And Eric attempted to sing for the last time the song of cold blue ice. And failed in his frustrated attempt to reproduce it.

It came out as a mournful howl, a moaning chord issuing from deep within his chest and up through his throat.

The janitor stared at Eric, frightened at first. And Eric fell silent. Then the janitor stopped staring at the patient and looked out the window. *Tell me again*, he requested.

And Eric tried to do better.

The janitor turned and smiled at him. He understood. *You were at my grandfather's place*, he said, and he turned to go.

There was darkness and blissful isolation again, for how long Eric didn't know. He arranged things in his mind, moved images about from one place to another. There was sound and bright lights and corners of comfortable darkness. Places of solace and disturbing chaotic areas filled with objects he could not name or understand. He had been "away" and he failed to find the path that led him into his own past. He could not know where or who he was until he could unravel where he'd been and who he had been.

Sometimes he thought it was the other way around. He had been home and *now* he was away. When his eyes opened, things were even stranger and more impossible than he had imagined. Yet his eyes seemed voracious for everything. They were starved, famished. They consumed the shape of the painting on the wall, the frame of a door, the cold hardness of the floor. Objects around him suddenly seemed very real.

Dependable. The people who came into the room seemed to exist in some other dimension. They tried to communicate with Eric but they didn't understand his sound, the song of ice still exerting its power over him.

Sometimes they adjusted the tubes running into Eric or the tubes running out of him. Sometimes a sharp thing went into his arm. He assumed it was by this means they hoped to penetrate the mystery of who he was. But soon enough, they became distracted and left him alone and Eric returned to the geography of things inside his mind. He returned to the fading but unbroken symphony of cold singing and he felt an ache so great inside that he thought he would break in half. He thought he himself might fade again and go away altogether.

Grandfather, the janitor addressed him when he bumped his pail and mop into the room. Much later Eric would learn that it was a word surrounded in a cloud of personal power, that it was a bit of a joke in a way but also a show of respect. The two could go together. Eric was beginning to see attachments between the sound of language and things around him. Even people. Like the man who cleaned his room. His name was Ray. Ray had smooth, tan skin and a long, dark ponytail that fell down his back.

Grandfather, you are awake today.

Eric followed his movements and thought he remembered him from somewhere. There was something about him. Something from the other side of the wall. The wall was important to Eric, especially now that the song was fading. When he was falling asleep now, he studied the wall more carefully. It had been there all along. Cold, tall and beautiful. Ice. A wall of ice inside his mind separating him from everything that had come before, keeping him safely away from whomever it was that he had been.

As Ray spoke, Eric could only blink his eyes and move certain muscles in his face that he hoped gave him an expression just like Ray used.

Eric was trying to smile. Ray laughed, a sound close enough to a song that it reminded Eric of something. He remembered that music came from more than just cold blue ice. Eric looked past Ray just then at the vessel of light that was the window and realized that it was somehow alive, in motion. Some kind of dancing thing. Round, soft, translucent shapes sliding. The whole surface seemed strangely alive.

Ray saw the look on Eric's face, the question.

"It's rain. I guess you didn't see a lot of that when you were up north."

Rain. Something shifted inside his thoughts. Eric closed his eyes quickly and tried to focus on the familiar things, the shapes and sounds that he'd begun to catalogue. He saw the wall in the distance and now realized that it too had an undulating surface like the window. It was in motion. And Eric now came to the conclusion that ice and water were of the same family.

"Gonna rain like that for a couple of days, they say."

The wall melted slowly in one place and language began to flow over the top, spilling into the place where he lived. At first he thought he would let it flood through him and take him wherever he had to go, but then he was afraid. He shut his eyes tightly and could not hear the song of ice at all over the torrent. So he gathered together his will and prepared to repair the wall, soliciting the ally of cold to help mend the damage and restore it.

Opening his eyes again, however, he saw Ray mopping the floor. And then he asked, "Where am I?"

Ray stopped his work, turned slowly. Behind him the rain drummed against the window now. *Rain and wind.* Words welling up in his mind. "I don't know where I am." And, to him, it seemed far more important to know *where* he was than *who* he was.

Ray walked over to Eric. He smiled and Eric wanted to count the man's teeth.

"You're south. You're in Ottawa."

"Ottawa," Eric repeated. The word meant nothing to him. Instead of sounding puzzled, he must have sounded discouraged.

"Hey, don't sound so disappointed. But I know how you feel. Man, no one wants to be in Ottawa."

CHAPTER TWO

HER CUSTOMERS WOULD SAY THAT MOLLY had a way about her. She seemed to know things. Understand things. Whenever the sky grew dark and heavy outside the store, she'd look up and away into the clouds, then back down at a pile of old books in front of her. She had an expression on her face that said she had just learned and understood something. Just like that.

Men walked into Molly's Books to buy a used copy of Helen Creighton's *Bluenose Ghosts* or maybe a nineteenth-century book on fly fishing. They couldn't help but study her. Her face, her hands. Molly wasn't the sort of woman who drew male readers' attention to her body. It was a good body but not a magazine body. She was thirty-five but might as well have been nineteen. Or ninety.

Men looked at her. And so did women. They looked at her because she made them feel calm. Molly had the only truly calm face in Halifax. Here towards the tail end of the twentieth century, Halifax had belatedly and sadly become a modern city. And that meant everyone was in a hurry and confused. People were always in a hurry and that made them confused. Or they got confused first and then hurried on to do the next thing on their list and, of course, there wasn't enough time. And so that was confusing too. There was plenty of confusion for such a small port city on the Atlantic, a city north and away from the worst of the stuff happening down the coast.

So the men who were patrons in Molly's little used bookstore read paragraphs about haunted houses in Amherst, or they mysteriously lifted a wrist into the air to practice a forgotten fly fishing manoeuvre that had never made it past 1876 and then they inevitably looked over at Molly. Maybe the sun had come out and it helped brighten Winslow Street all lacquered with rain. Molly touched her cheek with two fingers and then took a deep breath. She breathed in the smell of her bookstore and the people in it. She also took in the smell of the rain on the asphalt if the door was open. The chemistry of those smells plus the shiny black pavement, plus the feel of the cover of the trashy pirate novel from the 1950s in her hand — it all added up to something. Molly knew it was a poem but she also knew she was not required to write it down on a piece of paper. It was enough for what it was. And it showed on her face.

People were drawn back to Molly's store on the forgotten end of Winslow Street because of those moments. Sometimes they leafed through books on subjects they weren't interested in: ancient Mesopotamian law or diseases of sheep or cowboy novels by Zane Grey. Once in a while someone bought a book out of a sense of obligation or support for Molly and her little, quirky, used bookstore. A teenage boy once bought an old textbook on the Russian language when he stumbled into the store to get out of the rain. He fell in love with Molly, although he didn't think of it as falling in love. His name was Griffin, although hardly anyone called him that except for his mother and maybe his father when Griffin had done something bad.

Griffin stole things from stores. Gum, running shoes, cantaloupes sometimes. He stole things and was caught only five percent of the time and he got off because he was a kid who always said he was sorry and he had a chin that seemed to mean it and an Adam's apple that bobbed up and down to support the apology. So Griffin had come in out of the rain and here he was in a bookstore, a used bookstore yet and

Griffin wasn't much of a reader beyond maybe *TV Guide* and sports pages. But now he was lingering, hoping to stay dry for a while and he had picked up a book. The book about Russian. *Nyet. Da. Dos Vidanya.* He looked up from the book and there was this lady, this Molly person, who had just pulled together another one of those poems that would never be written or recited: rain, the musky wet-hair smell of a teenage boy in a store reading a Russian book, a bouquet of old PEI and Newfoundland maps in front of her. Road maps with crayon lines tracing some of the roads that a family had taken on a summer vacation. Then there was lightning and thunder and the power went out. It all fit together somehow so Molly slid her fingers across her soft cheeks with more satisfaction than you would have expected.

That was it. Griffin fell in love with Molly in the way that only a troubled, sensitive, shoplifting teenage boy could fall into love. And he knew he would always remember Molly even though he assumed he would probably not ever speak to her.

But he would do this: he would not steal anything. He would buy the book on the Russian language and stay up at night with his bed lamp on and study it. Griffin cleared his throat and purposefully walked towards the counter in the darkened but warm bookstore afternoon. He slid *Russian Made Easy* towards Molly. She opened the book to read the faintly pencilled price: $5.

"Hmm," she said. "It's pretty dog-eared. Two-fifty will do."

Griffin slid a five along the same path that the Russian textbook had just taken. Molly punched open the old style non-electric cash register and it made almost no noise at all as the drawer opened like a really smooth baseball player sliding into second base on a summer afternoon. Molly gave Griffin his two-fifty in change and put the book in a recycled bag from a store named Bargain Harold's.

That's when the rain stopped and Griffin went outside. The traffic lights weren't working and that seemed to make people in cars start being nice to each other at intersections, waving, saying *you go, no you. After you. I'm in no hurry.* Griffin had been infected by Molly's way of looking at the world and he didn't have a clue as to what was going on in his head. But he liked it and he couldn't wait to start learning Russian. *Nyet. Da. Dos Vidanya.*

A year later, Griffin would go to university, and discontinue shoplifting forever. He would major in Russian and graduate, move to St. Petersburg to become a successful art dealer and a sometimes not-so-bad painter. Molly would never know any of this.

On a sunny morning in the first week of September in 1998, a half hour before the store opened, Molly was rereading E.B. White's brief introduction to the very short but influential book, *The Elements of Style,* by Strunk and White. If Molly had gone to university, this small book might have been assigned as part of a basic English course but she'd never attended university or sat in any classroom. The island where she grew up taught her everything she ever needed to know and then some. The island had been assisted by her parents who were uneducated, at least in the formal sense. The island didn't believe in schoolhouses or classrooms but approved of books. There had been rock formations on the island, upright sheaves of shale squared off by forces of erosion, that looked exactly like books on a shelf. "Tomes" her father had called them. Her father's name was Henry but his wife liked to call him Hank.

"Omit needless words," *The Elements of Style* shouted out to her when she accidentally flipped the pages to the ever-vigilant "Rule 13." Her mother had come from the no-classroom school of Rule 13, not that the woman had been silent, tight-lipped or stingy with words. She just had a belief in the power of words and never used lazy ones like "nice" or "cute." Her mother used to say things like this about the end of a summer day. "It was a very tender day." Of winter, a day might be "rugged," "vengeful" or sometimes "discreet," but it was never simply cold or damp or windy. And there were almost never any days that were ugly. Sullen, perhaps, even vindictive or despondent. Her mother tried to find some meaning, even some semblance of beauty, in days of wrath. And that was her way.

In his little pre-introduction (which came before the real introduction) to *The Elements of Style*, E.B. White said the following: "I think Professor Strunk would not object to that." Molly had read that line many times before, of course, but it seemed rather acute to her mental ear on this day. She rooted around the store until she came up with nearly a half dozen copies of the Strunk and White book and set them on the counter, then popped the cap on one of those magic markers that smelled like artificial raspberries and wrote, "Special: 25 cents — Today Only." She would not get rich on the proceeds but it seemed like a very Strunk and White day and she was certain Professor Strunk would not object to her promotion.

It was natural that *The Elements of Style* reminded her of her mother. And thinking of her mother also took her back to the island where she grew up. Devil's Island. The original name was Duvall's Island, named for a dead Frenchman, but the local fisherfolk way back had slurred the name so many times in drunken conversations that it eventually became Devil's and then, with a name like that, there had to be stories to go with it. Plenty of stories with ghosts and shipwrecks and murder and treasure and, like so many stories of history, almost none of them were true. But it didn't matter much because you shaped your life around what you thought was true, not what actually was real, anyway.

Devil's Island was located at the mouth of Halifax Harbour. That's why there was a lighthouse on the island

and why Molly's father, Hank, had a job keeping the light to guide the ships that were heading towards Halifax. But Molly's childhood home was a world away from Halifax and the mainland.

The house beside the lighthouse was three stories tall and had more rooms than the small family needed. Hank named all the rooms. He liked making finely crafted wooden signs for everything, especially rooms. He had careful, elegant handwriting like people used in the seventeenth century and he used a specially trimmed seagull feather to paint the letters. Almost everything man-made on the island had a little plaque with a title. Northpoint Workshop, Deep Cove Boat Storage, East End Garbage Pit. And so forth. In the house, every room had a name and a plaque. The plaques were always shellacked to a lightning gloss. Hank shellacked the heck out of things, especially the plaques for rooms: Captain's Den, The City Room, Knitter's Corner, Central Kitchen, Molly's Haven, God's Attic, Guest Quarters, Atlantic Dining Room.

When Molly was three, her father had brought over two rabbits from the mainland. These were pet rabbits, one black, one white. Molly named them Black Guy and White Guy and the names stuck. Molly remembered the day the rabbits arrived. Her father was having one of those conversations where he was mostly just talking to himself but she was allowed to listen in. "Over there, ashore," he said, pointing east towards the mainland, "all the Passage People looked at me kind of funny as I put the two rabbits into the dory. Oh, sure I had other supplies. Kerosene, a bag of oats for oatmeal, sugar for your mum, a tin of molasses, figs, flour in a gunnysack, a fistful of wicks. But then they saw I had these here two rabbits. Rabbits for my little girl, Molly, I explained. No, heck, not for cooking. Not rabbit pie. Just a couple of pets for the kid, give her something to take care of. Oh, those Passage People, always thinking we're a bit odd, a bit off, maybe loony even, living on what they think is a haunted island because of the name and all. There I was with my two rabbits running around on their own now in the bottom of the boat. One feller says to the other, 'Old Hank. Look at 'im rowin' his rabbits to Devil's Island.'"

Three-year-old Molly looked up and away towards the south where the Atlantic Ocean took over and, sure enough, it was smiling a sparkly smile like it had a thousand glittering crystal teeth and had just brushed them good and clean with the sun.

It turned out that Black Guy and White Guy didn't like the chicken-wire cage Hank had made and didn't give a hoot about the fact that it had its own shellacked and wired-on mahogany sign that said Rabbit Hotel Deluxe. The two rabbits dug their way out of the Hotel Deluxe and, instead of living in frustrated luxury, spent their days racing each other around the entire expanse of the island. Hawks swooped towards them but could never catch Black Guy or White Guy. Sometimes the rabbits dived under the Boat Shed or squeezed into crevices near the Tomes. But mostly they just wandered, got fat, and mowed away at the salty island grass and the beach peas, sea rocket and orach.

Within a year, there were dozens of rabbits — black ones, white ones, and mixed black and white ones. There were even a couple of grey rabbits running around the island. Hawks did eventually snag a few and that could not be helped. After a few years, Hank sometimes rowed some of the little ones ashore to give away to kids on the dock. "Rowin' his rabbits from Devil's Island, the sky above the sea a smilin'," Hank sang to the thrunk and squeak of the oak oars in the rusty oarlocks.

Chapter Three

ERIC HAD NOT INITIALLY WANTED TO go to the Arctic to die but his desire for death grew within him the more he thought about the trip. At first, it seemed adventurous. He wanted to undertake some kind of purposeful, elemental Thoreauvian experiment. An academic dropout was not a bad thing to be. The University of Ottawa would plod on without him. Besides, he was dead tired of teaching Canadian history.

History was a sad well to drink from, a deep one too, perhaps bottomless. Historians had it all wrong and would never get it right, never plumb the true dark depths. The only reality of history had to do with the dullest aspect: facts. When some notable person had been born. When he had died. The truth, though, was elusive, a matter of opinions built around dates and artifacts.

The Arctic had been a clean and lonely place and in that regard it reminded him of Ottawa. And by then he had become enamoured with the idea of ending his life there. Almost dying had turned out to be a cleansing and not altogether unpleasant event. Having come so close to death, he now saw death as an enviable option contrasted with much of what he had been living. Giving uninspired lectures about early Canadian history from dog-eared notes he'd taken in graduate school. Coming home to an empty house at night with no one to talk to.

Early retirement had been a hopeful alternative to the drudgery that was his lot, and he had taken it. Eric gave himself permission to finally stop teaching Canadian history to undergraduates. History, he had come to realize, was mostly a matter of recording men's mistakes and reporting them to other generations. Eric had lost interest in political history entirely but had maintained a keen enthusiasm for stories about northern explorers as well as issues related to the sea. White men cruising the seven seas on sailing ships or sliding across the northern wastes on dog sledges. Maybe he thought he could be like one of the great explorers if he himself went north.

He was poorly equipped for it in many ways despite his hefty investment in the proper equipment. Eddie Bauer had profited from Eric Walker's early retirement. But like the Buddhists said, the problem with travel as a form of escape is this: wherever you go, there you are. And Eric had stopped liking himself some time in his mid-forties. If only he were capable of travelling as someone else, the prospects would be even more desirable.

After the divorce. After publishing two very well-received academic books on Canadian history. There was some gratification there but it soon faded away. And when he discovered how few copies the publisher actually sold, it was most disheartening. Then, after a rueful self-examination prompted by reading too many Joseph Campbell books and books about Joseph Campbell. After a thorough assessment of who he was and what he had done with his life. After all that, he gave up on the struggle to see himself as likeable or worthy. Other people, including his students, liked Eric, but Eric had simply stopped liking himself.

The day he left the hospital in Ottawa, he felt he was back to square one. Ottawa was still Ottawa, after all. His house in the Glebe was tidy and clean, and this fact made him feel more hollow and lonely than anything he had felt while alone in the north.

The old maple tree in front of his house was enormous and it greeted him with its canopy of leaves. That tree, he decided, was the only thing about Ottawa he liked. Eric knew that Ottawa didn't deserve what he was feeling towards it. He wasn't mad at the current government or the Houses of Parliament, the Ottawa River or even the Museum of Man. Eric touched the rough bark of the maple tree as he passed it. Nothing to look forward to but an afternoon nap. Wherever you go, there you are.

Eric noticed the ants running up and down the ridges of the maple tree. The tree was a kind of Trans-Canada Highway up and down from the solid earth to those dancing, celebratory leaves on the ends of branches. He looked up and saw the sun filtering through the curtain of green and red leaves. This emblem of beauty was the only good thing about Ottawa, he kept thinking. And then he let go one of those ho-hum sighs of total resignation — like an arctic explorer adrift on an ice pan, sailing south on a current towards warmer water, melting the ice and leading to a satisfactory death at sea. It was that kind of resignation that led the disheartened Ottawa explorer to an afternoon nap on a chesterfield purchased from an Ikea store in Nepean.

Eric woke up thinking about Radisson and Grossiliers, two French explorers backed by English merchants, who sailed to the Canadian north in 1668 and found wealth in the form of fur-bearing animals. The Hudson's Bay Company was created when it became obvious somebody could make a lot of money. An English carpenter named James Knight became the governor of the Hudson Bay region and was convinced there was a somewhat southerly open water passageway, the legendary Strait of Anian, leading to the Pacific Ocean. On Knight's ill-informed hunch, mapmakers redrew North

America. No one knew anything about the Rocky Mountains in those times.

James Knight, he knew, had gathered up what faulty, optimistic maps he could muster and sailed off from England to a place now called Ross Welcome Sound. His misguided enthusiasm led him to another Northwest Impasse and then something got him: probably scurvy, the disease where your gums get soft and you pluck your teeth out one at a time as you die. Eric admitted to himself that he would not want to die of scurvy.

Knight had hoped to make money for his financial backers and achieve glory by finding the elusive shortcut to China. Knight's ambition, however, had somehow inspired a politician back home, one Arthur Dobbs. Dobbs didn't have a clue as to what was in the Arctic but he was certain you could sail into Hudson Bay and, indeed, there would be a navigable river that would take you on a quick and easy route straight to California. And the beauty of opening up this route was that you could sell English manufactured goods — in particular, English teapots — to Californians.

Dobbs was a politician who dealt in dreams, not reality. Nonetheless, the government of England bought into his delusion and sent a worthy seaman, Christopher Middleton, and his crew off on a ship called the *Furnace*. Their job was to chart this convenient water passage to the Pacific. Middleton's accompanying ships were manned by crews commandeered off the seaport streets — volunteers had proven hard to come by for doomed arctic expeditions that year. Along the shore of Hudson Bay, Middleton's men dutifully followed the usual itinerary: starvation, scurvy, frostbite and amputation. In 1742, what was left of the crew headed back to merry old England after encountering ice-choked dead ends.

Eric found himself sitting upright on the couch, staring at the lines in his hand. A map of sorts, probably something more accurate than what poor Middleton had going for him.

He studied his lifeline that snaked down around his thumb. The palm reader at the Exhibition had told him he'd lead a long and happy life. Long, yes, perhaps. Despite all odds. Even the hungry Arctic that had consumed a thousand English optimists could not do him in. But happy, that would remain *terra incognita*.

The *Furnace* hobbled back towards port, its crew decimated. The bad news was put to Dobbs, the indefatigable spin doctor, but Dobbs told the world that Chris Middleton had actually found the passage. They'd be selling teapots and tea cosies to Californians in no time. More money was raised and two more ships sent off. A candle aboard the *Dobbs Galley* nearly burned her down at sea but the sailors plodded on, only to be impeded by (what else?) ice. Only seven men died on the venture and one daydreamer who returned told Dobbs that the Arctic was a kind of labyrinth. All one need do is study the tide and currents and you'd come out near Mexico.

In order to get further funding, Dobbs falsified documents, bribed witnesses, and slandered anyone who opposed him. Fortunately, the public, as well as Parliament, grew weary of Dobbs and, in 1753, he was dispatched to become the governor of North Carolina, where he spent the rest of his days. And the rest, as they say, is history.

In the soft, late-summer afternoon Glebe light, Eric's feet found their way to his old kitchen. Eric plugged a kettle into the wall and found a packet of instant miso soup. The water boiled, the dust became soup, and steam rose up like whirling sea ghosts around Eric's nose. At that instant he drifted back to his own arctic experience. The peace he had felt when he made his decision to let the cold take him. And now he could feel a tingling of pain in his once-frozen hands. He suddenly found himself crying.

CHAPTER FOUR

FEELING SORRY FOR ONESELF AFTER NOT properly dying in the Canadian Arctic was not something that was written about in any of those supposedly helpful self-help books. On the north side of his downhill slide, Eric had read some of them. He bought them on the sly at big-box bookstores where no one knew him. Bookstores on the outskirts of Ottawa. Eric knew he was in trouble and part of the trouble, he had concluded, was that he had somehow misplaced his soul. He had lost it and didn't know where to look for it. So he started with the self-help and pop-spiritual books that filled the shelves of the suburban stores.

Eric knew he wasn't alone in his dilemma or his search. He knew other people had lost their souls, or misplaced them or whatever the hell was going on, and they too were out there questing. Browsing up and down the self-help aisles in whatever sterile suburban town this was. All entering through the big glass doors and marching straight to New Age and Self Help.

Chicken Soup for the Lonely Middle-aged College Professor might have been the book he was looking for. Or *Save Your life with Music*, or maybe it could be books of poetry by ancient Chinese sages. He knew he wasn't alone and that should have been worth something. But it didn't mean squat. Nonetheless, he bought a handful of the hopeful books and disliked them immensely, sending them out with the newspapers to be recycled.

Eric truly didn't know who or what he was anymore and pretty soon he didn't give a flying fuck one way or the other, except for the fact that he knew he was not happy. Being well-read and self-aware, he knew too that this was not an uncommon state of affairs. But he was a tall, thin grey man in a tall, thin grey city.

With all the world going grey, Eric thought about trying to write another book. This one would be about the history of truth. It had been Arthur Dobbs that got him going on truth. Dobbs had no interest in truth, only political power, financial success, mercantile dominion, and selling the public on foolish notions. He was the adversary of truth.

But instead of taking a first stab at writing the truth book, he sat down at his computer and drew up a list of the mistakes that may or may not have led to his present predicament. The list went like this:

1. Not paying enough attention to his wife;
2. Not paying enough attention to his own inner voice;
3. Becoming an expert in Canadian history instead of something more enduring like the history of ancient Greece, China, or Japan.
4. Not taking his father's advice, which was, "Optimism is always the best working hypothesis";
5. All of the above. And more.

Eric's father, the game plan optimist, had also told him, wisely if obliquely, one day while they were climbing rocks in the Gatineau Hills this pearl of wisdom: "The best you can do, son, to achieve happiness is to figure out that you don't really require happiness in order to lead a rich and fulfilling life." His father lost his footing at that point and his attentive teenage son had grabbed his wrist with one hand while hanging onto the root of a near-dead pine tree with the other.

If he had fallen it would only have been a tumble of maybe two metres onto a small plot of wild lady slippers. They had not been a family of great mountain adventurers, just weekend hill hikers. Nonetheless, there might have been a sprained ankle or a broken elbow.

Sitting at the kitchen table alone, wrestling with truth and the history of the world, sustained by sushi for the soul, and pondering the advice of a long-dead and much appreciated father was the very cocktail that led to a bad decision: to fly north and hike alone into the wilderness of Baffin Island. A bad decision is better than no decision at all, Eric imagined his father to have said. (In truth, his father, who had worked at Indian Affairs for most of his career, would have never said anything so stupid.)

But Eric knew that pivotal events in the world had come about as the result of pilgrimages. Jesus into the desert, Buddha into the wilderness, Trudeau into the snowstorm. Big empty spaces were necessary. And that's what his nation could do best.

Eric remembered that in the fourth century B.C., Hui Ssu, a minister for the King of Wei, blurted out at a cabinet meeting (where someone promptly wrote this down): "Love all things equally. The universe is one." This line stuck in Eric's head, not because it was lofty but because it was handwritten on a piece of handmade paper by his wife the day she left him to pursue everything she had been putting off while pretending to be a happy university professor's wife.

Eric's father had his own compendium of quotes that found their way into father-son conversations, although Eric did not always see the connections to the conversations. They often seemed to be non sequiturs. "Always remember Wendell Berry's advice about what to do in a house where there are mice, Eric. 'Tread softly.'"

His father had in his own way tried to tread softly in the world and do no harm but late in his career at Indian Affairs, it had sunk in how badly government-sanctioned, church-run residential schools had treated the very people the government of Canada was supposedly protecting and assisting. Soon after that, madness started showing up as an uninvited guest at evening meals and in the quiet evening times with the television off. Mother and son watched a good man deteriorate like a healthy tree plagued by disease. A big, virulent Dutch elm of the Glebe, losing itself to a seemingly determined (not random) destructive game plan of nature. Around that time, Eric's father began reading thick, popular histories about Germany and World War II.

The cost of the civil servant's treatment at the "rehab centre" was covered by the government as was the way in Canada. His doctors advised against any more biographies of Hitler or Goering. He had to be restrained in bed at night. No one would ever say why. And in the day, his wrists had very loose terry cloth bindings that kept him seated in front of *As the World Turns* and *Days of Our Lives.*

When he died of a respiratory infection, his mother found a copy of Anne Frank's *The Diary of a Young Girl* under his mattress.

And now all of this and more was finding its way into the book Eric was writing about the history of truth.

CHAPTER FIVE

EARLY IN THE AFTERNOON, MOLLY LEFT the store to go visit her friend Grace's nephew in the Izaak Walton Killam Children's Hospital. Because Grace travelled so much for her job, she said she was feeling guilty about not being there more herself. Grace had come by the shop. Molly had known her for a couple of years but she'd never seen Grace so upset about anything. Molly said she'd be happy to visit and try to entertain the boy any way she could. His name was Todd. It sounded like such an old-fashioned name.

Molly hadn't been inside a hospital for a long time and she felt like a nervous but hopeful explorer going off on a strange adventure. There was no telling what she might find there. There was probably a lot of death going on but she expected it was kept well hidden. There might be sounds of babies crying and hallways full of worried parents. She didn't know if there was a special sort of language to be used in hospitals around sick children and parents of sick kids. Perhaps *The Elements of Style* would be of some help. On the way over she would recite some of Professor Strunk's rules as reminders of good language use. That couldn't hurt.

"Avoid fancy words."

"Do not affect a breezy manner."

"Do not construct awkward adverbs."

But first there was the matter of leaving the store. A very rotund man with a closed umbrella draped over his wrist was running his finger down a page of print. It appeared to be a book about the history of Chinese laundries in Canada. An elderly Black woman with those half-glasses used only for reading was studying a book on Asian economic policy and a completely nondescript-looking male university student was browsing the shelves in a sanguine manner, Molly observed, like a summer deer grazing in a salt marsh.

Molly wrote a message on a piece of cardboard and propped it by the cash register: "Had to leave for a while. If you want to buy anything, leave the money in the tin. If you don't have the proper change, take the books you want and come back later to pay. Thanks. M."

There was all of seventeen dollars and ninety-three cents in the cash register and she would leave it there. If anybody wanted it, well, they could have it. And if anyone wanted to steal books, well, that would be the way it would be.

No one even noticed when Molly left the store on the forgotten end of Winslow Street and walked out into the September afternoon.

"Place yourself in the background," Strunk had admonished generations of youthful writers. Molly understood the nature of background. She was an island person. She was grey skies and blue seas and cold, wet boulders slapped by waves in winter. Birds and fish, and in Molly's case, rabbits, taught island people things and became part of their personalities. Island people had thoughts that scattered on the wind and then collected on waving stalks of sea oats.

It was a good walk to the hospital. "Do not take shortcuts at the cost of clarity." Molly did not take shortcuts. Clarity was everywhere. September was beginning to have its way with the leaves on the trees just as it had in 1749, right before Edward Cornwallis landed at the harbour's edge to send his men forth cutting down those trees, getting drunk, and trying to transform the wilderness into something British. Today, the ravens spoke in strong vowels from those trees, discussing the randomness of the summer past and the intentions of the coming winter. A door to one of the old houses opened and a man and woman stood there arguing.

"But all the computers are going to seize up on the first day of the year 2000," the man said. "It's all going to grind to a halt. Nothing will work. Civilization is going to come to a complete halt. It's going to be awful."

"Bullshit," the woman said. "Complete bullshit!" And she slammed the door in his face. He turned around and saw Molly half smiling at him with the look of a person who knew she was only background for a September day walking itself around the city. He seemed a little embarrassed but you could tell he was not going to change his mind. It *was* going to be the worst thing that ever happened to them all, this Y2K business, and even his own wife wouldn't listen.

A raven bobbed his head up and down and coughed out syllables that sounded like a dolphin trying to laugh.

The Izaac Walton Killam Hospital For Children was large and white and set back from University Avenue. It pretended to be a sturdy, well-engineered symbol of health and control. Cars jockeyed on the street for places to park. The original Izaac Walton (without the Killam) had been the famous author of *The Compleat Angler, or The Contemplative Man's Recreation*, first published in 1653. It was a book about fishing but not really about fishing. Izaak Walton Killam, on the other hand, had been the wealthiest man of his time, although he lived a quiet life and shied away from publicity. He had been a financier and, as far as Molly could understand, a financier didn't really do anything. He just moved money around so that it made more money. You had to have your own money or somebody else's and then be real clever at moving it this way and that way so that it landed in the right place at the right time. Or to put it another way, it was like fishing. You had to cast your line into the right pool at the right time with the right bait until you snagged a big roll of hundred dollar bills.

A man with the unlikely name of Lord Beaverbrook had taught the young money fisherman which were the best pools to go fishing in. When Killam died, a big whack of his money ended up going to art, to universities and to this hospital for sick kids. Molly knew of Killam and his life but still didn't understand the ebb and flow of capital. She'd once read *Das Capital* but found the writing stiff and unlikeable. Karl Marx had not read Strunk and White: "Do not explain too much."

The glass doors swung open and Molly entered the Killam Hospital. Inside, the path to Todd's room was colour-coded. "Blue to the elevator, get off at red, and follow the hallway until it connects with green," the receptionist said. Along the green hallway, she found the boy alone in a room with one empty bed. He looked pale and forlorn and wore a Boston Red Sox cap over his bald head.

"Todd?"

"Hi."

"I'm Molly. From the bookstore."

Todd was fourteen years old but he looked younger. And he looked too sick to be fourteen. His body had betrayed him in some way he still didn't understand. Molly suddenly felt a little woozy. Colours suddenly switched around in her head and mixed into muddy swirls. She swallowed and closed her eyes briefly until she found the hard blue edge of the horizon. "I didn't know you'd be so sick," she blurted out. An honest statement but a silly, wrong-headed one. How could she let such language slip out like that? It was completely out of character.

Todd blinked once. "And I didn't know you'd be so pretty."

"Oh, boy. Thanks," Molly said, her words feeling fuzzy and loose in her throat. "How are you feeling?" As soon as the words were out, though, she regretted them.

But he surprised her with the answer. "I've been better," and then, realizing Molly felt embarrassed, he smiled at her.

"Sorry. I guess everyone asks that silly question."

"Don't worry. But I'm cool with it. There's no way to ignore the fact that I'm a really sick kid. But I'm copacetic with it, as they say."

"I haven't heard that word for a long time." Molly touched the side of her cheek and realized that she felt strangely cool, as if a pale November wind had just brushed her face. "Do you really think I'm pretty?"

"I don't lie. I only tell the truth now. I don't want to mess around with bullshit."

It was the second time that day the word had come up. "While I was growing up I didn't know if I was pretty or ugly. I didn't even know it was something to worry about. I spent most of my time with rabbits — black ones, white ones, and some different shades of grey. My parents treated me like I was an equal and I didn't know that mainland parents treated children like, well, children. I had a hard time at first adjusting to life off the island."

"Wasn't it boring?"

"No. Never."

"That's the way I feel now. I used to be bored a lot. Time sucked. There was too much of it and not enough exciting stuff to do. Then I got sick and things got weird. Ugly and weird. But it wasn't ever boring. Do you know my parents?"

"No. I know your mother's sister — your Aunt Grace. When she told me you were here I said I'd come to see you. Do you want me to bring some books when I come back? Grace said she probably wouldn't be able to drop by this week. I think she's in Toronto on business." But Molly knew it wasn't just that. She'd seen the look in Grace's face. Grace was having a very hard time coping with the visits to her nephew.

"You'll come back?"

"If you want me to."

Todd changed then. His face changed. Some switch inside him was thrown and he became a different person. He stopped being sick somehow for a brief instant. "Yeah, I could definitely use some company."

"I will then. But I'm here now. That was not a goodbye. You know how people sometimes say goodbye without saying it. *Nice talking to you. Keep in touch. I'll let you go.* It wasn't meant like that. I just got here. Tell me more about you."

Todd took a deep breath. He turned to the wall as if he had to read something from a cue card and then he turned back. "I like breathing. I like the air going in and out of my lungs. I like it better now that I know it won't go on forever. When I was a kid, I thought I'd live forever."

"We all do. Immortality is like a flag we wave around when we are young."

"I like the way you put that. I was sure I'd be, as you say, immortal. I swam in the lakes in New Brunswick and I played a lot of hockey in the winter. I never liked playing inside but I liked the ice on the lakes. I liked it when it was clear and black and when there was snow on the spruce trees. I liked the way ice made that booming noise as it shifted and cracked. I liked playing hockey at minus twenty degrees when the air felt clean and cold. And I liked skating hard, being tough with my friends. We always slammed into each other. Hard. I took a puck in the face once and we all talked about that for a long time. Another time I smashed up my knee and that was pretty all right too. Once I even fell through the ice with my friend, Dill. We were in Kilkenny Lake in January up to our armpits. I got us out because I had fingernails and Dill didn't. His were all chewed down. Mine still worked. I dug into the ice with my fingernails. My body felt like lead but I got up on the ice and then I pulled Dill out. Dill thought he was going to die and that surprised me. I was sure I was going to live forever. Dill wasn't so sure. That's why he had been chewing his fingernails down during school. If I didn't have fingernails back then, we both would have been screwed."

Molly sat silently and waited for more. She liked Todd immensely. Part of her ached with an intense pain, however, over the reality that he was so sick.

"And then this happened. I don't think I'll ever play hockey anymore."

"It doesn't seem fair."

"Why should anything be fair?" Todd said but there was no hard edge, no skate blade of sarcasm in his voice to go along with it.

"It should be, that's all. Even though I know better."

"Fair is one of those things you think should be, but isn't. We never played fair in hockey. I liked it that way. I'd trip Dill if I could and Dill would trip me. Sometimes we'd smack into whoever was dumb enough to play goalie against us. We treated goalies pretty bad but most guys didn't seem to mind. We weren't into fair out there on Kilkenny Lake. Not much seems to be fair when it's twenty below and the wind is whistling through the treetops and the sun going down. We wanted the day to last forever. But it was ending. It wasn't fair but it was all right."

"You miss it?"

"No. I'm okay with hockey. Aside from that hockey stick in the corner, the rest of hockey is back home in my closet. I'm done with hockey. I've hung up my skates. It's other stuff."

"Stuff?"

Todd turned to read the script from the pale blue wall again. He spoke this time without turning back to her, as if the paint had ears. "Maybe we can talk about it sometime."

"Whenever you like."

"I guess I avoided some of the more complicated stuff."

"I can understand that." Molly instinctively knew he was talking about girls.

"I thought tripping Dill on the ice or playing street hockey on a summer night beneath the streetlights was what was important. Somebody should have hit me in the head with a sledge hammer and told me to wake up."

"You were young."

He finally turned to look at her. He was angry. "Yeah, and now I'm friggin' fourteen."

Molly had to look away from Todd. She wondered how she had gotten in so deep so quick. She looked through the window out at leaves near the tops of the Halifax trees — mostly green but a few golden and some burnt orange — and above them now a grey, granite sky. She was in the icy, deadly waters of Kilkenny Lake in January, scratching at the ice with her fingernails. She and Todd and even the nearly-invisible Dill were there, him with his nails bitten to the quick with worry about his mortality. Maybe now she'd have to be the first to heave herself up onto the ice.

"When you got out of the lake, you and Dill, how did you feel?"

"Alive. I felt very much alive."

"But you must have been scared and cold."

"My pants froze first. Like boards. I could barely undo my skates, and my socks froze like concrete right away. Then my coat. Dill was crying. I didn't blame him. I had to help him get his skates off. It was dark by then and we started running. Staggering really. He still thought we were gonna freeze to death."

"You didn't."

"No way. I looked like Frosty the Snowman by that time. My fingers were numb, my toes. I couldn't feel a thing. But I kept us moving until we made it to my backyard. I made Dill stop crying before we went in. I told him I'd leave him to die in my backyard if he didn't stop crying first."

"But you didn't mean that?"

"No. I was just doing him a favour. I never told a soul he was whimpering. I never even told anyone else but you that I got out first and then pulled him out."

"Why?"

"I don't know. I'd already had my reward."

"Which was?"

"Going into the lake. And scratching my way back out. The way I felt. Nothing could kill me. That was my flag."

Todd was still waving that flag, even though he knew otherwise. He took a deep breath. "What were you like when you were fourteen?"

Molly realized she was far away, looking south out the window of the hospital, off towards Devil's Island where she had been born. She fumbled with the keys to her memory but couldn't find the right key for the door to that room.

"I was young, like you."

"And?"

It was a simple conjunction. The eternal one begging for completion but never satisfied. "And it was the year that something changed."

CHAPTER SIX

ON MOLLY'S FOURTEENTH BIRTHDAY, SHE SIMPLY thought the upcoming year would be like all the other years. Life on an island was full of endless surprises but *she* had always believed that she was a constant. She didn't really much consider she'd end up an adult like her parents or like the adults she'd met ashore at Eastern Passage. She didn't even exactly know where those adults came from or how they got to be adults. Well, she did really, but she just didn't want to admit it. She preferred to think they just suddenly appeared fully grown, or maybe arrived from other planets circumnavigating distant stars. Like the stars in Orion's belt.

So there was this fourteenth birthday on the fourteenth day of January. She got up at what must have been four o'clock in the morning, although she didn't have a clock in her room and all she knew really was that it wasn't morning yet. It was dark. She wanted fourteen to start as a dark thing and then get brighter as the hours passed. She hoped for more surprises, not just because it was her birthday but because it was another magnificent day in her young life.

It was incredibly cold out and a thin scimitar moon cast down an aluminum light that brought out the best in the frost on the shingled siding. The back doorknob felt shockingly cold even from inside the house.

But Molly wanted to look up for Orion. Orion was a familiar constellation with three stars for a belt. Molly didn't know much about stars except for what her father had taught her when she was quite young and it went something like this.

"Well, you got your North Start." Hank always pronounced a "t" at the end of it, like it was a place of beginnings. He said it was because of the way his father had spoken to him as a boy. It was his father's language sneaking through into his own.

"Then you got your Big Dipper and Little Dipper. The big one's easy and it helps you find your North Start if you need it. The little one gets all fuddled up in the Milky Way, though sometimes, so I just pretend I know where it's at. Don't much matter if I get it right or not. I just know it's there."

On a moonless, childhood night, the sky would be a profusion of mingling bright points of light. Almost nobody could find the darn Little Dipper on a night like that and those nights came often to the island. "Scientists could tell you which star is which and why, but I only have a handle on two or three of my favourites. I stick mostly to constellations: bears and dogs and queens and such, but I even lose track of most of them after I locate the buggers."

"What's that one up there?" Molly asked, pointing to a very bright sparkling star.

Molly knew her father would have an answer for her whether it was real or made up. It didn't matter much to Molly when it came to stars. "Oh, that one? The one that looks like a, um, great blue heron?"

"Yes, that one."

"That's Jack Daniels."

"There's a constellation named Jack Daniels?"

"Yes. They were all named by the ancient Greeks, you know. Great sailors, the Greeks. They fought a lot, which got 'em into trouble but they were pretty good sailors and sometimes would steer their ships by the stars so they knew all the constellations like personal friends. There was a story for each of them."

Molly could distinguish Jack Daniels now, a magnificent starlit heron, clear as day now. "What did Jack Daniels do?"

"He saved the earth from melting when it started getting too close to the sun. He had to sort of tie a rope onto it and tow it away."

"Close call."

"It was indeed."

Around that time, some high, thin clouds came over and cancelled out a big piece of the Milky Way and half the stars in the sky. "What's the one with the three stars in a row and kind of a big box around that?"

Molly already knew the answer but she wanted to hear it from her father. "Those three stars form the belt of Orion. You can see his shoulders, arms, and legs. I don't know about the head but the Greeks didn't worry about Orion's head."

"What did O'Brien do?"

"It's *Orion*, honey. He was Greek, not Irish. But I'm sure he wouldn't mind if you called him O'Brien now and again. Orion was a hunter."

"I don't like hunters. They shoot the geese and ducks in November. How come Orion had to be a hunter?"

"Truth is he was a lousy hunter. He hated killing animals, too, but there he was, stuck in the sky with that big belt and square shoulders, and Zeus or Jupiter or somebody said he had to go hunt things."

"That's not fair."

"That's exactly what Orion thought. So he took his bow and arrow — at least I think it was a bow and arrow — and just shot his arrows off into space where they hit nothing at all but, instead, travelled for, oh heck, millions of miles. All the other constellations saw Orion's arrows shooting around space and laughed at the poor silly bugger but he didn't care."

"I've seen O'Brien's arrows but they never last long."

"That's right. He shoots one and it's gone. The queen, Cassiocamelia or whatever, can sometimes be heard laughing at him."

"I think I like O'Brien."

"So do I, Molly. Everybody likes Orion. He's a good-guy kind of hunter that doesn't kill anything. He wanders around the sky according to the time of year and sometimes the poor bastard disappears altogether and you can't see him."

"Clouds."

"Sometimes clouds. Sometimes he just falls down into a hole and can't get out. Sometimes he falls into a lake or the sea and no one's around to get him out. Silly old sod gets stuck and he doesn't know what to do. He gets cold and hungry and nearly gives up, but then, suddenly, you'll see him back up in the sky. Three stars for a belt. Big, square shoulders."

"How does he save himself?"

"Nobody knows. Somebody or something comes along to help — hauls his sorry ass up out of the pit he's fallen into, or dives down and pulls him back up from the bottom of the ocean where he's turning blue from lack of oxygen, feeds him some lentil soup or fish chowder, and Bob's your uncle."

So, of course, Molly wanted to greet Orion on the dark morning of her fourteenth birthday. She knew it was bloody cold outside and bundled up, putting on one of her mother's coats over her own. She wore her father's big, galumphing insulated rubber boots and her feet rambled around inside them as she walked.

The sea was a plate of blue steel. All the renegade rabbits were snuggled up asleep under the house or in the shed with the spare parts for the lighthouse. The crescent moon looked thin and dangerous. If Molly reached out to touch it, she was sure she'd cut herself and bleed bright-red blood on the frozen grass. There was no snow. It hadn't snowed yet this year except for several days of blubbering, mushy sleet that slopped into the sea and melted on rooftops. Looking up and away, she wondered, where, oh where, was Orion?

North Star, Big Dipper, Little Dipper — maybe were there or maybe not, according to how you felt about it — but clearly, there was no Orion. Fourteen years old and no sign of Orion in the sky. There was a heavy sadness that came with the sudden realization that childhood was slipping away for the first time — perhaps in every thread of visible air she exhaled into the night. Something would have to be done about Orion.

The fourteenth day of January brought a pale, weak sun that was still somehow bright enough to blot out all the stars, except for the lingering flashlight beam of Venus that remained until nearly eight-thirty when it too vanished. To Molly, it looked like it should have been a sunny day, a cold and crisp day with the sound of boots crackling over frozen stones. But by ten o'clock or so, a northeast wind arose. It warmed a little in temperature but felt colder because of the wind and damp. That ugly wind snagged onto everything, found corners to hide behind and surprise whoever was coming up on the other side. It thrashed at the windows and spit sea water up over the ledges. It wasn't a good wind for a birthday.

Woodstoves worked double time. Molly's mother retreated to her private "studio" where she was working on a whirligig of a leprechaun milking a cow. Molly began to read *The Catcher in the Rye* for the first of many times in her life. Holden Caulfield was not happy about something. Molly fell halfway in love with the messed-up Holden.

By the afternoon, the weather was awful. Snow arrived finally, but not the kind of snow you want to make friends with. Wet, hard, pellets of ice, wind shifting from north to east and back and, at every shift, getting colder — bone cold. Now the temperature dropped. Hank fussed back and forth from house to lighthouse, checking on this, checking on that.

"Stop wrestling with the weather," her mother, Lea, told her husband. "Give it up and just let it be."

"Gotta tie things down. Gotta check on the light. Generator might go at any time. Gotta be ready."

Father out the door into the snort of winter, mother clucking her tongue and bobbing her head. "He's always the same, Moll, when the wind goes like that. It gnaws at him, gets him going. Never seen a man take weather as personally as your father."

As the afternoon got worse, Lea persuaded Hank to stay inside and listen to how bad the weather was from the reports on the marine-band radio. He could sit there and stew and mutter to himself if he liked, but at least he'd be as warm and dry as the rabbits all piled up on top of each other, fast asleep in the burrows under the porch and the shed.

Molly decided to write a letter to Holden Caulfield after reading a truly sad part of his story. She was amazed at how complicated people's lives must be on the mainland and was coming to realize that, someday, she might have to deal with those kind of people. It never occurred to her, though, that she might one day move off the island and live among them. Her world was a fixed place. The geography of the years ahead was solid footing, all right here on the island. Seasons might change in any number of whimsical ways, but the island was forever, fixed in a sea of permanence.

Inside the wind-thrummed house, her father was up to his old tricks. One minute he would be sitting beside the radio, listening to scratchy radio reports, reporting to whoever was listening about the wind on the island. He'd be teasing a hole in the toe of his wool sock, working at the threads until it was three times larger than when he discovered it, and the next minute he'd be gone, vanished. Molly was sure he had not gotten up out of his wooden chair, and certainly no doors had opened. Nope. Hank had just vanished as he was prone to do now and again. She wondered if he had done so for her entertainment. Or had he heard something on the radio?

She slid a small clamshell into the despairing life of Holden Caulfield to mark her place and looked out the window to observe her father, coatless, walking into a now-easterly wind, purposefully heading to the shore that faced the open sea. The people speaking on the radio seemed almost unintelligible, as usual, but she wondered if there had been something her father had heard. The radio voices sounded like they were wrestling with electricity. Then the static smoothed as silky as a satin blanket on your bed. Finally a Coast Guard radio man came on: "We got a plane down in the water, we suspect, south and west of Devil's Island. Prop job coming in from England. Not sure how many people on board. Anybody out there at the mouth of the harbour? Over."

Static screech, the yowl and yelp of devils and wild animals on the air.

"Repeat. Looking for any visuals from anybody off Devil's Island. Over."

Molly's mother walked into the room then. She'd felt the news come right through the walls of the house. She'd only heard part of the message. It was the snap and grind of the unanswered question that bothered her most.

"Your father?"

Molly looked out the window. Hank, walking direct to the shore.

Lea picked up the microphone. "Coast Guard, it's Lea on the island. Hank went to see if there's anything out there. Can't see much. No boats out in this mess for sure. Over."

"Copy, Lea. Smart day to stay ashore. Can't send any aircraft. Maybe get a rescue boat as far as Bull Rock but reports of seas running twenty foot plus. Don't look good. Tell us if you see anything. Over."

"Right. Over and out."

Molly's mother sat down now and stared at the ghostlike image of her father walking the shoreline, waves, smacking onto the boulders just inches from where he stepped, sending cascades of sea water vaulting up into the sky. The wind vamped up while mother and daughter waited by the radio for Hank to turn and head back to the house. He seemed to disappear in a volley of wet snow before he reached them. When visibility returned, he was nowhere to be seen and Lea stood up, scowling, then wrestled on her winter coat and barged out the door, Molly in her wake still clutching *The Catcher in the Rye*. On the harbour side, the downwind side of the island, Hank, now wearing his old shaggy woolen coat from the shed, was slipping the knot from the dory and beginning to tilt it down the icy spruce planks into the tiny bay, blocked on all but one side by the big mushroom-shaped granite rocks they called the Gates of Hercules.

The dory seemed surprisingly anxious to return to the sea before spring and Hank had her halfway to the waterline before he was knocked off his feet by his wife with a blow to the back, a two-fisted thing that Molly had never ever seen. It was like she was chopping down a tree with an invisible axe. Henry was all of oak but fell quickly to the wrath of a woman on a day when the venom of a northeast Atlantic storm seemed not to faze him at all. He fell on the stones and cut his forehead, then looked up in amazement at his wife, her coat and skirt flapping in the wind like some insane, frenetic whirligig.

Molly herself was running through the cold, the wind stinging her ears and knifing through her blouse. She felt tiny and vulnerable and didn't know that she was much stronger than her mother when it came to saving the life of her father. Hank was trying a second time to join the little boat and guide it out from the minuscule bit of placid waters into the swaggering catastrophe of the harbour and sea beyond.

Lea gripped her invisible axe and was ready to fell the tree again but Molly had come up behind her and stood staring at her parents. Just then, a single vindictive wave wrapped itself like a cold arm around the east side of the island, slammed up and over one side of Hercules, raining cold, salt water down on them all. Hank wiped blood and sea from his small wound and licked it from his finger, then looked helplessly at Molly and that was enough. He stood perfectly still, as if himself turned to stone, an impotent ragged ghost of a man. He watched as his wife reattached a line to the glazed capstan and wound the boat back to its proper rest.

Molly's father took off his coat and wrapped it around his daughter, wiped snow and ice from her brow and led her home with Lea following behind. An hour later, as darkness joined forces with wind and calamity, they listened to a young Coast Guard man report to anyone listening that the rescue boat had not even made it much past McNab's Island before it was swamped by a wave. Engine trouble, relentless seas, and a sandwich of fear and common sense had forced it back to the dock. The sea would do whatever it had to do to finish a bad plan on the part of some pilot foolish enough to tempt a Maritime winter storm.

Chapter Seven

It was a bad night and no night for a birthday anything. A fire roared in the wood stove. The old oil stove in the kitchen sang the same old song, the song of a cold, windy, island night. Tonight it was a Rachmaninov stove because somewhere outside in the violent storm people were dying.

"Bloody hell," Molly's father said. He stared at his hands and seemed to be angry at them because there was nothing he could do to help whatever poor bastard was drowning a horrible death just beyond his island.

"Nothing to do but wait, now, Hank," Lea said to him. "Listen to that wind. Nobody can do anything in a terror like that."

"Bloody wind."

Molly tried to get interested in Holden Caulfield again. Holden was trying to figure out girls. He didn't understand them and seemed to be all worked up about it. What's there to understand? She thought of herself as very normal, very simple even, and easy to understand. She thought any person would be able to sit down with her and read her like a book, a book much less complicated than *The Catcher in the Rye*. She wondered why Holden was so worried about everything when he didn't hardly seem to have anything to worry about. Maybe that's the way boys were, she thought, because she'd had so little contact with boys. Maybe they worried and fussed and made a big deal about nothing — like trying to understand girls — which was probably the easiest thing in the world.

The winds kept thrashing the thorny branches of a big, wild rose bush against the window. It sounded like angry fingernails on the glass. "Godforsaken storm," said Hank. "Felt it in my bones this afternoon, felt it comin' on like the wrath of God."

Lea clucked her tongue. "You did not, Hank. Be still. Find something else to do other than sit there and stew over the mess outside."

"Bloody wind."

Molly's mother was shellacking one of her whirligigs. The room smelled of shellac in an intoxicating way. It was a whirligig of a pair of geese whose wings would flap in the wind. If it had been mounted outside tonight in the storm, the geese would have been wingless by now, wings ripped off by the blast of sea wind. Lea's other whirligigs were probably out there getting wrecked. Little wooden men were chopping wood so fast and furious that axe handles would fly off, metal pins for shoulder joints would chew through the wood. Among all the other damage of the night, there would be whirligig wreckage.

And then her father did his famous disappearing act again. Neither Molly nor Lea noticed, of course, how he did it. He was that good. He was there one second cursing the storm in a gnawing repetitive pattern and then *poof*. Lea looked up at the door and saw that the inside hook-and-eye latch was still holding. Certainly, he had not gone out into the godforsaken storm. It turned out that he had just gone off to bed.

Molly and Lea were both a little woozy from the shellac fumes and Lea put the brush in some Varsol, then tapped the lid down on the shellac can with a small ball-peen hammer. "Sorry about the smell, girl," she apologized to Molly.

Molly went to bed, turned on the small light on her bedside table and began a short letter to Holden Caulfield.

Dear Holden,
I know I haven't met you in person yet but I wanted to tell you that you're probably not as screwed up as you think you are. I wouldn't worry so much about trying to understand girls, if I were you. Girls are pretty simple really. If the others are like me, then they are interested in things like smooth, whispering summer skies, sparrows dangling on the side of ripe sea oats, patterns in bedrock licked clean by the sea, tiny red spiders threading between loose stones on a beach, and watching rabbits munching on tufts of wet morning spring grass. Once you understand that, you pretty much know all there is to know.
Your friend,
Molly Willis,
Devil's Island, Nova Scotia, Canada

Molly wondered if Holden Caulfield even knew where Devil's Island was. She hoped he would open a big atlas at his library and look it up, maybe even find Devil's Island marked at the mouth of Halifax Harbour. Molly never once considered that her advice about understanding girls was probably not at all relevant in the complicated, neurotic mainland world of Holden Caulfield, wherever he was.

Sleep was not the word that could properly be used for what anyone in the Willis family was doing that night. The wind continued to rage. It tore at the house, slipping loose shingles from the roof and sending them into outer space. It slammed with powerful fists into the east wall of the sturdy old three-story, wood-frame home. It bullied and barged at the sea until frothy grey midnight waves, tall as chimneys, crashed down on the fortress of natural rock that had provided protection from every war the weather had waged against this tiny island since the days of the glaciers.

Poplar trees fell and small spruce trees lost branches and a few taller ones were even completely uprooted.

And then, at three o'clock in the morning, it was as if someone had thrown a switch. On one minute, off the next.

Molly dropped off to sleep and dreamed she was walking through a very large, dimly-lit house with an infinite number of doors. The doors did not have signs like those in her real house. There were noises coming from behind each door. One sound was like the voice of the wind. Behind one door, fingernails scratched and scraped at something hard. Behind another, fists pounded. Behind another was the pure moaning of wind. Molly was looking for the door to summer in her dream. As she turned a corner, she saw someone else, an almost featureless boy her own age who looked confused and beleaguered. She was reaching out to take his hand and lead him to the doorway to summer that she knew she could find. And then she woke up.

Her room was cold, but she liked waking up in a cold room. She slept on cotton sheets beneath a heavy, wool blanket and several quilts filled with goose down. She always felt buried and safe beneath her mountain of blankets, tucked inside her cocoon the way a girl should be. But now she remembered the news of the downed plane.

Molly heard her father's bare feet hit the hardwood floor then tromp down the stairs to the kitchen. Molly opened her bedroom door to listen. Loud static now filled the warm kitchen below, as if her father had just disturbed a hive of August bees. There were electric, crackling sounds like amplified frying bacon. Then Hank was on the horn to the Coast Guard.

"Willis here on Devil's. Anything yet? Over."

There was a pause, and more bees than bacon. A pop and a whistle, then some animal growling through a distant screen door.

"Coast Guard here, Hank. Storm's moved out and away. Bad night all around. Nothing on the plane. We'll try to get a helicopter in the air and rescue boats again at daybreak. Our guys are pretty sure that if the plane went down, it was pretty close to Devil's. Did you see anything?"

"Nothing. I'm gonna go out and look around. Over and out."

Molly found yesterday's clothes and slipped them on, topped up with the clothes from the day before that. Out in the bloody awful cold, layers mattered. Hank's hand was on the doorknob, just as his wife and daughter found the kitchen and bundled themselves into large heavy coats and wrapped long wool scarves around their necks and faces. Hands and feet found mittens and gumboots.

The west door opened to the shed and then the frozen latch that led outside required cursing and kicking before it would let them out. A war had been and gone. Everything was battered. Boards had been jimmied from the tool shed. The paint had been stripped from the lighthouse. Frozen kelp and seaweed lay in heaps and coils. The sea itself had been up and over sections of the so-called front yard. Boulders bloomed where once flowers grew. Salt water was freezing everywhere in puddles and pools. Hank held onto family elbows, trying to keep his girls upright as if they were made of china. One slip on the slick, bony rocks, he feared, and they might fall and shatter.

It was dark, but a pale timid partial moon, shrouded by leftover storm clouds, provided a modicum of light. It was still well below zero. You could feel it in your breathing, the way the air had its own teeth of ice. The ocean thundered now as they walked closer to the seaward side of the island. It sang a simple chant of *Doom, Doom, Doom* that Molly thought was unnecessary and intimidating.

Suddenly the clouds overhead parted. A few stars and the fat, curved blade of the moon appeared. The newly glazed island was a magnificent platinum surface under such influence and it even tasted like some strange metal in Molly's mouth. *Doom* went the cannonade of waves.

Hank, Lea, and Molly surveyed the corrupted waters. Plumes of dirty froth girded rock outcroppings. Waves, like huge moveable tents, loomed dark and travelled in all directions. The family knew where to look for anything that would have come ashore. To the west was a stand of loose rock. Anything coming shoreward would be driven by currents around the big boulders of the front headland and pushed west, then driven up on the stretch of sandy shoreline. In the soft, nurturing summers of her fourteen years, Molly had spent many days happily sitting alone with the sea, admiring it, talking to it, taking part in discussions with small blue-green waves, making castles out of sea urchin shells and driftwood, or pretending to be flying up above with the shearwaters and gulls. There was no connection between that memory and this scene before them. Molly suddenly felt that there was no thread of time, no continuity at all. Her only comfort was that her parents were there with her. Her father was still holding onto her elbow. When he slipped on a peel of kelp he nearly brought his whole family down, and good thing he had two agile women on either side to keep him from cracking his ribs on the rocks.

Molly had been looking right at the body for several seconds and had not realized what it was. She thought it was another bundle of seaweed, not the carcass of a long-haired woman facedown in the sand. The moonlight revealed that she still wore a long, dark dress and one high-heeled shoe. Molly was suddenly terrified that, after this, nothing could ever be the same in her life again. The scene before her made her feel small, sad, and oddly selfish. Before she spoke, she silently begged the light-giver moon, the one with the cruel, sharpened blade of light, to prove she was wrong. *This is not a woman*, Molly prayed. *Please, just let this be another hump of seaweed, rolled, threaded, sculpted into something that appears human, and tossed ashore.*

Lea and Hank saw the woman's body now. Lea unlocked her elbow from Hank and walked forward, knelt, removed her mittens and touched the long hair, the hair itself inter-woven with delicate icy souvenirs of rockweed, dulse, and Irish moss. Hank inched forward, past his wife, close enough to stumble and slide into her slightly, then recover and stagger on to the next victim, a man wholly curled up on his side, as if he just happened to fall asleep there, tired after a long day of doing something unimportant on the little beach. The man wore some sort of uniform. He had been the pilot, perhaps. Molly noticed he had no shoes on at all. The sea had kept his shoes but given up the body.

"Froze solid," Hank said.

There was a heavy-set, bearded man with hands locked on the handle of an unfurled umbrella. Molly almost felt giddy when she saw the umbrella. A man in a plane is told that there's a storm ahead. They are flying over the ocean. The man takes hold of his umbrella inside the plane thinking that if it should start to rain, all he needs to do is unfurl his umbrella to ward off the elements.

Hank and Lea had moved further west down the beach, looking for more victims. Molly thought about leaving her parents there and walking back home, going to bed. She craved sleep and warmth. She looked up into the sky at the confused stars. None of them seemed to be in any of the right places. The storm had jumbled up all the stars somehow. No Cassiopeia, no bears, no serpents. Not a dipper in the whole whack of them. And the familiar North Star was not where it should have been.

And no Orion. The hunter was lost at sea. Molly blinked hard, observed all the stars in the heavens wobble, and then she wiped away the tears that were so cold now on her cheeks. Looking up, she tried again, tried to piece together a simple rectangle of a hunter's frame from the points of light. Nothing. Then she tried in vain to find the three bright stars of Orion's belt. No. Orion was not up there tonight.

Molly came back to earth and took a few tentative steps beyond the rocky outcrop. She fell to her knees on the soft, sandy shoreline. She looked seaward to face the brutal waves again and then saw the last victim of the night. A young man, completely naked, with blue-white skin, the colour of the inside of a clamshell.

Chapter Eight

THE PALENESS OF HIS SKIN SEEMED surreal in the silver moonlight. Like driftwood. The body was floating back and forth near the shoreline, first sliding up onto the smooth, cold sand and then tugged back into the white, foamy claws of the sea. As the naked body rolled back into the sea, the arms flailed in the water almost as if he might still be alive. Naked and unconscious in the winter sea, but alive.

Another wave snapped down hard this time on the young man, making him bounce, then float, as the water shoved him further up on the beach. Molly ran at once and found her feet sinking in the soft, wave-punched sand. She touched the hand of the young man just as another wave began to retreat and draw the body back out. She held onto the cold, bony hand as the sea tried to take him back.

Molly tugged him up to where the sand was hard and frozen and turned quickly, looking for her parents, but Hank and Lea were looking after their own dead. This one was hers. *Maybe he is alive*, she tried to convince herself. Her hands were wet now, stinging from the cold. Her face burned. She removed her wet gloves, turned the young man onto his back. His eyes were closed. Maybe he was just unconscious. She would pry open his mouth. She would open an airway. The jaw dropped open without resistance. The skin was cold, no motion from the chest. She wanted desperately to know who he was, to have a name she could speak.

Molly knelt beside him now and touched the bony ribs of his chest, put a hand over where she thought his heart might be, closed her eyes tight, and willed him to come back to life, to come back to her. She held onto that silent prayer for several seconds without breathing but, when she took a breath, she realized that such hope had slipped away forever. It seemed incredible that he was completely naked. Had he stripped off his clothes to try and swim in the maelstrom? How could it be that one man washes up still clutching an umbrella, while another younger man is pounded ashore by unforgiving waves that have stripped him bare? If she had seen her father without clothes, it had been a long and accidental while ago, and it had left almost no impression. Here was a startling and gruesome education and she couldn't help staring at the chest, the arms, the poor, shrivelled genitals. Shaking now, she arranged his arms flat against his sides and studied his face. He was young. Seventeen, eighteen maybe. Not really a man, but still a boy. He had a strong face, a head of dark, soft hair and now it was all freezing into long, thin needles of black ice. She lowered her face to his until she could hear herself breathing.

More waves thundered and then clawed at the sand as if they were trying to get at her as well as the violated man. The sea would have to suffer disappointment. A small defeat, but enough to boil in the belly of that sea and ferment into who knows what.

Molly tried to move him several ways — dragging at first, then lifting him in her arms, but she was not strong enough to carry him like that, like a child. And then her father saw her, called out her name, and stumbled towards his daughter. "Let me," he said, and quickly hoisted the boy over his shoulders.

Molly walked beside them as they trudged back towards the house, occasionally trying to steady her father when he looked like he was about to fall.

Once inside, he gently lay the boy down on the carpet near the wood stove. He stared at him, disbelieving, then looked at Molly. "Stay here. I have to go back out."

Lea arrived home then and put an arm around Molly. "I'll put more wood on the fire," was all she said as Hank headed back out into the night.

Her father next carried the woman into the house and swore that he could not go back to get the others, even as he was changing his wet gloves and coat and preparing to go out again. After his next journey out into the night, he came back in puffing hard, bringing with him the one who must have been the pilot. Hank looked lifeless himself, torn inside, depleted, as if some heavy hand had reached down his throat and pulled some essential part out of him. Hank took a drink of tea from a cup Lea thrust at him. He drank rapidly and then threw up in the sink. Took a second drink and stared at his image in the frosted glass of the dark window until he built up enough anger to go back out again.

He was longer coming back this time and hauled the next victim over cobbles and debris. He had taken the wooden wheelbarrow from the shed. It was the heavy-set man clinging to the unopened umbrella.

Lea had already reported the news to the Coast Guard.

"They'll be picked up in the morning," Lea told her husband.

"We'll put each one in their own room," Hank said. "It's only right." His daughter and wife nodded.

The man, still clinging to his umbrella, was put onto the large bed in what was labelled "The Captain's Chamber." The pilot was put into "The Government Room" and the woman was settled upon the colourful quilt in "The Sunset Suite" to the west end of the house. In each room the windows were pried open to allow the full strength of the cold to preserve the bodies. For some windows, Hank had to use the wooden handle of a hammer to tap the frame to break the lock of the ice outside.

Lea had wrapped an old towel around the young man's loins and he too had his own bed in what had been whimsically labelled by Hank as the "Room of Least Intentions." It was a small, narrow room with a child's bed, the one Molly had outgrown. Hank had wrestled with the dead man's knees to place him there, and pried another stubborn sash, accidentally cracking the glass.

Then Hank and Lea had sat up with tea and rum in the kitchen while Molly retreated to her bedroom. She looked into the mirror and saw dark patches under her eyes.

A voice deep inside her skull suggested that she could remove herself from this. She would get into bed, get warm, fall asleep, and dream herself back into summer. Pretend none of this had happened. She had practiced this many times before in winter, but no winter night had been anything like this. Yet before she could retreat to the sleepy safety of summer, she understood for the very first time in her life that she too would some day die. Maybe not like the people from the plane but die nonetheless. Molly could not fall asleep. Instead, she slipped out of her room and went down the hall and entered the Room of Least Intentions. The young man lay there on a white sheet, with enough moonlight coming in the room to paint everything the colour of aluminum. He lay on his side with legs bent, one arm bent behind his back. Hank had gently readjusted the boy's limbs to make him appear more normal. The room was bitterly cold. A slip of a breeze made for a slight flutter of curtain, enough to give Molly a chill. Hank had not pulled blankets up over any of the guests. But the young man seemed to be asking her to pull the top sheet and blankets up over him. Molly did just that and tucked him in, smoothing the sheet, then fussing over the blanket and the quilt, handmade by her own grandmother from scraps of old flannel shirts.

She turned to go but couldn't quite make herself leave the room. Whatever the family had done tonight to prove its compassion, it had all been an abysmal, pointless failure. Molly touched the dead boy's cheek and held her hand there for a few seconds. She felt the terrible cold of his skin. As she pulled her hand away, she stared out into the dark night and then got up to close the window. There were extra blankets in the closet. She added a third blanket to the bed and curled up in an upholstered chair with a faded quilt around her.

Molly awoke sometime before sunrise. She was not startled to find herself in the room with the young man. She got up and walked over to him and traced a finger over the bones of his cheek. Then she kissed him lightly on the neck and walked downstairs to huddle for warmth by the cook stove.

In the kitchen she found her mother and father slumped over the kitchen table, snoring. The oil stove murmured, but it was a tuneless, inanimate thing. It was still very dark in the room, and so boots and a winter coat were found by lifting the lid on the stove and letting the red, inner flame illuminate the kitchen.

Outside was a dark and windless world. But up above, the stars had returned. Molly pulled the collar of her father's coat tight to her neck, scanned east, west, north. Big Dipper. Little Dipper. North Start. They could be detected among the starry confusion if one focused a bit, squinted to ignore the lesser stars.

But looking into the heavens was not enough to comfort her. She felt that her understanding of the world was a great, stupid, sad lie. A myth. Everything she believed and understood, all of the great wordless, unspoken truths were reduced to nothing. Orion was nowhere to be found in any quadrant of the sky. False Orions, flickering imitations, but not the staunch shoulders, no star-studded belt. The failure of Orion seemed somehow worse, more sorrowful than all that had come before. But she would not give up just yet.

She looked to the east, the direction from which the storm had come. She could see the first grey shades of sunlight and slightly to the north two bright stars near the horizon. She closed her eyes and willed those stars to rise up from the dark shoreline of Eastern Passage. She coaxed and pleaded. And when she opened her eyes she was certain they were higher in the sky. She closed her eyes again and made fantastic, impossible propositions with God, with nature, with the stars themselves. And when she opened her eyes again she was rewarded.

The three, bright, unmistakable stars of Orion's belt hovered over the treeline of the shore. Had they been there all along? She tested her powers one final time as she felt a small thrill of cold air on the taut skin of her neck.

The new light of the sun had begun to burn the weaker stars from the sky. Orion was well above the horizon now, however, and any amateur stargazer could have picked him out. The gentle hunter had been lifted up and given back his rightful place in the sky.

Molly turned and went back into the house as the sun began to bring colour back to a grey world.

Chapter Nine

ERIC WONDERED WHY HE WAS SO damn healthy after nearly dying in the Arctic. His brain was trying to convince him he was a ghost, a thin vapour trail of a spiritual entity wandering from one room to another in a brick house in the Glebe. People did not come to visit him. He suspected they didn't know what to say. "Cold up there, eh?" "Death, what was it like?" "Were you really dead?" "What does it feel like to die?" "To come back?"

Dead as Disney or Kennedy or Genghis Khan. Dead as a doornail, as they used to say. Oh, he'd received a card from his old department chair, and it was signed, Dr. Sylvia Minot. The dean had sent a get-well card, too, something from Hallmark. He wasn't surprised his former colleagues weren't queuing up along the maple-lined street to visit him. He'd dug his own grave, so to speak. It was a cold and private place with little pleasure. He was nearly dozing off when the phone rang.

"Grandfather?"

"Ray?"

"You sound tired."

"I am."

"I'll call back."

"No. Why are you calling?" It came out sounding like an insult but he didn't mean it that way.

"I was finishing work. I had this feeling in my gut I should call you. When no one was around, I looked into your file. Are you doing okay with yourself?"

"No. There's a lot of confusion."

"You need a shrink."

"I don't want one."

"What is it you want?"

"I want to know more about what happened. All they tell me is that I went hiking out of Pangnirtung on Baffin Island. There was a storm and I became lost. Someone found me, thought I was dead, but took me back to town across unsafe ice. At the hospital they decided I was alive, did what they could and sent me south to Ottawa once I was stabilized."

"They didn't tell you who found you, did they?"

"No. I don't understand that. Why?"

"I don't know who it was but it was someone from the community. Maybe one of my relations, I don't know."

"Why wouldn't they want to me to know?"

"Who knows? Folks up there know how white guys fuck things up. Maybe he thought you'd fuck things up if you tried to show your gratitude. We like to hold our tongues sometimes, y'know, keep a low profile so things don't get more fucked up than they already are."

Something about the way Ray said this reminded Eric of his father sitting in a wheelchair in the mental hospital, his wrists tied loosely with old terry cloth towel, the weight of history sitting like a cold stone on his shoulders.

"Would you come over and tell me about your grandfather some more?"

"That's why I called, professor."

Eric blinked at the sunlight when he opened the door. He felt weak and weary again, ghostly and insubstantial. There was the smell of fallen leaves already decomposing on the ground and it entered into him like a powerful intoxicant.

"Some neighbourhood," Ray said.

"Come in."

Inside, the house filled up with an awkward silence. Ray looked around him like he had just stepped into a museum. "So this is where you live?"

Eric led him to the living room. "Sit down, please."

"You don't got a TV."

Eric shrugged.

"You don't like to watch the people fight on *Jerry Springer*?"

Eric wasn't sure he knew what Ray was talking about. He cleared his throat. "I'm having a hard time adjusting to a lot of things, I think."

Ray seemed to understand. "I'm no shrink."

"So why did you come here?"

"I don't know why it was me, man, who was standing there with the mop when you came back to this world, but I figure there was a reason for that." Ray seemed to be studying the four corners of the room.

"You called me grandfather."

"I don't know. It's a game we play on each other sometimes. I had an uncle who thought I was his great-grandmother. I was a little boy and he would always address me as his great nanny. Very embarrassing. Not all of my people hold onto these notions. Television has taken a lot of it away. Television and Ski-Doos and bingo. Bingo is killing the north."

Eric suddenly thought he understood something — that he'd found a thread at least to lead him back. He could remember leaving the lodging that day. Remembered the breakfast of Arctic char and scrambled eggs cooked in what he thought must have been seal grease. He remembered the sunlight. Was it June twenty-first, the longest day of the year? The sun would not set. But on that morning, after all the planning, he didn't know exactly why, as he started walking out of town and out into the wilderness, he was there on Baffin Island. "I'm still trying to piece my life back together, Ray. I don't have much to work with, it seems. I want to know about your grandfather."

"He died when I was twelve."

"How old was he?"

"Not much more than sixty. But it was his time. That's what they said."

"How did he die?"

"Maybe we get to that later. You wouldn't happen to have any Kool-Aid or CuppaSoup or anything like that?"

"Juice?"

"Just a glass of sugar and water will be okay. Point me to the kitchen."

Eric pointed, sat back and waited for Ray to return. "I used to steal sugar when I was little. I'd steal it and mix it with Kool-Aid, water it down to get a lot of mileage out of the Kool-Aid pack. Grape was my favourite. My friend Niebold and me would drink Kool-Aid down by the dump and feel like a million dollars. Those were the days.

"My grandfather told me our ancestors came over from Siberia, that we were all really, deep down, fuckin' Russians. He remembered the old days of hunting seals. He'd show me the remains of homes from the old days. The frames were made from whale bones. Man, that was spooky. But you know the thing my grandfather was famous for?"

"I don't know. He loved to hike? He knew the wilderness like the back of his hand?"

Ray sipped the sugar water. "No, you're way off. My grandfather wandered off a lot and got lost. Maybe it was like Alzheimer's or something. We didn't know about anything like that. He'd get lost just walking to town or down to the dump. He'd always pretend he knew where he was going but he didn't. He'd come home late after wandering for many hours. 'Where you been, Grandpa?' 'Out on the land,' he'd always say. Funny guy."

"So what was he famous for?"

Ray held out three craggy rocks. They looked like pieces of slag that you used to find down by the railway tracks. Ray held them out to Eric and Eric accepted them. "These were in your dresser back in the hospital. I borrowed them. They were in your pocket when you were found, man."

"I don't remember." Eric couldn't identify them at all but then he had a habit of picking up many things and putting them in his pockets.

"They're meteorites. Rocks from space, as my grandfather would say. *That's* what he was famous for. He had the biggest collection of meteorites, like you wouldn't believe."

"So, this is why you think I'm your grandfather?"

Ray sipped at his sweet water and blew bubbles into it like a little kid, smiling. "No, professor. It's not exactly like that. I told you, calling *you* my grandfather was a game, like, you know, ping-pong or Trivial Pursuit."

"I don't get it."

"It was my dead grandfather found you or he led someone from the community to find you. Where I come from, dead men hover. Women too. Nobody just goes away without leaving part of themselves behind."

"Metaphorically speaking," Eric added.

"Pardon me?"

"Sorry. It's part of your belief system, right?"

"Yes and no."

"Explain."

"I don't know. You may not understand. In the world I grew up in, almost everyone died with some kind of purpose. There was almost always a meaning to death. Down here, people live and die and don't know what for."

"You're still playing this game with me, right? Remember, I'm still pretty fuzzy on everything since I woke up. You may not be helping me."

"Like I said, I'm no shrink. All I know is that there is some connection going on with you and my grandfather. Why else would you end up in my hospital way the fuck down here?"

Eric shrugged. "In your world, as you said, things have purpose, reason. I come from that other world, the one that gave you TV and Ski-Doos."

"And syphilis and bingo, but I'm not holding you personally responsible." Ray was smiling. "But like I was saying, my grandfather, he had a big collection of these rocks from the sky in his little house. In the old times, he said, our ancestors knew how to melt them down and make knives for working hides and tips for spears. These were made from gifts from the sky, as he'd say. A rock expert, a white man geologist, came up from the south once to see my grandfather's collection and he couldn't believe it. Some of those meteorites weighed over fifty pounds. A couple of smaller ones, my grandfather had melted down with an acetylene torch. He liked the flame of the acetylene torch and thought it was one of the best things the whites had come up with. But they didn't tell him to protect his eyes. He lost part of his eyesight from staring at the blue-white flame. But he made some damn nice knives and a lot of spear tips for his friends."

"I would like to have met your grandfather." Eric thought the room had begun to orbit but he knew it was only that he was very tired. He needed to sleep now but he didn't want Ray to leave.

"You look pretty wasted, man. I hope I'm doing the right thing by telling you this. They'll be pretty ticked at the hospital if they find out I looked in your file and then came here."

"It's okay. I'm interested in all you're telling me. I really am. It's just that I don't know what to make of it. But then I don't know what to make of anything these days."

Ray finished his sugar water and there was a thick residue of sticky, white sludge on the bottom. He kept the glass tilted up until it drifted like a small, sweet avalanche down the glass and into his mouth. "The last time I saw my grandfather, it was in the evening — sun going down on a very still day in early June. Maybe eleven o'clock at night. I was out looking for him, thinking he must have got himself lost again. I was out on the ice, even though my mother told me never to go that far out that time of year. I was a bad kid, hardly ever listened to what I was told.

"So there I was, far out on the ice and afraid I wouldn't have enough light to get back but I had this feeling, you know. So I'm hopping over jumbles of ice ridges, sliding across big, flat pans of smooth ice and then I see him, not far from where the water opened up. He had a seal-oil lamp. I smelled it first, the familiar smell of his home. Smelled the burning oil, then saw the flickering flame. And there he was, sitting on the ice by the lamp inside a circle of his rocks from space around him. I don't know how he could have carried them all there. Must have been over a hundred pounds.

"He seemed very happy to see me and I kept asking him what he was doing way out here. 'Don't worry about me, Raymond. I know what I'm doing.' He had this goofy smile on his face. So he asked me to walk with him and I thought he meant to walk back home. Instead, we walked around the outside of the circle of stones and then once inside the circle of stones. Very slowly. Very purposefully. 'The lamp is the sun, these are all the planets, the rocks in space. We are the travellers.' It was so quiet out there, except for a couple of distant muffled explosions of ice cracking deep down. And the sky was this big, blue dome. The sun was down but it would be light for at least an hour. Three stars were up in the sky even though it was still early on. My grandfather asked me to pick three of his meteorites from his circle. I chose three small ones because I didn't want to have to carry the bigger ones back with me when we went home.

"I put them in my pocket. Then my grandfather walked back to the centre of the circle, sat by the seal-oil lamp. He pointed me toward land and told me to go home, not to run fast, but to jog a little and I would make it before dark. For some reason I knew not to ask him why he wasn't coming. I must have known what he was doing.

"I began to trot like a dog would across the ice. And I realized how far out I had come. I was frightened but I took the three stones from my pocket and held tightly onto them, all in one hand. Then I listened to the song of my breathing as I ran and I thought I could hear soothing voices. I figured they were the voices of my ancestors. If I ran too fast, though, the song would be harsh and raspy and I'd lose them. So I'd slow down until I could hear my ancestors singing in my ears again."

CHAPTER TEN

RAY HAD STOPPED TALKING AND WAS looking at the flat, open palm of his hand as if it was a beautiful landscape painting of an arctic sunset. His long, black hair was a dark waterfall spilling into the air.

"Why did you move away from there?" Eric asked.

"I ask myself that every morning I wake up in my little apartment. I think it's because I stopped loving the land. I don't know why that happened. It just did. Some day, I'll remember how to love it as much as my grandfather did and then I'll go back there for good. I know I will."

Then Ray stood up. "Gotta go, man. Back to work. You need anything, you can call me there. I got a beeper. Just like the doctors. Remember, you the ice man, so you'll always be cool."

Ray pointed to the three meteor rocks on the table by Eric's elbow. "I wasn't gonna keep 'em. Just wanted to carry them around for a while. You hang onto those things. Rocks from the sky. Think about it."

"Thanks, Ray."

"Take good care of my grandfather."

Ray was out the door and into the Ottawa afternoon. Eric felt like he'd been delivered some kind of a gift. He held a rock in each hand, closed his fists over them and stared at the one meteorite left on the table. For the first time in many days, however, he began to feel shooting pains in his fingers and his toes. The doctor had told him to expect this — leftover nerve damage from his exposure to cold. He got up and went into the kitchen, found the painkillers he'd been avoiding and washed them down with tap water.

He settled back into a deep chair in the living room and closed his eyes. Off in the distance, he heard children playing. Eric felt old beyond his years. An ancient thing, but featureless, unfinished. A boulder of granite on a tundra, aeons of weather wearing it down. Eric wondered again why he could not remember what happened on that morning after he left the lodge on Baffin Island. He pondered again exactly how he'd been saved and why.

There was a map on the wall, an inaccurate map of North America that was a reproduction of a seventeenth-century map showing a river that ran from Hudson Bay to California. The continent had been mostly unknown then. North America was a thin, variegated island and Newfoundland was a little larger than it should be. Nova Scotia was enormous, a small continent unto itself. Arthur Dobbs would have loved this map. Eric wondered how many of the personal maps that he'd been consulting all his life were distorted or downright wrong.The painkillers had done their guerrilla warfare on the nerve endings of his fingers and toes. Now they felt slightly numb.

Soon Eric was drifting off to somewhere on what felt like a three-whiskey high. Eric tried to focus on the map again and he found himself following a water route from Baffin Island down Davis Strait into the Labrador Sea, sliding ever so gracefully through the Strait of Belle Isle into the Gulf of St. Lawrence, until his way was blocked by Nova Scotia. He saw the Highlands of Cape Breton looming up before him as he fell asleep.

Eric had become a great fan of sleep during the days of the dissolution of his marriage. He had one of those marriages that had just fallen apart. Eric and Elisse blamed no one for their predicament, not even themselves, but adopted a clinical, almost academic, wait-and-see approach. They convinced themselves they were incapable of repairing the marriage and waited for nature to do what it had to do.

Eric grew depressed and slept a lot. Elisse, on the other hand, made the best of a bad situation and found a women's awareness group to rescue her. But there was no such help for Eric. After the break-up, there was the matter of divorce, a rather businesslike ceremony with two agreeable lawyers who treated the event like an afternoon billiards game. Eric discovered he could still teach classes, but he was just going through the motions. And then he returned to his Glebe homestead to sleep for twelve to sixteen hours at a stretch. He loved sleep the way some men love hockey or booze or chasing women. Eric had settled on one of the more passive addictions that a man could latch onto. He was a sleep junkie.

In an attempt to recover from somnambulism, Eric went north in June to where it would be daylight nearly around the clock for a few weeks. He had only the vaguest rumour of a desire to recover from whatever depths he had sunk to. Threads of history still interested him. He was most passionate (if that word could be stretched to its undernourished lower limits) about the study of wrong-headed history, the history of misinformation and blunder. It was on Baffin Island, for example, where Martin Frobisher had fooled himself into believing he'd found a mountain of gold. It was the perfect destination for Eric. The plane ticket cost more than a trip to Patagonia, but he had so little interest in the value of money at that point that he bought a first class ticket north. He slept all the way there. He had to be awakened by the airline attendant after they'd landed in Pangnirtung when everyone else was already off the plane. He checked into a lodge and slept some more. And after that, he had apparently found the will to head out on his solitary field trip with no intention of ever coming back.

So, after he was saved from the elements and returned to Ottawa, Eric was forced to continue to mull over his own existence and some plan for his future, however dull it would be. Eric knew that not all great men lead exciting lives. Not that he thought himself "great" by any stretch of the imagination, although one naive, misguided academic reviewer had called him "brilliant" for one of the books he had written. This review came from a scholar, he later discovered, who was hoping to get a teaching job in Eric's department. The candidate failed to get employment and later wrote Eric a nasty letter.

Eric knew that other fine men had come to lead sedentary lives. Darwin, for example, after circling the globe on the *Beagle* and concocting brilliant theories about the origins of life on earth and evolution itself, spent the bulk of his remaining days in his own house. Karl Marx wrote books that caused world revolution and then holed up in the British Museum. Emmanuel Kant never ventured more than ten miles from where he was born. Painkiller sleep turned out to be quite good, Eric discovered. Here on this Ottawa afternoon, Eric could sink deep into it. And then, for the first time in many months, he dreamed.

He heard a plane flying overhead but he could not see it.

Where am I? he wondered. The ice, of course. He was on the ice, and the ice was slowly moving. It felt glorious. He stood alone in the middle of an island of ice the size of a hockey rink, floating off to somewhere. On an arctic river draining to California? Or some other route. And then he noticed he was standing in the middle of a circle of stones. The grandfather thing. No, he would not believe he was Ray's grandfather, but possibly dreaming that he was seeing through the eyes of

Ray's dead grandfather. And this, he knew, even in his sleep, had been prompted by Ray's story.

So there he was on the Ottawa afternoon, not just snoozing into oblivion but embracing another world. He stepped out from the circle of stones and walked to the perimeter of the ice. The sky was a big, blue-pink vault above his head. There was no wind. He saw other islands of ice around him and, in between, water so blue it made his teeth hurt. Eric admitted to himself he felt much better. He felt alive, and that what he was experiencing was something very powerful and even real.

Close to the edge of the ice, he sensed the movement more acutely. Judging from the position of the diminishing sun, he guessed the ice was moving southward. Naturally. Davis Strait. Greenland off to his left, Baffin Island to his right. He was sailing an acre of ice down into the Atlantic. The only sound was the engine of the plane overhead but he still could not see it. And then he discovered he was wrong about the sound. It was not the engine of a plane at all. It was a boat engine, its captain threading his way through the ice field in a ship, a two-master piercing the blue sky. But there were no sails. No wind.

It was clearly a boat from the twentieth century, and the roar of the engine grew louder as it approached. Eric waited until the strange craft was a mere twenty metres away and the captain cut the engine. He saw the lettering, RCMP, on the side and almost laughed at the thought of Mounties showing up in his dream like this. Cops.

A man with a beard stood by the gunwale and waved.

A single gull flew low between them and Eric heard its wings slice the clear air.

"Where are you going?" Eric shouted.

"Halifax," the man yelled back.

"Where have you been?"

"All the way through," the bearded man said. "And yourself? Your destination?"

"South, I suppose."

"Well," he said, "you're going the right way."

He waved again, stroked his beard once, and then fired up his engine. Chunks of ice burbled about in the water as the boat moved on, leaving Eric alone again beneath the cold, blue sky, breathing oxygen so pure, sniffing the scent of polar ice so intoxicating, that he found himself feeling happy for the first time in a long, long while.

CHAPTER ELEVEN

WHEN MOLLY FINISHED HER STORY, TODD said nothing. Molly leaned over and touched her lips to his forehead very lightly, then squeezed his hand. "I'll come back again," she said. Todd nodded. And then she left.

Todd had paid very close attention to every detail of the story and it became not just part of his memory, but part of who he was. His temperature was going up and he fought the accompanying dizziness. His medication was wearing off and there were small restless armies of pain in his body rousing and preparing to do battle against him. He could not fight off those soldiers and he grew weaker until he knew he had to reach over and press the sensor which would allow more painkiller to drip into his blood system. A cocktail of pharmaceuticals was coming to his rescue, but it was no cure.

Todd despised being tethered to machines and chemicals but he understood why it was necessary. He even understood that the pain helped to bring him closer to the things Molly was telling him. He was amazed that this woman would tell him such a personal story. He couldn't help but love her. He knew she was not really an older woman. She was still fourteen. She was still living on the island. And it was winter.

The drug soothed and cooled him. Somewhere in his head he was swimming in large, dark, foamy waves. He tasted salt. Todd closed his eyes and tried to thank Molly but realized she had already left. The unsaid words were small, puffy clouds lifting up and away in a cool wind. The pain was going away. The soldiers had found their weapons were jammed: rusted or frozen. They wouldn't work. They'd lost the battle but knew they'd win the war.

Todd chased after the words but the entire vocabulary of the English language was slowly vanishing. It was if another language filled his head, Italian maybe, but he couldn't pronounce any of the words out loud and he didn't know what they meant.

Outside, September pretended that the world would go on forever. September in Halifax keeps to one tense: the present. Molly's feet knew their way back to Winslow Street. Todd's story had taken Molly off into another world, one that was not her own but yet so intimate and real that it might have been *her* story. Todd did not leave her as she walked through Halifax. He became part of her. And she wasn't at all sure what to make of that. But there was no place to go except back to her bookstore and the familiar smell of old books.

The little bell rang when she opened the door. A Black woman was there, sitting in a chair by the front window, reading Robert Burton: *The Anatomy of Melancholy.* She looked up when Molly came in. "I hope you don't mind," she said. "Mr. Burton and I were just getting acquainted."

"Of course not," Molly said. "Stay as long as you like." She nodded at the book the woman was reading. "Why don't you keep it."

"I want to pay for it, please," the woman said.

"Five-fifty should cover it, then." Molly listened to herself speaking but she was still some other place, far away.

"Those are a lot of words for such a small sum. A person could get lost in the pages of a book like this and never come out."

Molly nodded. The word "lost" seemed to fill up her mind. She looked around the room. She noticed that someone had left fifteen dollars in the cookie tin. The big man or the student, perhaps. The rest of the cash remained in the till, of course. "Thanks for keeping an eye on the store."

"You were gone a long time."

"Yes." Molly wasn't even sure she was back yet. She hadn't thought about that winter night for so very long. And then there was Todd. Molly still didn't know how she was going to fold those feelings back into her life. But there it was.

The woman paid with a ten and accepted the change. "My name is Elsie Downey. I'll come back soon," she said.

"Please do."

"I'm reading all the classics now that I'm retired." The word "retired" was said with more dignity than one could expect from seven letters arranged on a straight line. "I was principal at Albert T. Barton Memorial Elementary, you know."

"I grew up an island and never went to school."

Elsie's eyes flashed, her fingers twitched on her purse.

"How was such a thing possible?"

"I did home-schooling. I read a great deal."

There was a nod of approval, congratulations, a tinge of new admiration.

"And now you have all this."

"I've lived a great deal of my life inside books."

"Nothing wasted in that," Principal Downey said and Molly could tell by her eyes that Elsie was remembering something difficult from the past, something about her job at the school. "I've seen lives wasted, you know. I learned to detect lives going the wrong way at the earliest deflection from the proper childhood path."

"Is that possible?"

"Oh, yes. Sometimes it's a sign as simple as chewing gum. I know it sounds foolish. But I've seen a good boy start out fresh with a keen intellect and a fit body and one day someone gives him a stick of gum. In no time at all, he's lost interest in literature. He has other interests."

In her mind's eye, Molly could see a classroom with all the desks and chairs turned upside down. She could see Elsie and her staff surveying wads of multicoloured gum glued to the underside of many of the desks. Elsie herself would be taking notes as if at the scene of a murder. The janitor was on hand with a hammer and chisel to remove the ossified gum.

"Anyway, I will be back for more of the classics after I consume all of what Mr. Burton has to say."

"Bye, now."

To Molly, it seemed that Elsie Downey disappeared as soon as she left the store. An old woman and her book became part of the landscape of the forgotten end of Winslow Street as the sun illuminated the afternoon with a coppery light.

It was very quiet in Molly's store for a while. Molly wrote a few cheques to pay bills and then dusted a shelf of foreign-language dictionaries with a feather duster. She sorted a box of old westerns brought in yesterday by a young boy who didn't look a day over ninety. She discovered a couple of first edition Zane Greys in hardback.

And then it was time for Dumpster Teeth. Molly looked forward to the arrival of Dumpster Teeth each Thursday at four-thirty. And here they were.

Leggo arrived first with his Ibanez guitar in a gig bag and his homemade practice amp made from plywood, stereo speakers, and the recycled guts of an ancient Fender Twin Reverb head. "Yo," he said.

Dart was behind him with his fretless Gretch bass. "It never worries," was Dart's proverbial introduction to his instrument if anyone asked. Trailing him was a big old Kustom amp on a skate board. A car stopped at the front door and a drum kit was hastily deposited onto the street; Sabian cymbals and high hat parts were scattered at the curb with the frenzy of jangled, brass flying saucers crash-landing in Halifax. The car sped off as the liftgate was slammed down and Reg collected as much percussion as he could and shovelled it through the front door of Molly's store and then hastily went back to the street a couple of times to get the rest.

"I'll make some tea," Molly offered.

"Try this," Leggo said. "I brought some red zinger. Thought you might be out."

"That was thoughtful."

Thoughtful was a most appropriate word. Dumpster Teeth was a very thoughtful alternative band. They broke the mold when it came to young, hip, and angry. They wore skater clothes and famous skateboard scars and wounds to go along with them. Their classmates at Queen Elizabeth High called Leggo, Dart and Reg "skids." Leggo had artificial red hair that was trimmed flat on top like a suburban lawn. Dart had a teenager's dark goatee, black moustache, and dark weasel shades that made him look like evil incarnate. Reg had three piercings in his lower lip, pale cadaver-like skin, and a mouth that turned downward as if he were forever making unfavourable judgments about the world around him and the people in it. They all wore baggy, ragged, ripped, and shredded T-shirts over long-sleeved, flannel shirts, with sandals and tie-dyed socks for their feet.

Molly plugged in the kettle by the sink located in the heart of the Canadiana section. Pierre Berton and Farley Mowat were there side by side with Charlie Farquharson and Michael Ondaatje. Molly wondered why she had never finished reading *The English Patient*. She turned away from the shelves to watch the band set up. She knew that, in a few minutes, the quiet little bookstore would explode with the ragged euphoria of distortion guitars, slap bass, the thunder of floor toms and kick. All to accompany songs about a world revolution of vegetarian good will.

That was the odd thing about Dumpster Teeth. Their politics. Diehard vegetarians, Dumpster Teeth lovingly cooked up mountains of meatless Indian dishes and served the food once a week from a rented van on Blowers Street to homeless kids and adults. Organic apple juice was served with handmade chapattis and curried dishes of rice, most of it cooked at Leggo's house.

Dart had explained to Molly that a lot of things were destroying the planet and Dumpster Teeth was making a musical stand against those things. Child labour in foreign countries sucked. So did CFCs. Genetic modification was worrisome and Dart was into saving "primitive seeds" so that when all the modern hybrids of grains and vegetables really screwed over the world's food basket, he'd have some of the old genuine stuff: stunted wheat, sea oats, crab apples, and stuff like that. They had a song about it called "Weeds Will Save Us" that everyone thought was pretty cool because listeners thought it was about smoking dope.

The kettle boiled and Molly served the red zinger in an earthenware teapot.

Dumpster Teeth was probably the only alternative band in Halifax that practiced in a bookstore.

Dumpster Teeth drank it straight without any sugar (what Leggo referred to as "white death") or dairy products. They had once shown Molly a master list of things they would never put in their mouths. They didn't chew gum either, and if Elsie Downey had been around, she would have been proud of these young men. It wasn't that Dumpster Teeth thought gum in and of itself was a deadly multinational plot. As Leggo explained it, they just thought gum was a waste of money that could be spent on whole wheat pita bread, hummus, or tahini.

Molly sorted Pierre Bertons from Farley Mowats and tucked Michael Ondaatje off in a corner with Mazo de La Roche. She was thinking of Todd, of course. How different a young man's life can be — compared to these boys in her store. And then Reg kicked his bass drum: *one, two, three, four.* And off they went.

The band was pretty raucous sometimes and neighbours would occasionally complain about how loud Molly's bookstore was on Thursday afternoons. It just didn't seem right to some people, living on the forgotten end of Winslow Street, that three skinny vegetarian kids would have to cause such a distraction while they were trying to watch *Oprah* or the afternoon soaps.

Molly was the best diplomat in the history of the world, though, so she could always smooth over ruffled feathers with neighbours or with the police. Besides, she never caused any real trouble except for condoning some occasional vegetarian noise.

After some serious jamming, Dumpster Teeth was ready to play its first anthem for its favourite audience: Molly and a bunch of old books. The song was called "Random Kindness." It was way too loud for all the neighbours trying to watch their silly televisions but the Teeth didn't care and neither did Molly.

As the song was barrelling towards its momentous conclusion, Molly looked up to see a Halifax police car stopping by the curb. She walked towards the door and peered out the glass window. A patrolman wearing a bulletproof vest was getting out of the car but then he saw her standing by the door. She had that look about her. He shook his head, attempted a friendly smile in her direction, and then got back in the patrol car and drove off toward the far south end of Winslow Street, and that was that.

Dumpster Teeth was safe and sound, free now to finish another practice session unmolested by authorities but, despite the volume, Molly was not the attentive and appreciative audience that she usually was.

CHAPTER TWELVE

ERIC AWOKE AT NINE O'CLOCK IN the evening, reached for a notepad, and wrote down his dream. He could figure out part of it — the ice pan and the arctic landscape, nothing too mysterious about those origins — but the man on the RCMP boat, that was something else. He made a sketch of the boat and the man, not a very good sketch but something to keep the image fresh.

When he stood up, Eric felt an overwhelming sense of purpose. A clarity of things. His mistakes were clearly in front of him now. This clarity of vision was not such a bad thing. Eric discerned he was one of those men who appeared to be quite successful, but deep down he was unfulfilled. That was why he had gone north to die. But he had botched that somehow as well. He had ambled towards death rather than running straight towards it. His purpose in dying had not been clear enough. Having failed at a good arctic death, he was certain now that his only option was to embrace life, despite the fact that he didn't think he had the tools, the gumption, or the courage.

There were a handful of clues before him, however. They were seemingly random, but enough to start with. There was Ray and his grandfather. There was the dream, the ship and a man with a beard who had spoken to him. He tried to sketch again what he remembered of the man, the captain of that funny-looking ship. The eyes, the nose, the beard.

A cool evening breeze swept into the room through the open window. It had rained. There was the sound of car tires slurping at the water on the asphalt. It was a clear, rich sound, and there was the smell of wet pavement too.

In the morning, Eric headed for the National Archives. First he walked up to the front doors of Parliament, for no particular reason, other than the fact that it was there. As was common, protestors were shouting near the front steps, facing the building as if those very doors and windows were somehow responsible for the problems they were angry about. What was it today? Unfair unemployment insurance rules? Income tax? Fishing regulations? Eric envied the protestors their passions and wondered if he might find something to get really angry about, if that might help him in some way.

A long, black car pulled up and the prime minister got out. Jean Chrétien waved to the crowd of protestors as if they were his fan club, while they booed and hissed and allowed themselves to be held at bay by the Mounties. Eric studied the faces of the RCMP officers to see if one of them was the man he had seen in his dream, but none of them looked at all familiar.

Chrétien was ushered into the Parliament Building beneath the grey sky and, as if on cue, it began to rain. The protestors huddled together and lit cigarettes as if that was thing to do to ward off the weather. Eric walked back to the street and dodged large bullets of rain by ducking under store canopies until he made his way to the National Archives. He showed them his university ID and his archives pass, and then walked to a familiar room that smelled of old books, stale documents, and failed dreams.

Eric was an efficient researcher and he was ably assisted by a young woman in a pleated skirt and white blouse who wore her hair in a bun. Eric had met her once before. She was someone who was undoubtedly very attractive but had purposefully made herself seem less so. Eric liked her and wanted to give her a compliment but didn't quite know how. Instead, slightly embarrassed, he showed her the sketch of the ship in his dream. She asked if she could take it with her. Eric said yes. She disappeared and left him with a pile of old books to root through.

When she returned, she brought with her a photograph of a ship, a rather unpretentious two-masted sailing ship of some sort. Eric looked closely and squinted: *St. Roch* was painted on the bow. Eric asked the young woman if there were any other pictures associated with the ship. He discovered she had already pulled the full file for him. There were more pictures of the boat, at port in Vancouver, amidst ice fields. And then a mug shot of her captain: Henry Larsen. The ship and the man didn't perfectly match the ones he had seen in his dream. But they were damn close.

Eric thanked her profusely and left. Then he went into the reference library and looked up *St. Roch* and its captain, Henry Larsen, in the *Oxford Companion of Ships and the Sea*. There he discovered that on the twenty-third of June in 1940, Henry Larsen and his crew had sailed the *St. Roch* out of Vancouver, north to the Bering Strait, and then east through arctic ice fields. He did not arrive at his east coast destination port until October 11, 1942. He had left Vancouver and taken the hard way to Halifax, through the Northwest Passage. That was what Larsen was doing in his dream. He was sailing — the first man to ever accomplish the task — west to east through the Northwest Passage. He was heading to Halifax over the top of the world.

Eric had never in his life been accused of being impulsive. Even his trip to Baffin Island had been well planned. But this decision to move to Halifax was entirely different. On his departure date, in the dim morning light of his bedroom, his brain snagged once or twice as he was about to put his two feet on the floor to pursue the impulse . . . or not. Eric was lying in bed with the sheet pulled up over his head. Waiting for an answer.

It arrived.

Not thunder, not lightning, no quivering of the mortal planet, or blast of solar light into his room. Instead, the surprisingly powerful thud of a small bird flying directly into the glass of his bedroom window. This, apparently, was enough to make a middle-aged man in hiding decide it was time to act. There he was, up and breathing deeply, two feet on the floor, and ready for anything. Legs into pants, bare feet padding down the hall and outside, around the back. The air smelled surprisingly sweet with the perfume of damp grass, fading flowers, and leaf mulch. He spotted the bird. It was a vireo — yellow and black. Eric picked up the sorry traveller and held it in the palm of his hand. He felt like he was about to cry.

Then he realized he was being watched. A neighbour's Siamese cat was studying him from beneath a backyard hydrangea. Ancient eyes, hunger. "Sorry, you can't have him," Eric said.

Eric cradled the bird in his cupped hands. He turned and walked around the house. As he put one bare foot upon the cold concrete of the front step, the bird stirred within his warm human cage. Feet scratched, wings fluttered. Eric opened his hands and the vireo stood up on wiry legs and looked at him. Then the bird flew rapidly up into the sky, disappearing almost immediately into the clouds.

Eric looked up into the sky with wonder. A smile began to appear on his face. The very next intake of air into his lungs felt somehow different. He turned and walked purposefully back into his house. Once inside, he phoned a taxi and then ate half a bowl of cornflakes. Ten minutes later he heard the taxi's horn. He grabbed his wallet from the top of the fridge and he was almost out the door before he decided the only thing he lacked was reading material. He grabbed three dusty books at random from the hallway shelves and stuffed them into a plastic Loblaw's bag.

The Lebanese taxi driver was listening to rap music — Puff Daddy. He turned it down from a massive urban thunder to something that reminded Eric of a washing machine spinning a very unbalanced load.

"No luggage?" the driver asked.

"No."

"Usually people going to the airport have some kind of suitcase or something."

"Just this," he said, holding up the plastic bag. "I like to travel light."

"Good plan. I try to convince my wife of this."

"Usually, I take too much too. I plan things too well. Not anymore."

"Sometimes it's good to prepare yourself for whatever."

"Oh, don't worry, I'm prepared." Eric suddenly realized he was smiling again.

And he was still smiling when he walked up to the ticket counter at Air Canada.

"The next flight to Halifax is in forty minutes. We can still get you on if you like."

"Great." He slipped the ticket agent his Visa card and when all was done, he was amazed at the cost of buying a last-minute ticket for an hour and a half flight. He walked straight to Gate 23 and onto the plane. He sat down in his assigned seat and opened up the Loblaw's bag to see which books he had selected for the journey. And what an odd trio he had grabbed: *Finnegan's Wake* by James Joyce, *Moby Dick* by Herman Melville, and *Bleak House* by Charles Dickens.

Once they were aloft, Eric felt buoyant. He was thinking about Davey Crockett. When he was a kid, he had become obsessed with the American frontiersman. Disney had put Davey Crockett on TV. That had gotten the ball rolling. Then there were Davey Crockett cards. (Could he still taste the pink bubblegum in his mouth? Yes, he could.) He'd had a Davey Crockett, raccoon-skin cap that was worn to school with immense pride.

In his ten-year-old mind, Eric had *become* Davey Crockett and if you had asked him where he was born, the answer would have been, "Born on a mountain top in Tennessee." Not long after that, something or someone had murdered his imagination. Not any single event. Maybe it was just something about his environment that had vacuumed the life out of his imagination as effectively as if he'd had a lobotomy. What or who did this to him? Was it school? Fluoride in the water? Middle-class life in suburban Ottawa? But there would be no courtroom hearing, no medical inquiry. It was all in the past now.

The pilot came on to speak in that amazingly relaxed monotone voice. He sounded a bit like Margaret Atwood on Quaaludes. How relaxed do you have to be to fly a plane, these days? The pilot was happy that Eric and his travelling companions were flying Air Canada. He explained how high in the sky they were flying and that there was temperature and wind and that the weather was doing one thing or the other in Halifax. And he assured them it would be a pleasant flight.

It didn't much matter to Eric. Henry Larsen had been heading to Halifax and now so was he. Eric thumbed open the copy of *Moby Dick* and smelled the dust that had been residing inside the book with Ahab and the whale for many years. On a blank page near the back of the book — directly across from the epilogue with the quote from Job: "And I only am escaped alone to tell thee . . . " — Eric wrote,

Things to do:
1. Rent a small apartment downtown
2. Become a vegetarian
3. Buy some books
4. Live each day as if it is my last
5. See what else happens.

It was the "See what else happens" that pleased him the most. Eric read part of the epilogue of the novel. Somebody was floating around an ocean on the back of a coffin. Then he looked up and made another note to himself:

Item: catch up on ships and sea stuff – maritime history, pirates, privateers, famous gales, famous disasters, men of the sea.

Books would provide clues for him; he knew this instinctively, now that he had sloughed off the chains of reason and order that had been keeping him tethered to conformity all his life.

He closed Ishmael's story and opened *Finnegan*: "riverrun, past Eve and Adams, from swerve of shore to bend of bay, brings us by a commodious vicus of recirculation back to Howth Castle and Environs."

Below, the clouds supported the language of Joyce; they conferred and approved and pillowed it so it need not fall to earth but could comfortably shadow the DC 10 on its direct route to Halifax. *Riverrun the sky*. Another note:

Item: books, language, circuitry of imagination, maps, pathways to elemental things, buried objects/buried ideas, incommodious excess to be tossed to the winds at thirty thousand feet.

Joyce was placed beside Melville as if the two were old chums on the empty seat beside Eric. In his now nimble mind, Eric reshuffled titles: *Moby Wake* and *Finnegan's Dick*. Yes, why not.

He almost laughed out loud. Eric's eyes grew misty with a kind of warm insanity lighting up small campfires of euphoria inside his head. He wondered if this was what it was like to lose one's mind. And he began to think about his father again. And then one more note:

Item: pilgrimage. Let the guides be the winds, the words, the nomads, and the explorers who have gone before.

CHAPTER THIRTEEN

MOLLY FELT SOMETHING AKIN TO A religious experience each time she approached the door to her store. It was, after all, her world. It was her literary island in a sea of non-literary otherness. The feel of the cold, rain-wet, brass door handle sometimes made her think of the cold, wet stones of Devil's Island on a summer day. And that made it feel even more like home.

Inside, as Molly was straightening a stack of books, she watched through the window a woman approaching her store. The woman paused. She was not looking at the store or up at the sign above. She was looking straight ahead, down the road, but Molly knew she was considering the possibility of going in and something was preventing her. The woman looked to be seventy or older. An old woman in good health, by the way she carried herself. An old woman with something on her mind. She wore a long, lady's coat, despite the warmth of the day, and it seemed like a coat from another century. Dumpster Teeth referred to old people who wore clothes from way back as Time Travellers.

And then the old woman turned suddenly, put her hand upon the brass door handle, and entered the store in one quick thrust of herself as if she were a gunman about to rob the place. She surveyed the room, eyes darting to all four corners, before settling on Molly whose hands rested like small doves on the open pages of a book.

Molly understood that this was not simply a customer looking for a guidebook to Halifax or a French-English dictionary. The woman had a strong face, dark eyes, shadows in the hollows of her cheeks. She seemed determined, a little arrogant maybe, but then, as she tried to speak, she appeared bewildered, lost.

"Can I help you?" Molly asked politely.

The woman seemed frantic. Her hands fumbled with the catch on an old, black leather purse, opened it, took out a card. "Harriet Fitzhenry," it read. The older woman said the name rather loudly and with a British accent.

Molly thought it was the name of an author the old woman was looking for. The name didn't ring any bells. "Do you know the title of the book?"

The old woman shook her head emphatically, seemed annoyed now. She put the card back in her purse. Having regained her composure, she spoke aggressively. "*I* am Harriet Fitzhenry. I know I appear foolish at times. But I forget my name. It takes me a second to remember to look into my purse and when I do, well, you saw for yourself."

"We're all a little forgetful," Molly said. "Could I get you a cup of tea?"

Harriet fixed Molly with her piercing eyes. "This is not a social call." The accent was even more pronounced, the voice almost belligerent.

Molly was puzzled. She didn't understand why the old woman was being rude.

"Forgive me," Harriet Fitzhenry said. "I'm here to see you about a very grave concern."

Molly had not a clue as to what that concern could be.

The purse clicked open again and the old woman's pale hand, with its pale flesh, rigid knuckles, and blue prominent veins, reached in and pulled out a newspaper clipping. Harriet moved forward and laid it on the counter, meticulously unfolding it, smoothing it with her ancient hands.

The clipping was yellow and partially disintegrated. It was a photograph of a young man beneath a headline that read, "Son of Financier Dies in Plane Crash."

Molly stopped breathing. She reached out to touch the piece of paper but it seemed so very far away. She had not thought about that incident for such a long time. But then something about being with Todd had made her tell the story. And now this. As if the revealing of those events had brought this strange woman into her life. It had to be more than coincidence. Molly didn't know what to say.

"The headline was misleading," Harriet said. "Leave it to *The Times* to put it that way. As if there was not a mother, only a father."

"Your son?" In Molly's mind she was young again and fighting with the breaking waves to keep Harriet's son from being pulled back into the sea.

"And it was your family who found him, I believe."

Molly swallowed.

"Was it your mother or your father? Which one pulled him ashore?"

"I did. My mother and father tried to help the others. I found him."

"I lived through the scene many times, but I always thought it was a man who found him. You must have been just a girl at the time."

"I was. It was unlike anything . . . " She trailed off, not sure if it would be good to explain.

"What did he look like? When you found him."

"He'd been in the sea quite a while."

"I'm sorry. I've lived with this for so long. I've harboured images that crowd out other things in my mind. I can walk in here and forget my own name, but I can never forget how I imagined the death of my son. The storm, the crash, then alone in the cold sea. And washing up. All I knew was that he was found by the family that kept the light."

"My parents are both gone now."

Harriet set her purse on the floor and rubbed her temples with the palms of her hands. "Parents have a habit of doing that to their children. I'm sorry they have left you. About my son, did you learn his name? Did they ever tell you his name?"

"I read it in a newspaper someone brought out to the island a few days after. Bertrand Fitzhenry."

"Did that seem like an unusual name to you?"

"It did at the time. Very formal."

"Stuffy, you mean?"

"A little."

"I picked the name Bertrand, like Bertrand Russell, you know. Perhaps you have some of his books here. Fitzhenry, of course, was my husband. The financier." She pronounced the word with some malice. "A better man with money than with family, but I have no great complaints of that. We both knew what we were getting into when we married."

"Is he in the city with you?"

A shake of the old woman's head — an almost frightening motion of a such a delicate thing. "Gone. And I have the sad fate of having descended from a line of long-lived antecedents. Eighty, ninety, with my luck I'll live to be a hundred. Nothing is fair, is it?"

"Let me get you that cup of tea."

Harriet picked up the newspaper clipping. She put it into her purse, closed it, looked away and then opened it again. Took out the little card with her name written on it and placed it on the counter. "I should go."

"Not yet. You didn't come all this way just for that."

Molly led Harriet to the comfortable, worn chair by the front window. She gently settled Mrs. Fitzhenry into it, studying her, looking for similarities to the young man who had washed in on the waves. Molly went for tea and when she returned, Harriet looked rather peaceful in the sun with a tattoo of prism light across her cheek.

LESLEY CHOYCE

"I wonder if you'd be willing to do an old woman a favour."
"Certainly."
"Tell me about that night. Every detail you can remember. This may seem perverse of me but I want to know the truth for once."

And so Molly brought the tall stool out from behind the counter and told Harriet what she needed to know.

She described the discovery of the dead for a second time and again explained how they were brought into the house and put into beds. In the morning, the Coast Guard ship came to carry away the bodies of the air crash victims. Molly felt she had said all there was to say, except for the fact that something about Bertrand had haunted her all her life. She believed it had something to do with why she had had so few relationships with men and why she'd never married.

"Had he survived," Harriet began, "had Bertrand survived, he would have done great things."

"I'm very sure of that." Molly now remembered the treacherous mental whirlpool she had fallen into after the Coast Guard boat had loaded those dead bodies wrapped in canvas. It had almost drowned her, this whirlpool. *Had he survived* . . . he would have fallen in love with her. They would have lived on the island. Nothing else would have mattered. Sometimes she had fantasized that Bertrand was *supposed* to have survived the crash — the only survivor. She was *supposed* to save him but she had somehow failed.

That's what literature had done to her. Stories. In purposeful fiction, everything meant something. Not like the random chaos of real life.

Outside, traffic seemed to have gone into slow motion. There were no more customers that Thursday afternoon.

"Had he survived," Mrs. Fitzhenry continued, "he would have accomplished great things. He had insisted on coming to Canada to study. Here at your Dalhousie University. He wished to do a degree in geology. He had a passion for stones

· 92 ·

and for rocks. He said the rocks of the UK held no interest for him. But the rocks of Newfoundland, or Nova Scotia, or the Arctic, well, that was a different matter. His father tried to persuade the boy that making money was far more intriguing — 'more challenging' my late-great husband would say — than cracking open old stones.

"I myself was glad Bertrand was leaning away from a life in the financial district. He seemed to care very little for money or even the things it could do — aside from sending him to Canada to learn about rocks. Do you know what he told me? I remember this as clear as if he were in the room right now. He said, 'Mother, when Gondwana split up, most of it shifted east millennia ago and became Africa. But part of it was left behind and converged with North America.' It was not a point I could see any excitement in, but Bertrand did. He said to me that the slate beneath the Nova Scotian soil is the exact same slate as that beneath a mosque in Morocco."

Molly remembered the cold, wet slate: the bedrock above the reach of the waves. It was easier to skid the body across that smooth, flat stone than to lug it along the unstable, sinking sand. Bertrand had left England with its boring geology and arrived at both North America and Africa at once. "What is an island for?" her father had often asked of himself out loud and then answered himself as well. "An island is a refuge for things. A place for things to wash up on, a place to put a light and warn sailors of danger, an asylum where one can live sensibly apart from his fellow man and all the madness. A place to live a life with your own worries instead of the thousand worries of your neighbours. What do you think an island is for, Molly?"

He had asked her this in the style of a family ritual over and over again through many years of her life. Molly changed her answer continually to entertain both herself and him. "An island is to walk around. An island is for rabbits. An island is for feeling scared and lonely and being afraid it will be swallowed by the sea. An island is a natural studio where the sea sculpts the stones into art."

"Bertrand's father scoffed at Bertrand's preoccupations as he called them. We were at the dinner table. 'What have we done, Harriet?' he asked. 'Have we raised ourselves a young Victorian rock hound with a penchant for geological trivia?' But it was not trivia, of course. Bertrand took himself and his concerns very seriously. He had other interests as well: anthropology, medieval literature, philosophy. He was truly named for Bertrand Russell. I wasn't kidding. That was my idea, although I never owned up to it to His Majesty."

"Do you miss your husband?"

"Some. Enough to travel with his remains, I suppose. A scoop of ashes in a sealed urn in my suitcase. It must mean I miss him deeply, despite his shortcomings."

Molly poured some more tea, and now she saw the aura around Harriet. She saw something that made her seem illuminated from within. Molly believed that everything had some sort of energy field; at least that is what she had convinced herself. "I'm so happy you came to see me," Molly said with conviction.

"My husband was very good at making money. He said he did that for me. It was a bit of a burden, really, and now I let others take care of the details. Sometimes it can be a chore even to give money away. But the sad irony, or perhaps the beautiful irony, I don't know which, is that Ethan, so very full of himself and his success, proved to be even better at making money after he was dead than while he was alive."

"We all have our gifts," Molly said.

"He blamed himself for the crash. It was a private plane carrying one of his business friends here to Halifax. Bertrand could have gone first class on British Airways but preferred to go in a smaller plane with Ethan's friend who had the shipping interests here."

Molly understood now that it must have been the portly man with the umbrella.

Harriet Fitzhenry opened up her purse yet again, as though she was about to reveal some powerful secret she'd been toting around all her life. The woman's old hands gingerly dipped into the purse and drew out a document. "Bertrand might have become a fine writer if he set his mind to it. You know how some people have writing in their soul — it's just there, and the language spills out. That was Bertrand. He wrote this essay for one of his classes at school, but his instructor said it was too fanciful. Bertrand refused to rewrite it and received an F. I thought it was his best work. That's why I've kept it with me all these years. Would you care to read it?"

"Certainly," Molly said. Harriet held out the folded yellowed pages. When Molly touched the paper, she felt a small thrill of electricity race down her spine.

"Would you mind if I just sat here and rested for a little bit?" Mrs. Fitzhenry asked. "The sunlight feels so luxurious." The word *luxurious* had never been spoken before in her shop. Molly was certain of that. She felt the sound of the syllables do curious things to the surroundings. The whole place did seem more elegant now, with old books and sunlight and a fine elderly woman from England. And then Harriet Fitzhenry closed her eyes and fell asleep, her teacup still in her hand, the silver spoon glinting ribbons of light. Molly removed the teacup, even though it looked as if Harriet could wield it through sleep. And Molly sat down on a bench beside Harriet and began to read.

Chapter Fourteen

Martin Frobisher
by Bertrand Fitzhenry

Martin Frobisher was born in 1535 and when he was only fourteen he found himself on an expedition to West Africa in Her Majesty's employment. Martin was a quick learner and a quick-tempered, violent young man. He learned all there was to learn about sea life — swearing, cheating, hard drinking, and some useful things about how to sail a ship a thousand miles from port if need be, how to keep from puking when the seas got rough, how to endure the worst things that indifferent nature could send at them. In West Africa, the young Frobisher nearly met his death, and as death began to put its first mask of comforting darkness over his face, he felt an odd sensation of cold welling up inside him. The darkness and the cold were somehow beautiful and familiar and he greatly preferred it to the heat of equatorial climes. And then something had wrenched him back to consciousness and he lost track of what he had found in those brief seconds, except for the fact that he believed he had "gone somewhere"; he had sailed off to some place far and away and that he would return there if he could.

Frobisher grew into a proper sea dog, an Elizabethan "adventurer" who did not object to taking orders, especially if it involved plundering an innocent ship flying the wrong colours on her mast. He sailed well, fought hard, collected admirable scars on all parts of his anatomy, suffered valiantly through numerous diseases of sea and land, knew fevers and madness and sometimes good, stolid health. He cultivated his own magnificent indifference to the plight of those who suffered or those he made to suffer. The sea itself had taught him to be indifferent, uncaring of the damage that could be inflicted on the spirit and well-being of any man.

By 1576, Martin Frobisher had garnered considerable military favour and some authority around the influential circles of court. Along with other naval captains, he had studied a wide range of maps with imperfect renderings of seas and islands and coastlines and knew that he must sail to the west and discover whatever was to be found in those smudged territories of *terra incognita*. Many a mapmaker of the day had gone ahead and sketched out guesswork coastlines and imaginary islands, whole continents of possible shapes and sizes, and embellished their maps with inaccurate pictures of porcupines and ridiculous-looking sea birds and land animals with six feet and long snouts, or frightening, giant, fierce mammals with fur and tusks. And if you believed these maps, the seas were filled with dragons and fish the size of houses and crazy impossible things with eighty tentacles and evil eyes.

Nonetheless, in June of 1576, Martin sailed off north and west towards unknown lands in a ship called *Gabriel*, named for an angel. In his mind's eye, he saw a passage north and west, a navigable route between islands and land masses that would take him directly to China and bring him fame and, of course, fortune.

When Frobisher first spied the ice of the Arctic, the jagged white peaks like crystalline sailing vessels, he fell madly in love with their beauty. West of Greenland, he sailed north. He saw the coast of Labrador and its snow-capped mountains and advised against going ashore there. He later claimed it was peopled by fierce pygmies who sharpened their teeth to knife points, but his men knew he was lying. Frobisher had no fear of men with sharpened teeth, sea dragons, cataclysmic storms, God, or the devil. The truth was he wanted to find his route to China, or sail off the end of the earth doing so.

It wasn't until August that he and a handful of men rowed ashore on a craggy island that he believed was some remote part of Asia. He climbed a hill with a small English flag on a pole and surveyed this bright, barren Orient with a feeling of pride and power that stirred his blood. It was a cold, clear day. Frobisher was far from home and savoured the sensation of everything here that was new and different. As he walked back down from the hill top, he met the citizens of that place. Their skin had a coppery hue. They wore the furs of animals and wielded weapons with stone tips. The first exchange between two worlds of men went fairly well. No one was killed. The Inuit were polite and cautious. Frobisher saw no dwellings about, no houses, no towns, no sign of civilization. He wondered if God had dropped them down out of the sky on that afternoon to challenge him.

From his pocket, Frobisher pulled a small gold coin and held it out. A gift. One of the copper men with a heavy brow reached out and took it, smiled cautiously with unsharpened teeth, and passed it on to the other three in his hunting party. Then the Inuit man surprised Frobisher by squatting down and poking about in the soil with the tip of his spear.

The man plucked something from the earth and stood upright, spit on the rock he had found, rubbed it to dry on the fur of his garment, and handed it to the Englishman. It glinted in the afternoon sunlight and Frobisher now knew that he had not only found a new route to China but that he had discovered an island made of gold as well.

Back on board the *Gabriel*, Martin sent a man named Chris Hall ashore to bargain with the Native population. Hall packed off with mirrors, small cheap toys from London, and jewellery like one would find on a woman of the streets. With such gifts, several Inuit were lured back to the ship and came aboard. A handful of Inuit hunters were persuaded to help guide the *Gabriel* even deeper into waters unknown to the English, and five sailors rowed them back ashore to prepare for their first voyage on an English ship.

When the sailors did not return, Frobisher assumed they had been tricked. The copper men must be cannibals after all. When a lone Inuit hunter appeared by the side of the *Gabriel* in his kayak, the captain had his men snatch him aboard.

Martin Frobisher locked up the poor man, and fielded suggestions from his men about what to do next. In his private quarters he pondered the several golden rocks in his possession and considered his three victories worth preserving: discovery of a clear route to China, a human specimen of an unknown culture, and the discovery of an island of gold. They would return home.

Audience was arranged with Queen Elizabeth herself and she marvelled at the copper man, applauded Frobisher's expeditionary prowess, and became enchanted with the idea of an entire island of gold that would be in the possession of her empire. The Spanish monarch, plundering the rich, gold store-houses of the southern Americas, would be ever so jealous.

As far as everyone in London was concerned, Martin Frobisher had found the Northwest Passage. Mapmakers furiously reshaped the known world on paper and sketched in illustrations of Frobisher's fur-clad hostage, already dying from contact with European diseases.

Frobisher basked in his fame but didn't get the satisfaction he expected from his fortune. He cared little for the soft, decadent life at home. Meanwhile, greed had fired the imagination and loosened the purse strings for another voyage back to what would one day be known as Baffin Island. So he was more than glad for the opportunity to sail off again with 120 men under his command in 1577. Onboard were five unlucky miners who would chip and chisel away at the New World until two hundred tons of it became healthy ballast for the trip home to England. Wealth beyond dreams was the freight that Frobisher would sail into English waters. But not before one sharp-eyed Inuit hunter, equipped with bow and arrow, planted a razor-edged, stone-tipped arrow into Frobisher's right buttock.

The heavily-laden ships sailed their precious freight back to England, but the experts there claimed that there seemed to be no way to extract the pure gold from the ore. The usual methods of refining had failed. The gold of the Northwest was of a strange breed with magical powers that would not allow it to be unlocked. It was not affected by heat or acid. But nobody was about to call Frobisher or the Queen a fool despite the massive load of worthless iron pyrite that had been hauled across the Atlantic. Instead, the lure of the newly-found lands infected the gentry, stimulating literature and conversation alike.

Unable to get the bloody gold out of the damnable rocks, Frobisher unwittingly bankrupted his loyal patron, a man named Michael Lok. Nonetheless, Frobisher's reputation as an adventurer remained unscathed. After a while he decided to go back to what he did best: plunder and murder. So he threw his efforts into helping the ruthless Sir Francis Drake sink portions of the Spanish Armada in the West Indies and slit the throats of Spanish sailors onboard ships and on beaches in whatever corner of the world they could be found.

Such unbridled violence, murder, and mayhem brought him more glory from the Queen, who rather fancied Frobisher's bloodthirsty ambitions. She held no grudge whatever about the stubbornness of Frobisher's gold. Instead, she knighted him for bravery. Martin Frobisher continued to fight his Spanish adversaries until infections to a wound received at the Spanish fort at Crozon finally sent him to his deathbed in 1594.

When Frobisher first felt the familiar tingle of cold beginning to consume the fever that was devouring him, he may have remembered his first close encounter with death in Africa. And as he closed his eyes, he must have envisioned those distant mountain peaks of white-blue ice and felt the cool, pleasurable chill of arctic waters seeping into the veins of his arms and legs. There was an island of gold, he believed, a million tons of it, still waiting there for the taking, unguarded and unclaimed by anyone but him and his Queen. And he tasted his own blood as he bit his tongue and found it salty and cool. As he swallowed, he felt both proud and calm and as he closed his eyes more tightly, he sailed off into a pure arctic dimension of white where pain and pleasure were one, a place where cruelty and kindness blended into a single, perfect, frozen union.

Molly blinked as she looked up from the pages of Bertrand's essay. It was an odd piece of history, and one that incorporated plenty of the author's own musings. But what, if anything, did it reveal about the young man who had written it? And why would his mother carry it around in her purse with her long after her son had drowned? Proof that she once had a son who had a mind of his own and a fascination with the past?

In the back of Molly's mind there was an imaginary conversation arising: the one she might have had with Bertrand had he washed up alive on her island on that dreadful winter night. The one that would have begun with Molly saying to him, "Nothing is ever as it appears . . ."

When the door burst open and Leggo galumphed into the store with his practice amp, his guitar and a hockey bag of gear, Molly suddenly remembered it was Thursday and four-thirty at that. Leggo saw the old woman asleep and tried to make less noise. He set his gear down and whispered a hello to Molly.

"She's asleep."

"Time travellers look cool when they're asleep like that. My grandmother falls asleep in a chair just like she does. My grandmother knows more about stuff than all my teachers in high school combined."

Dart and Reg arrived after that and none of Dumpster Teeth knew what to do about practice since there was an old lady asleep in the bookstore. And Molly had never once told Dumpster Teeth to cancel practice or go somewhere else.

"We could cancel," Leggo said.

"But we do have the gig at the Café tomorrow night," Dart reminded him.

"Nobody can tell if we're at our best or not," Leggo said. "They don't even notice mistakes."

"Still, we have a reputation to keep up."

And then Leggo had an idea. He hauled out of his gig bag a small mixer and a ganglion of earbud earphones. "We do this," he said.

"What about me?" Reg asked.

"Miniature Octopads," Leggo said, rooting around in his hockey bag. "My mother bought them for me. Here, plug them into the mixer."

So there it was. Reg could pound on the eight rubber pads, Dart could thump thunder through the mixer, and Leggo would play raunchy guitar chords that only they would hear.

Dumpster Teeth fussed and finagled with chords and headsets and effects units. Reg had a hard time getting himself comfortable until he sat up on a stool behind the cash register and put the Octopads down on top of two small pillars of *The Elements of Style.*

"I can just mime the lyrics," Dart said. "Nobody listens to our words much anyway."

And so they tuned up, warmed up and played a silent set to the bookshelves as Harriet Fitzhenry slept in the sunlight.

"This is incredibly weird," Dart whispered.

"Weird, but cool," Reg added.

Molly sat by the front window pricing books:

The Creative Process $2.50

Drugs: What You should Know $1.95

Tristram Shandy $5

A hardback edition of Michener's *Hawaii* $4.50

The Viking Portable Emerson $7.50

People walking by probably didn't quite understand why three teenagers were miming alternative music inside a bookstore, making no sound at all, while a delicate old woman slept in a stuffed chair by the front window. It was pretty weird for sure, but Molly noted that a couple of art college students stopped to watch from outside and they probably thought it was some kind of performance art.

CHAPTER FIFTEEN

As ERIC WALKED THROUGH THE AIRPORT in Halifax, he was surprised to see that an airport could be such a happy place. Security guards looked like they were on Prozac picnics. Mild-looking men in business suits with Buddha faces stared into the screens of their laptops. There were dark men in African robes and pinkish European faces too — German maybe or Swiss, with shiny skin stretched over balding skulls. Everybody seemed to be happy. Laughing gas pumped through the ventilation? What was it?

But after a few minutes, he began to realize that the euphoria he thought he had been witnessing was not really in the people around him. It was *his* euphoria projected onto them. He was the one experiencing this intense joy.

The sounds of families and their rolling luggage carts was downright symphonic to his ears. Surrounded by the mass choir of human noise and all the accompanying orchestration of the airport, Eric thought he could again hear the sound of the Arctic — the sound of cold singing in his ears. The bright blue notes, the song that been with him when he was dying, a beautiful sound that he had grown to assume only arose at the portal of death but now he appreciated how wrong he was. The sound of cold singing was also the sound of living: this place, this soulful, droning, harmonic song of nomads. He picked up a newspaper left by a fellow traveller. The pages were folded back to the classifieds: houses for sale, apartments for rent. He let his eyes rove down the columns until he saw this: "Quiet one bedroom apartment for gent or lady, one block from downtown library."

The library made it seem just right. He walked to a payphone and punched in the number. A man with a Newfoundland accent assured him the apartment was just what he wanted. "No drugs or dogs, though. None of that stuff."

"No, I promise. When is it available?"

"Nothing stopping a person from moving in any time. It's not spic and span if you know what I'm saying, thanks to the fella who left 'er that way but I've swept it up and opened a few windows."

"I'll be right there. I'm at the airport. Where shall I tell the taxi driver to go?"

"Grafton, near Blowers. He'll know that. The room is right across from the church. It's just above a store called The Black Market. You'll need to leave an extra month's rent if you want to move in right away — security deposit. Ya know how that is."

Ryan's Taxi took Eric downtown. The driver, Oscar Ryan, according to his ID card on the dash, claimed to have been a roadie for the rock group, Rush. He wondered out loud if the world was getting more fucked up or if he just wasn't as optimistic as he used to be.

"I never could get used to the nineties," he said, condemning an entire decade with a look into the rear-view mirror. "Or the eighties for that matter. The sixties were okay and so was a fair part of the seventies. Then came disco and bad television and . . . I don't know, maybe it's just me. Sometimes I feel like I was born into the wrong century."

"I know that feeling well," Eric conceded.

"'Angels and demons dancing in my head / Lunatics and monsters underneath my bed.'"

"Excuse me?"

"It's a line from a Rush song. What is it that brought you to Halifax?"

"I haven't fully figured that out yet. Ever hear of Henry Larsen?"

"Hockey player?"

"No. Sailed a RCMP boat to Halifax from Vancouver through the Northwest Passage."

"Nobody ever told me this. Was this like recently?"

"In the forties."

"I think I might have liked the forties. The music was good. People had attitude. But they had that fucking war. Still, it was probably better than the fifties, what I remember of it. So you gonna link up with this frostbitten Mountie, or something?"

"No, I think he's dead. He's just part of some kind of pilgrimage I'm on."

"Why come here? Why not India?"

"All the indicators were pointing towards Halifax."

"You must be into some heavy shit."

"Know of any good used bookstores in Halifax? I'm going to do a lot of reading. Stuff on the Arctic. Maybe I'll luck onto something about Larsen's voyage."

Oscar Ryan scratched his jaw in a ponderous, clinical way. He tilted his head back towards his passenger. "You believe in angels?"

"I could."

"After you get settled in, go down to the south end of Winslow Street. There's a bookstore there. You'll walk right by it the first time. It's like fucking invisible, I swear. Very low-key. But go in. She'll be working there. She's read every book in the world, I think. Knows everything. She'll find something on your man Larsen. I went in there once looking for a book by Leonard Cohen. I was going out with this ageing, hippie chick who went nuts over anything by Leonard Cohen. The lady in the bookstore quoted me the entire lyrics from 'Famous Blue Raincoat.' I'll tell ya, I was losing interest in my

Leonard Cohen fan by the time I left. But I never went back. She was out of my league."

They arrived in the city which seemed to hum with a gentle urban resonance. The cab stopped in front of the store, The Black Market, which turned out to be a kind of throw-back to the sixties. "You need a hash pipe? That's the place to go to," Oscar offered. "You say your apartment is upstairs?"

Eric looked up the face of the two-story brick building. The windows were open, a curtain sifted out into the city air. "It looks like I'm home." Across the street, skateboarders were launching themselves from the metal hand railing leading up to the church and landing with a loud *thwack*.

"You sure this is the place you're renting?"

"Yep. I like it. It fits the pilgrimage."

Eric paid the driver and Oscar flipped him a card. "You need a ride or anything, give me a call. I'm not in the phone book. I operate on my own."

Chapter Sixteen

Todd's mother stays overnight sometimes, and she tries to cheer him up. He doesn't see his father that often, though, because of his work. But Todd still spends a lot of time alone. On bad days, he becomes part of the walls, the floor, and the furniture. On really bad days, he feels so sick he wants to be unconscious and so he'll increase the drip of the painkiller until he drifts off. Nobody talks to him about actually leaving the hospital anymore, but he knows that soon he'll end a round of chemo treatment and then he's supposed to begin to feel a little better. At that time, he's going to figure out a way to spend some time outside the hospital. He doesn't care what they say. He doesn't care if it kills him.

Todd will pretend he is not sick, even though he will look like a pale, walking, stick figure of a teenager. He thinks people might laugh at him. But he doesn't care. He just wants to get out there on the Halifax streets and go somewhere. He does not want to go back to Moncton. Ever. He does not want to see old friends and have to put up with them feeling sorry for him. He wants to be around people who only see the part of him that is still alive. Not the part that is dying.

Todd wants to hear loud music. He wants to smell the sea. He wants to eat a hamburger at Burger King. He would like to skateboard but doesn't think he can do that. Todd's got all this unresolved stuff about girls in his head, too. Sex is such an unfamiliar landscape to him that he doesn't even want to go there, not even with the right passport. But he'd really like to kiss the right girl. A truly serious kiss. But who would want to kiss a fourteen-year-old boy with cancer?

And then came the weekend. Both parents arrived and spent as much time with their son as they could. But then they left. They left behind some more cards from relatives. Some of the envelopes even had money in them. That seemed really weird to him but he didn't say anything.

Todd's first counsellor had been a woman. Tall, thin, and nervous. He liked her but she had quit after a week. "Gone to the States," they said. "Really good pay in Texas."

The new guy looked a little too much like a school principal and that kind of freaked Todd. "What do you miss most about school?" was the man's first question. Not a good omen.

"Lunch," Todd answered.

Todd was pretty tight-lipped around the counsellor. He was afraid that if he let on about his current obsession with kissing girls he'd get some kind of label and they'd think he was more screwed up than he actually was. Like his mental health really mattered all that much since he had such a short lease on life anyway. Why fix the mind if the body's gonna give out soon anyhow? He almost told his counsellor that much. But he kept his mouth shut. Once, the counsellor ("Call me Brad.") had walked in while Todd was listening to a new band called Glob. The earphones were on, the music was too loud. Why bother to worry about being deaf? But there he was, on this particular day, not feeling at all like hospital furniture or walls, Glob cranked high and him singing out very loudly — his new hobby to ward off dark, malignant thoughts. Really dumb, loud, angry lyrics: "It's cold, it's hard, looks a lot like dark and crazy. It's dead and red and crawling out of my head. It amazes me!"

Nobody could hear the music except for Todd, and his own karaoke to the track echoed far down the hall and he knew it, even felt a certain pride in having the audacity to be able to do it. This was thanks in part to the drugs he was on that day. He had come to the conclusion that the drugs were responsible for his loss of interest in country music. Garth Brooks, Shania Twain, George Strait just didn't synch up with Demerol, or whatever the new pharmaceuticals were. Glob, Toneknob, Styff, and Bolt Ugly went well with whatever he was on.

"It's cold, it's hard, looks a lot like dark and crazy.

It's dead and red and crawling out of my head. It amazes me!"

Those lines from the chorus sung at the top of his lungs eventually brought a cheerful visit from Brad who must have been in the building at the time. The painkiller drip had shuffled around the boundaries of real and not-real in a very convincing manner.

"Defiance is a good thing," Brad said.

Todd didn't hear him the first time, but then he removed the earphones, checked various reference points to see if the apparition was of this world or another. "Excuse me?"

"The music. Defiance. You are expressing your anger. Good ventilation." He touched his chest, saw the confusion in the boy.

"You're expressing your pain. You're letting it out."

"Was I singing?"

"You could call it that."

"You like metal bands?" Todd asked.

"Sometimes."

"Not all the guys in those bands are really as angry as they sound. Some of it is a put-on. It's like acting."

"I think I knew that," Brad conceded.

"Were you a fan of Kurt Cobain?"

"Not really. You?"

"Yeah. I really liked Nirvana."

Brad just nodded but he didn't say anything about it being too bad Cobain was dead.

Todd felt his eyes burning. "Next week when the chemo stops . . . "

"Yes?"

"I'll be off chemo for a while, right?"

"I think so but I'll have to check the chart."

"I want to get out of here."

"We can call your parents."

"I don't want to go out with them."

"I don't understand."

"I need a little freedom."

"You'll need their permission."

"Okay."

"And someone to take responsibility. Perhaps one of the staff. Maybe I can . . . "

"No. I mean, no offence." Todd looked at Brad's gaunt, sallow face, the ruled line of the cheekbone, and the bony skull at the receding hairline. Oh, yeah, right. An afternoon outing with this guy. Wouldn't that be sweet. "I have a friend. I'll call her."

"It's healthy to show this kind of initiative. You must be feeling strong."

"Yes. Yes, I am."

"Do you know why?"

"Could be the drugs."

"I don't think so. It's something from within you."

Like the lines in the song.

Brad looked at the phone sitting on the table. He picked up the receiver and handed it to Todd. Todd's hand was shaking when he took it. He knew the number by heart even though he'd only called her once before.

Molly was sorting through a dusty box of old Thomas Raddall first editions that had just come into the store. The dust made her sneeze. She answered the phone and was surprised to hear Todd's voice on the other end. She had been thinking about him, wondering why she had told her story to him in the hospital. And then the amazing, sudden appearance, not long after, of old Mrs. Fitzhenry.

Todd explained his brief holiday from chemotherapy coming up. "I want to come visit you, at your store. Maybe go out for ice cream or a hamburger or something. Maybe both."

"We can figure out something. I'd be honoured." She could hear his breathing on the other end, ragged, nervous, excited. As she hung up, she felt something curious in the shop. Not a presence, but an absence. As if a clock had stopped or all the people in Halifax had simultaneously held their breath. She didn't know what to make of it. She focused her eyes on the dust motes in the sunlight coming in through the window, then down at the open page of a book sitting open beside the Raddall pile: *The Canadian Atlantic Fishery* by Ruth Fulton Grant. Page 72: "After unloading at the end of the voyage, the fish are prepared for shore drying by careful washing to free them of all slime or other accumulations, piling to allow the pickle to drain off and then drying in the open air on flakes."

As the shop door opened, street noise spilled in around a man who blinked as he moved from the bright, outside sun into the somewhat darker store. Molly looked up and thought she recognized him. Maybe he'd been here on another occasion. But when he spoke, she realized she had never met him before.

"You wouldn't happen to have any books by or about Henry Larsen?" he asked.

CHAPTER SEVENTEEN

AT FIRST, THE NAME OF HENRY Larsen was like an echo in a long dark hallway. Molly looked up at her customer. A tall man, late forties. At first, his seemed to be an ordinary face but that was only what others would see. Molly's eyes traced a line up from his chin, along the salt-and-pepper sandpaper stubble of bearded growth on his jaw line. She studied the arc of his cheekbone and the daunting paleness of his skin. And then she noticed the eyes. Often, at moments like this, people meeting Molly for the first time thought she was a person with some mental problem: defective or dense or psychotic maybe.

Eric was a bit unnerved by the way she was looking at him, but he cleared his throat and said, "Larsen arrived here in Halifax in 1942 after sailing through the Northwest Passage." Here was at least a patient customer. A gentleman with a soft way about him, as if he had just dropped in by parachute from an earlier century. There was no hardness in his eyes, even though Molly could detect that he was someone who had suffered a great loss of some sort. She guessed he had felt some great defeat. "Do not take shortcuts at the cost of clarity . . . Prefer the standard to the offbeat." These were the words she heard in her head. She met his eyes and spoke. "I thought I saw something about the North when I was sorting Pierre Berton the other day. You say he was an arctic explorer?"

"Maybe explorer isn't the right word. But I guess you could say that."

"Funny how the Arctic keeps coming up."

"Pardon?"

"Someone had written a paper about Martin Frobisher. And I was asked to read it."

"I've written a bit about the Canadian North myself."

"Are you an author, then?"

"Mostly academic stuff."

"Nonetheless, an author, here in the store. We're honoured." Molly didn't know why she had fallen into the "we" business. His eyes fluttered like a little boy who had just been told his spelling was excellent.

"It was very dry," he said, as if commenting on the weather. "What I wrote, that is. I'm through with all that, though. And now I'm here in Halifax."

It seemed like an abridged biography. A kind of Coles Notes on a man's career, his life. Molly, having read several recently acquired volumes on shamanism, was of the opinion on this dusty afternoon that each volume in her bookstore was the repository of some part of an author's soul. This was not a fixed religious belief but a construct that she was working on in her head.

Molly knew immediately that her words were delivered in such a way that made her customer feel at home. She made a quick study of what she thought was the man's aura and decided it was blue or it could just have been the lighting in the store producing a corona of dust above him. She led him through the bookshelves, past Self-help, New Age, outdated Lonely Planet travel guides, and a rack of books about how to get rich without trying very hard. Then came history and the section on Canadian history. A whole wall of it. Both silently fingered the spines, searching for books on the Arctic.

"I believe the name of his boat was the *St. Roch*. Does that ring any bells?"

It was an intimate, narrow space there between a wall of history and a longitudinal shelf of English poetry. Eric was a full foot taller than she. He wore an ironed blue-jean shirt and he had a rather intriguing little Adam's apple that moved up and down like a little elevator car when he spoke. He was surprised to discover that his heart was racing.

"No, but we shouldn't give up. Let's try Biography."

They moved down the aisle, a small, sacred parade in a cathedral of words. As her eyes rested on one book or another, she moved in and out of texts, in and out of literary worlds: *Tristram Shandy*, Henri Bergson, Sir Thomas Moore, and onto biographies — Joan Rivers to Elizabeth Taylor, Wayne Gretzky and Nikita Khrushchev. It was a fine pilgrimage for the book they were looking for.

"Every life deserves a book," she heard herself blurt out.

"Some would be more interesting than others."

"Perhaps it's more in the telling of the tale than the tale itself."

"Yes, I think so, but still, there are those of us who would make very dull subjects for a book."

Molly suddenly felt a wave of sadness come over her. She stopped, turned, and surprised him as she put her hand up to his chest. They were breathing in each other now. She tried to look into his eyes, but he seemed nervous and looked away. Still, she detected something about him. Something that reminded her of Todd, but also of Bertrand. And then she remembered something else.

"Larsen," Molly said. "Henry Larsen, RCMP. My father spoke about the man. I grew up on an island at the mouth of the harbour here. It was Larsen's last stop before he came to port here in Halifax. My dad told me the story of how he came ashore, this big bear of a man with a Norwegian accent. There were dogs barking on his boat and my father thought it strange to have so many dogs on a boat. But they had been up north. Larsen rowed a dinghy ashore by himself and told the story of his journey. He left something with my father, something that he said belonged to the North and should not find its way to civilization. It was a very odd knife. Does this mean anything to you?"

"I don't know but I'm intrigued."

"I'm sure that my father said there had been barking dogs on the boat. My father was a great storyteller. And he could also make himself disappear when he wanted to."

"An amateur magician?"

"It was a hobby. If he had lived on the mainland, everyone would have thought him quite peculiar — crazy even, but on the island, there was just us. When you'd least expect it, he'd be there one minute, gone the next. If you took your eyes off him for a split second, a blink of the eye. Gone. Then back."

"What an odd thing. How did he do it?"

"He assured us it was a trick. Had to do with observing what other people were observing, 'slipping between the spaces of someone's preoccupation,' he called it. He didn't make us think it was anything more than a parlour trick, but sometimes I wondered if he had special powers."

"Why do you suppose he did it?"

"He said that sometimes a body just wants to know it's able to make itself... go away, when it wants to. Have you ever wanted to just disappear?"

Eric sighed. "Maybe I could have profited from your father's skill. Did his disappearing act ever frighten you?"

"Not at all. He always reappeared. Even after he died, he'd show up in my dreams when I'd least expect him to be there. I'm sorry, I'm rambling."

Molly moved her hand from Eric's chest and felt uncomfortable, the way she always did when she allowed herself to become intimate with someone she had just met. Her motivation was almost always intuitive. Afterward, she would understand the reasoning. Here, her motivation had been to heal this man of some unknown affliction.

She turned rapidly and reached out to a book she knew would be on the shelf above her head. There it was. *The Big Ship*. Henry A. Larsen. She pulled the book from the shelf, breathed in its dust of dark winter days, smelled its aroma of dogs asleep on icy decks and men sweating in their bunks below. She handed the book to her customer, and she remembered her father telling her the words that Larsen's boss had told him before his voyage. "Take her to Halifax," Larsen's commander had told him. "Over the top."

CHAPTER EIGHTEEN

ERIC WALKER PAID FOR THE BOOK and left but it wasn't a purposeful leaving. He drifted about the store first, almost sat down in the window chair to read, halted, traced his fingers over some books of Robert Browning's poetry on a shelf and then looked up at the ceiling. And then he smiled — at least Molly was pretty sure it was a smile, although he was clearly a man who had not been good at smiling. Then he disappeared into the afternoon.

Molly suddenly wished Dumpster Teeth would come to practice this afternoon because she wanted noise. She wanted Reg banging his Sabian cymbals. She wanted the clapping of high hats and Dart's soft fuzz distortion bass and Leggo's squealing guitar.

She grew restless and decided to go for a walk. She went down towards the harbour in time to see the fog pulling in.

She breathed in the air of the harbour; she studied the grey-green water, muted below the still, damp air as the massive wall of fog advanced from the sea. Devil's Island could not be seen but it was out there.

She was reminded of a warm summer day on the island with the sun high overhead, but off to sea was a dark curtain of fog advancing towards them. Soon the sun disappeared and did not return for days.

"Upwellings," Hank said. "Cold water from the depths rising to the surface. Meets the warm air. Bang. You got your fog."

"Light south wind," Lea added. "Ship to shore fog. Maybe I'll bake those muffins this afternoon after all." Rhubarb and wild strawberry muffins that tasted like summer itself.

Muffins were intended to be an antidote to fog. First you light the wood cook stove, then smell salty driftwood burning, close the oven door, wait until it heats to 375 degrees, and then bake the muffins. Baking was a precise form of alchemy. Muffins for fog, molasses brown bread for snow or rain, pies for sleet.

Sometimes the three of them would stand on the rocky outcropping that Hank called Old Edgar and watch the fog moving in. "It's a good trick when done right," Hank said. The fog was also good at making things disappear. "Welcome back," little Molly would say, pretending she was glad the fog had returned.

Then the sea disappeared and when they turned around their house had disappeared as well. And the lighthouse gone. Just like that.

While the women baked, Hank did odd jobs that needed to be done. He saved various fix-up jobs for fog. Hung a painting, varnished a doorframe, fixed the creaky back step. Later, Molly would wander the island in the fog and talk to the rabbits, study the droplets of water on the lichen, wonder what it would be like to grow up.

The island had secrets, she had always known that. Shipwrecks before she was born, military cruelty, ravages of history. But the island was not the haunted place that some on shore believed it to be. The island was a rock in the sea. It had a spirit, a soul. How could it be otherwise? It allowed for some sand, some soil, a chance for new life to position itself above the waves. It had no qualms about hosting a lighthouse built by men to both warn and welcome. *Come close to these shores but do not crash into us.* In the old days, lighthouses had lamps floating in mercury and a lighthouse keeper would breathe mercury into his lungs and it would eventually make him go mad, and then die. Fortunately for all, mercury had been abandoned. In Molly's youth, a great, electric light spun round of its own accord, powered by a well-balanced motor. Usually, you could hear no sound at all from the motor. But some nights, Molly could hear the faint electric hum of it. Years later, when she met her first Buddhist, he would try to teach her to chant one long sound — *Om,* and Molly would recognize this as the sound she sometimes heard on dark island nights, the *Om* of the light.

Molly allowed her mind to fill with images and sounds from her childhood and, once the fog had moved further up the harbour, erasing George's Island and then the Angus L. Macdonald Bridge, she turned and headed back home.

When she returned to the store it was empty. Molly sat in the chair by the window. Light filtered in, for the fog had not pushed further than the docks. The familiar dust motes rose up, those delicate particles dancing in the rising solar wind. Molly felt herself as light as the sunlight. The world was a gift given to her, everything about it. She was happier than most. She had this. This store, this life, this bit of Halifax. A small pool of calm in a much larger sea of turmoil and chaos — the confusion of living she'd seen in the people she met.

She thought of her father again — disappearing and reappearing. Once, at the dinner table when she was nine. Her mother wondering where the blazes he had got to now. Mother and daughter left sitting there with hot food in front of them: corned beef, salt fish, and biscuits out of the 375 degree cook stove. But a sudden empty seat at the table. No Hank. Then before Lea could call for him, he reappeared. He just seemed to have been dropped from the ceiling into his seat. Molly was astounded, her mother not impressed. "Your food is getting cold," she chided him but Molly smiled. His best one yet.

Molly looked up from the pile of books at her feet, saw her reflection in the window, the traffic beyond, and, in the distance, a great, tall machine with a wrecking ball dangling from a cable. Everything is so wonderful, she thought. And so brief. Her attachment to this life, to this here-and-now, this very moment was so strong that she wanted to cry. She found herself thinking again about the boy in the bed and a great sorrow swept over her. Closing her eyes she knew what she must do.

On her next visit with Todd, she listened to everything he had to say. She held his hand. She understood which part of what he was saying was true, and which part was the medication. She discovered that her plan to take him out, to show him the town, to introduce him to Dumpster Teeth, was not going to happen. She was fearful he was dying more rapidly than everyone had anticipated. Was Todd really going downhill sooner than the doctors had predicted? She studied him while he slept. She listened to his breathing, heard the music in it. She touched his face with her hand; sometimes it was cool, sometimes hot. She tried to cure him — half believing she could by putting both hands on his temples and singing to him: "The water is wide, we can't cross over . . . "

Sometimes he was awake and wanted to talk to her about hockey. She listened and learned about hockey. Sometimes he wanted to talk about his own parents — they loved him, he knew, but they did not understand him. They were so afraid of his illness that they were avoiding him now, telling him, and telling themselves, he would get better. He felt that they had abandoned him — trying to get on with their lives during the week but coming to visit him on weekends during the days and spending the nights in the Holiday Inn at the corner of Robie and Quinpool. "I feel so guilty that I'm putting them through this," Todd said.

"It's not your fault. Besides, I have this feeling that something is about to change."

"Like what?"

"I just know that everything is going to be all right."

"How do you know?" Todd asked.

"I can't really answer that. Words don't always explain things properly. So you'll have to trust me on this."

"Okay."

That was when Molly first noticed that Todd had fallen in love with her. A thin, icy thread of something slipped down her backbone. A small constellation formed a tight bundle of light somewhere inside her as well. Was it in her heart or in the well-protected room of emotion in her mind? Molly had grown familiar with the idea of strangers falling in love with her — or at least feeling enchanted by her. She knew she had this power over others but it was not a power that she ever wielded for personal advantage. She did not *use* it. The young man who studied Russian, the others, old and young, some men, some women. And she had always kept them at arm's length. She cherished her privacy. They would come seeking — like Eric had. She was never sure how they found their way to her but they did. And she always gave them what she had to offer, which was her serenity, her innocence, her grace, and her ability to reassure troubled souls that *everything is going to be all right*. They fell in love with Molly — in a way — and then eventually they saw the implausibility of who she was or they became distracted with the busy pursuits of their own complicated lives. They wandered off to search for fool's gold or to write books or to build condominiums or to teach from textbooks. But Todd would not do that. Todd could not wander off to anywhere.

Eric settled into his room above the so-called Black Market on Grafton Street. There were skateboarders again on the steps of the church across the street — twenty-four-hour-a-day skateboarders. He sat on his bed and read his books. He ventured outside periodically and bought a slice of pizza or a coffee or a travel magazine that he did not read. He went into the Book Room on the corner of Blowers and Barrington and found it to be a fine and friendly place but all the books were new and it reminded him how much more he liked a used bookstore, especially the one run by that unusual woman. He wandered off towards the south end of Winslow Street and found Molly's store closed — well, not exactly closed. There just wasn't anyone there. The door, he discovered, was unlocked and so he brazenly walked in and sat down in the chair in the window, noticed a book of poetry by Dryden there, one by Longfellow, and one on speech articulation. He was puzzled why anyone would have selected those from all the possible books in the published universe. There was a fourth by Emily Dickinson. That made more sense to him. He thought of Molly as a kind of modern day Emily Dickinson, only prettier and more optimistic, less isolated. "How dreary to be somebody! / How public like a frog." That was the line he found on the page of the book that was open. He breathed in the Emily Dickinson dust.

He wondered where Molly was. He was shocked at how truly disappointed he was that she wasn't here. Eric found himself smiling. Again.

That's when Dumpster Teeth arrived. Molly had forgotten that Leggo had phoned earlier in the week to say the band *was* coming on this particular day to practice for an "impromptu benefit concert for a new vegetarian political party" happening that night.

"Dude," one of the Teeth said to Eric as he arrived.

"I was just . . . " Eric started to explain why he was there but the teenagers didn't seem to care. Someone was hauling a drum kit in through the door. There was suddenly a lot of noise for a used bookstore. The ever-reckless Sabian cymbal fell into a pile of anatomy books. As they were arriving, it seemed that Dumpster Teeth was in the middle of a conversation or debate or something about ethics. Leggo was saying, "But that would be an end in itself."

Dart countered, "The ends justify the means."

Reg disagreed. "No, they don't. No way. Never did, never will."

Eric didn't know whether he should get up and leave or stay where he was. There was a rattling assemblage of drum paraphernalia, plugging in of amplifiers, unreeling of guitar cords and a seemingly random tuning of strings. The first tune they began to practice was called "Occam's Razor." It was loud and rambunctious and unlike anything Eric had ever sat through in his life. He liked it very much, though, and wondered if it was punk or techno or hip-hop or rap or something else.

When they took a break, Leggo offered Eric some hummus and pita bread he had brought with him for nourishing the Teeth. In an all-too-professorial manner, Eric asked them if their music was based on any specific belief system. "We believe in everything that's natural," Leggo said.

"That's not entirely true," the drummer added. "We don't believe in violence and that could be said to be natural."

Dart tried to bring things into a sharper focus by thumping a really inventive riff on the bass and then adding, "But the trick is not to become too linear in our thinking or to compartmentalize the world into neat little boxes." Dart formed the boxes in the air with his hands.

Eric left Molly's store, disappointed that Molly had not been there, but feeling pleasantly refreshed. Up until that particular encounter, he wasn't sure there were young people like Dumpster Teeth out there in the world. He wondered why they called themselves Dumpster Teeth. For at least the third time since he arrived in Halifax, the air around him seemed somehow transformed. Transformed into what, he didn't know, just somehow altered — the lighting, the colours tweaked up a shade or two, and, despite the mild ringing in his ears, sounds seemed a bit sharper. Could there have been drugs in the hummus? Not likely.

Stopping by the cemetery near downtown, he noticed the statue of a lion with the word "Sebastopol" on it. He studied it closely and noticed that the beast had apparently once had genitals but someone had chiseled them off. How curious.

All of the headstones were black as if someone had dumped soot on them and rubbed it in. Otherwise, there was a lot of green: the grass, the moss growing up the base of the statue of the lion. Sebastopol, he remembered, was a town on the Black Sea — under siege by the French, the English, and the Germans for nearly a year. Young men from Halifax went there as soldiers to die for something that most people had long forgotten. Even Eric, himself a historian, couldn't quite remember what it was they died for. What could it have been? A simple notion of empire? Honour for a queen? Or was it a king back then? He was pretty sure almost no one on the streets of Halifax could tell him what those young men died for. He thought of the noisy trio of Dumpster Teeth and was glad they wouldn't be persuaded to go into battle at Sebastopol or anywhere else. He hoped they could continue to perform their noisy philosophical music.

If you were going to die for something, Eric mused, you damned well better pick something worth dying for. History, he knew, was filled with people dying for crazy, illogical, ultimately unimportant and unremembered causes.

Chapter Nineteen

Ernest Hemingway ended his novel, *For Whom the Bell Tolls*, like this: "He could feel his heart beating against the pine needle floor of the forest." Eric remembered that line from a long time ago and, alone in his second-floor room, he thought it was an important thing to feel your heart beating against something. The softness of a pine needle forest floor would be like lying with a woman, he thought. He was thinking of Molly. It was not a sexual thing, he realized. It was some other thing. Magnetic, certainly, and a little like sex, but different.

His mind was like the needle of an old compass. It kept pointing him back to her. She kept reappearing in his mind. True north. Yet she was a warm thing, a being who had melted the ice in his veins. He had been a man who had been frozen. And now the body was thawed and he was warm with possibility. He still doubted that the psychiatrists had created exact names for his malady. But, whatever it was, he had come to Halifax to find the cure.

Todd's mother did not like Molly and she as much as told her so. She was spending three days a week in Halifax, sleeping overnight at her sister Grace's house. Sometimes Grace was there and that was comforting, but often she was away on business and being alone in Halifax made Joyce Kingsley feel sad and sometimes angry at the world for the plight of her son. And for her own pain. Joyce seemed to visit Todd at unpredictable times of the day. She arrived one day to find Molly reading *Lady Chatterley's Lover* to her son. Molly could tell by the scowl on the woman's face that she disapproved.

Mrs. Kingsley was a person who judged a book by its cover. She read magazines, anyway, not books, and did not know what it was about books that attracted people. She wore her hair short — cropped, because she said it was easier to take care of. Her everyday interests were prompted by television and women's magazines. She had two other healthy boys at home and secretly resented spending her time split between home and Halifax.

Joyce did not know what to do with her emotions concerning her son's illness. Todd was the middle boy, fourteen. While the other two had excelled at most things they did, Todd had always been what she considered average — which was not really a bad thing in her mind. She assumed he would finish high school, take up a practical trade, and go straight to work. Todd had been dependable and always remembered both her birthday and Mother's Day while the rest of her family was sometimes neglectful on those points.

Todd's cancer somehow felt like her fault. Something he had been born with, maybe. Something inherited from her side of the family. Something she fed him as a baby. Some hideous mistake she made somewhere along the line in his upbringing. Her anger made her self-righteous and a nuisance for Mr. Kingsley, who drove up once a week from Moncton. It was because of the special kind of cancer Todd had that the hospitals in Moncton had sent him on to Halifax to a specialist at the IWK. Joyce and Bartlett Kingsley had not even known what an "oncologist" was until this past year. Now, their lives were full of talk of cancer, pharmaceuticals, chemotherapy, radiation, and all the other new and seemingly unreliable treatments.

"Everything that can be done will be done," Dr. Jesperson had said.

Bartlett was working on his "solid as a rock" persona as his way of coping. Not that he was without emotion. He screamed out loud while driving alone through the back roads of New Brunswick. Windows closed, Garth Brooks on the radio. He could scream out as loud as he wanted and just stare straight ahead. And sometimes he'd cry so much his shirt would be soaked, and then he'd stop by a stream in the New Brunswick forest. He would wash his face in the icy-cold water, and sit on the forest floor and roll pine needles around in his hands. Then go home and see what Joyce had found at Zeller's that day.

Joyce did not have that kind of therapy to help her. She had things bottled up in her. On top of that was the fact that she felt guilty about *not* wanting to be with her son throughout the day. She hated the fact that she felt so selfish and sometimes hated herself for it, assigning ugly names to herself: heartless, insensitive, failure, bitch.

She knew that Molly was a friend of her sister, Grace. It had been Grace's idea. "Molly," her sister had said, "has a certain unusual quality about her. She's a little odd, runs a used bookstore, but she makes people feel good when they are around her. I don't really know what it is but I feel it myself. Maybe she can keep Todd company."

Joyce mistrusted Molly. And she was jealous of her easy, familiar manner with her son. She especially didn't like the way Todd smiled at her. He never smiled at his mother that way.

Nonetheless, Todd needed all the friends he could muster. Only none of them did much good. Two roommates had died already. This gave him a clue as to which part of the hospital he was in. Now Todd had a room all to himself. There was some concern on the part of hospital staff that waking up to another dead roommate would be a bad thing for a fourteen-year-old.

Todd had been losing interest in almost everything. In his head, he kept a short list of things he still cared about. He cared about food, even though he was almost never hungry. He liked the *idea* of food — remembered how hungry he'd been after a hockey game or at lunch during school. He loved hot dogs and hamburgers with everything on them. He loved spicy french fries. And pizza. He loved burnt pizza for some reason. He had some association in his memory of a really fine day of his life that had included an overdone pizza.

"Do you think I got cancer from eating all that stuff?" he asked Molly one day.

"No," she said. "You don't eat a lot of junk food and then suddenly get cancer. It would take years."

Todd also loved the idea of being home with his brothers watching television. Now, however, he almost never watched the television in his hospital room. Often he was all alone in his own private room, and it was too lonely, too weird, to watch TV on his own. It made him morose — a word he'd learned from Brad. "It's natural to feel morose," the counsellor had said. To Brad, everything Todd was feeling was "natural" but knowing it was natural didn't help at all.

There was always a foul chemical taste in Todd's mouth. There was a chemical smell to his room. The food that was served didn't live up to his hopes. Molly had smuggled in hamburgers and french fries from the Harvey's on Spring Garden Road but he couldn't eat it. Nonetheless, he looked at the food and he breathed in the smell of it and that made him happy. Then there was the pizza, burnt on the bottom as requested, from Tomasino's. Now that was therapy — but still it went uneaten.

Todd began asking Molly more and more about herself.

"Well, as you know, I grew up on an island in the harbour. Things washed in. My father, in his own way, was a magician like Houdini. I saw shooting stars at night and the lights of ships passing silently by. And, of course, there were storms."

"What did you watch on television?"

"There was no television."

"What did you do?"

"I read books. I kept a journal. I walked about the island — over and over. And it was new and different each time. I believed it changed around me day by day. I tested it once. I closed my eyes and walked out my back door. I knew where everything had been yesterday but it was changed. I bumped into the shed, then I turned, headed straight to what should have been the centre of the island."

"And you walked into the sea."

"How did you know?"

"I knew."

Molly told him stories about her father disappearing, about storms, about injured birds and seals. And she told Todd he was very handsome and this was the single most important thing anyone had ever said to him in his entire life.

What set Molly apart from just about every other grown-up in Halifax was the very fact that she had not truly ever become an adult. She had sidestepped that process — purposefully, hanging onto a childlike quality, a cultivated naiveté and optimism. It was in her features, in her beauty. And she *was* beautiful; there were few men who could deny that.

An island childhood had set Molly apart. It was who she was.

Todd saw Molly as an equal — she was a fourteen-year-old girl, his girl. When she was with him, she was altogether his, although he did not possess her, and he knew no one could. She was her own democracy, her own island, and her own reality. But, when she was with him, she was nowhere else and he knew that this was almost never the case with all the other adults who came to visit, even his parents.

Todd's friends, it seemed, had simply forgotten about him but he didn't hold them accountable — they were far away, still living their healthy, New Brunswick lives. Todd now had this new identity and he understood that he lived on his own kind of island, although sometimes he thought it was his own planet. Aside from Molly, he knew he was almost totally alone here and he realized he could live with that as long as she was part of wherever he was.

Todd's sleep cycle gave him four hours of wakefulness and four hours of sleep. He dreamed of life on an island. He was not alone there — ever — and there were storms and injured birds and seals and, at night, Orion above. The boundaries of the island shifted each day — sometimes it was huge, expansive. Other days it was barely large enough for two people.

On one occasion when Molly visited, Todd suddenly became strangely jealous. He wanted to know if Molly was in love with anyone. (He wanted to say "anyone else" because, on *his* island, in that wonderfully remote island that kept him sane and even hopeful, Molly was, of course, his.)

Molly understood what he was asking and why. She understood fully for the first time the monumental responsibility that came with befriending a dying fourteen-year-old boy. It swept over her like a rogue wave, unexpected, unannounced, overpowering. She saw the jealousy in Todd's eyes. Molly decided she would tell him about Jake.

Molly "came ashore," as she would refer to it, when she was nineteen. She rented a room in Halifax and convinced the head librarian at the Spring Garden Road library to give her a job reshelving books.

And then Jake came into her life.

Jake studied at the art college and painted canvasses of sailing ships in the style of nineteenth-century painters, much to the chagrin of his New York trained professors, who preferred modern and abstract. Jake was intense, and although he did not like impressionists or post-impressionists, he viewed himself as a kind of modern day Van Gogh. Manic about his work, intense beyond most others' tolerance of him. He fell for Molly like a stone dropping to the bottom of the sea.

Jake lived in an old weather-beaten fisherman's shack at the end of Causeway Road in Three Fathom Harbour. He had an old Ford with holes in the floorboards and he drove Molly out to his home on weekends. Jake was so in love with Molly that he trembled in her presence. Molly could not help but fall in love with him. Jake felt too much of everything. He had come into her life like a ferocious, unstoppable storm. Jake waited until Molly was ready to make love to him, and when the time came, the passion was volcanic. They consumed each other.

Molly had fallen in love with everything about Jake. The way he saw things, the way he described things even. "See that tamarack tree, the way it bursts into the sky." "Hear the sound of the waves, like a million miniature stars being dashed upon the sand." "I like the way your hair is so animated. It seems to have its own ambition." Jake's seed of discontent had been there from the beginning and that, too, may even have been part of what she loved about him. It was also what made them so different. Molly was satisfied easily. She had yearnings but they remained vague, vaporous things on the perimeter of her life.

Whereas Jake had sharp edges, Molly was round like a drumlin — not fat in any way, shape, or form — just that she had about her the soft curve of a seacoast hill, sculpted by the forces of nature. Not ravaged by storms, but tempered by winds, by waves, by soft summer rains falling with permission on her face, on her shoulders, upon her breasts.

The plan was to give up the city altogether, for them both to live in the fishing shack at the end of Causeway Road and for Jake to fish. He would drop out of art college and continue to paint. Molly followed him to Causeway Road and moved in with him.

Molly had given herself to Jake the way she had given herself to Devil's Island as a child. It was an act that was total and beautiful, not a thing of sacrifice at all. Instead, an intertwining. He was woven into her breathing life, moment by moment, as she inhaled and exhaled. He became part of who she was. She had not really considered what their future would be and she never concerned herself much with his past unless he wanted to tell her a story about himself as a boy. He rarely spoke of his family or of other girls he had loved.

While they had been together, Molly had established a life of present tense. Inhale, exhale. They made love elaborately and often. Each time seemed like the first time. Molly vividly remembered once when it happened like this. Near the end of an uneventful, calm day, a sudden and intense storm moved through and, afterwards, there was a complete change in the way everything looked under the clearing, prismatic sky. And then they fell into bed together.

Afterwards, Jake got up and put on his clothes. He grabbed his oil paints and a canvas and walked off down the sandy scallop of beach to the west to paint what remained of the day. He did not ask her to come along, but that was all right too. Molly was left in a dreamy state — she read (Fitzgerald, Stendahl, Hardy) and she wrote poems that she realized no one would ever read.

It would not be accurate to say that Molly had departed from the twentieth century. She just had very little interest in it. It would be hard to have found someone less informed about world events. She didn't try to avoid the news. It simply wasn't a part of her life. She expected some day the world would catch up with her. She was only barely attached to the mainland by that thread of man-made road that could easily be undone by a good hurricane or nor'easter.

Small things made her happy. A bag of lentils brought home by Jake. A sparrow clinging to a shaft of sea oats midmorning.

But Molly awoke one morning three months later to the soft grey fog of the Eastern Shore and Jake was not there. The room was cold and the paintings — the canvasses of sailing ships and storm-tossed seas — were slashed. Outside, the old Ford was gone and so was Jake. He did not write for five years. And then it was a postcard from Cornwall. A three-word apology written on the back of a picture of the remains of Tintagel castle, the apocryphal home of King Arthur.

A nineteen-year-old girl, alone in a drafty fish shack on a thin, crooked finger of land poking out into the North Atlantic. Winter. Driftwood cut up with a hand saw and fed into the old wood stove made from a barrel — a stove fashioned by hand by Jake. Molly bought fish from the local fishermen and occasionally accepted a lift from one of the locals to the old general store in Grand Desert, where she bought a bag of carrots, a turnip, some flour; an onion would be a frill. She bought and drank powdered milk, a white, pathetic powder mixed with water that she hauled from an old well high on the nearby headland.

Molly tried to unravel the puzzle of why Jake left her. Such unravelling led her into dark places in herself that she had never visited before. The pain of a shattered heart was entirely new to her. It was a deep, frightening chasm she had not known was even there before and she had fallen into it head first.

She blamed herself at first but then, gradually, she put the pieces of the puzzle into place and realized that it was Jake; part of Jake's "way" was that seed of dissatisfaction within him. It expressed itself in his art and in the way he talked about the world with a kind of yearning, a wistful what-if-ness that he couldn't leave alone.

Molly realized she'd lose her mind if she stayed there living alone on the Eastern Shore. So she returned to Halifax and went back to work at the library. She eventually saved enough money for a down payment on a rundown little shop on Winslow Street.

Chapter Twenty

Molly's story had been interrupted several times, once when someone checked a chart, once when the nurse came to adjust the IV drip, and another time when a doctor spent less than three minutes with his patient before he moved on.

The visits were daily now. Molly and Todd had woven their lives together. It was his doing as much as hers.

"Todd, do you think they would let me take you out of here? Even if it was just for an hour or so. Is there some way we could go out into the city?"

Todd knew there wasn't. He had tubes. He had good moments but plenty of bad ones, too. He knew he was losing strength by the day. He knew he was worse off today than he was yesterday or the day before that. When he closed his eyes, he saw light behind his eyelids. "Sure," he lied. "I bet if you ask real polite, they'll say okay."

"Should I ask your parents first?"

"No. My parents are afraid. Right now they're afraid of everything. Especially my mom. She's mad about all this and she tries to be nice to me but I can see she's angry at me even though she doesn't want to be. She'll make things complicated."

"It's because she loves you and this makes her very confused."

"I know that."

Molly went to find Dr. Jesperson.

"You're not serious?" he asked.

"I thought maybe there was some way. It would mean a lot to him."

"He's worse than he looks," he said.

"He looks pretty bad."

"Well, like I said, he's worse than he lets on."

"How long?"

Two hands in the air. Vague, ambiguous, imprecise but accurate enough. Palms up, fingers pointed towards two opposite walls. A doctor's hands — pale, somewhat beautiful in a feminine way, and undoubtedly skilled, but incapable of some things, unable to deal with some stuff.

Todd was falling into one of those dreamy, drug-induced states when Molly returned to his room. He knew what the doctor would say and it had ripped away at him, at who he was, the safety zone he was living in inside his head. He understood he was dying and that was clear as a bell but one part of him was insisting that he would continue to live on — he had images in his head of himself at sixteen — kissing, making love to a girl he would meet. He clearly envisioned himself driving a car, going to university, playing hockey in university, falling madly and irretrievably in love. And after that, he saw himself living an ordinary life. And that story shone like a star inside him.

Whenever the pain came back, it tore through that fantasy life and stole every ounce of energy left in him. Then he settled into a fog as thick as any that stole up into the harbour and curled like a smoky cat around the city of Halifax.

Molly sat down and said this: "Just let your eyelids close and imagine a silver thread coming out of your imagination, out of your head — a thin, silver thread, like a fishing line maybe. You can follow it up into the sky and see where it takes you."

"It's taking me to the island where you grew up."

"I know. The sun is out, isn't it?"

"There are big rocks along the shore. The sea is so beautiful. The grass is green."

"Are there rabbits?"

"A few. No wait. A lot."

"People?"

"No. No people. But I see the house."

"That's where I grew up."

"And the lighthouse. I can see the lighthouse."

"How do you like travelling without your body"?

"I like it a lot."

Molly stayed as Todd slipped off into sleep. She hoped he was still tethered by the silver thread to the sunlight and the island. She would encourage Todd to explore whatever he could encounter outside his physical confinement, even if others thought her crazy. She knew that one of the nurses had already said something unkind to Dr. Jesperson about her. She knew that Todd's mother did not trust her. Those were all factors far outside of herself that she could not deal with. So she would not trouble herself about them.

When Todd's eyes eventually opened, she asked him if he had stayed on the island very long. He nodded yes. His mouth was very dry and Molly helped him sip water. "I stayed there a long time and I became a keeper of the light."

"All alone?"

"No," he said.

She was surprised he used the old expression "keeper of the light." Maybe he had picked it up from her. She decided she should tell him more about her former home and about lighthouses. "You could see the other light on Sambro Island from where we lived. That is the oldest standing lighthouse in Canada. We felt connected by the thread of light we could see from Sambro."

Molly told him of the older times, the stories of times before she was born. "Sometimes island people made bonfires on headlands to warn ships of coastal dangers. And at times, nasty people made bonfires in the wrong places intentionally to misdirect vessels onto the rocks where they were smashed to smithereens so that the greedy people along the coast could harvest whatever washed ashore. They were as bad as the pirates and privateers who plundered the ships at sea.

"Yet the men and women who kept the lighthouses understood their sacred and necessary occupations. They used simple candles with mirrors at first, then oil lamps — fish oil and seal oil, vegetable oil or the oil of whales until Abraham Gesner came along and gave the world kerosene.

"In the late nineteenth century, lighthouse keepers often went mad from breathing in mercury fumes that destroyed the cells of their brain. In those days, the light itself floated on a pool of liquid mercury. Isolated, living in pairs as husband and wife or alone even. Sometimes it was the woman left to tend the light after the man had died from mercury poisoning. 'Keeping the light' in many centuries, meant isolation, despair, and madness.

"I grew up with electricity and all I had to worry about was to never look directly into the light itself or I would go blind. Sometimes on a warm summer night, I'd walk around the base of the lighthouse. I would keep the revolving beam above me as I walked around, slowly, around and around. After a while, there was a path in the grass, a perfect circle about the lighthouse made by a little girl with nothing better to do than keep pace with the light."

Todd fell back to sleep again, possibly returning to the island and resuming his job as the keeper of the light. A nurse entered the room and brought with her a replacement bag for the drip going into Todd's arm. She also brought with her a chill that made Molly shiver slightly before she stood up and touched the forehead of the sleeping boy. Then Molly left the hospital room and found her way back out into the city.

Chapter Twenty-one

Eric had gone to Molly's bookstore a total of seven times since he'd arrived in the city. Four times she had been there, three times not. Each time he bought an old book. Usually a book about some aspect of Nova Scotia history. Each time Molly was there, she remained slightly out of reach. He was, if he'd admit it to himself, falling in love with her.

The total freedom that Eric had granted himself had its own problems, as did the room he was renting above the Black Market. The noise of skateboarders across the street on the steps of the church no longer bothered him, however. The sound of skateboarders skidding their boards down the railing and then falling was almost constant through the day, although it did not begin until eleven in the morning. Apparently, the skateboarders of Halifax slept in. After that, they carried their skateboards downtown and found railings and steps on which to practice their injurious sport. Skateboarders did not seem to enjoy cruising their skateboards down smooth, paved hills anymore like they did in the old days. Eric assumed there must be a lot of scarring among skateboarders. Skill came at a cost.

Eric put a positive spin on his current state of affairs. He was still confused about many things but felt himself to be in a state of grace; anything could happen if he let it. And that was a good thing. He knew he had been given some clues. This business about Henry Larsen, for example. So far, his reading of the book had not offered any grand insight but perhaps it was a bit too early. But Larsen had led him to Molly and Molly had sold him the book. And told him the story of Larsen stopping on Devil's Island and talking to her father. Was that true, or did she just make it up? One day soon he'd have to go to this island. Maybe he'd take sailing lessons and sail there — with Molly, of course. Eric had a quick breakfast at the Mediterraneo downtown and walked uphill to the town clock. The clock reminded him of two things: Prince Edward, who had ordered the construction of the clock, and the unreliability of time itself. J.B. Priestley, in one of the books he had purchased from Molly called *Man and Time*, had written about "ordinary time," "inner time," and "creative time." Ordinary time was like the time it took him to eat his two eggs and drink the dark coffee at the Mediterraneo. The second, inner time, was where he lived most of his day — inside his head, daydreaming, fussing with ideas, or compressing and expanding things of trivial or monumental importance. But it was creative time that interested him most. Priestley suggested that something happened to people who were involved in creative endeavours. Writers fell into this other mental dimension of time. So did painters and sculptors and maybe even skateboarders. A person in this creative state could almost live outside of time. The old rules of the clock need not apply.

To that end, Eric thought he must take up some form of creative work — writing, perhaps, even though it seemed so fraught with pitfalls. He would speak to Molly about this. Eric had the feeling that she was a woman of some extraordinary talent.

Eric walked up the steep hill of Prince Street and stood before the skateboarders' favoured steps leading up to the old clock building. Eric liked some things about it but other things he did not. He didn't particularly like the fact that its construction came at the bidding of Prince Edward, fourth son of George III of England. That particular prince had come to Halifax in 1794 and started ordering soldiers and workers to build all kinds of things. He had his century's fondness for timepieces and the Old Town Clock was his monument to English time, a rather fixed form of time that suggested an hour was an hour and a minute a minute, despite all the experiential evidence to the contrary.

Prince Edward thought his military men should be on time for everything and, if everyone did their job on time, you could run a bloody empire that way and win wars against France or whoever you decided your enemy to be. Bill Fenwick, the royal engineer of the day, helped Edward design the clock. Actually, the prince did none of the work. He just said, *Build a clock and make it pretty, accurate, and symmetrical.* He told them to make the clock faces on the east and north big while the south and west ones should be small. The larger clock faces were facing the people more important to the prince while the smaller faces were directed towards people of lesser interest. The military and the well off got time with big arms and numerals, and the poorer people of Halifax had to squint if they wanted to know what time it was, though many of them didn't give a damn about the exact time anyway.

A cannon still went off in Halifax at noon each day to remind the citizens that this was as good a time as any to have lunch. It also helped to wake any late-night revellers still abed with hangovers.

Eric walked up the legendary steps that ascended the hill above the clock and found a bench halfway up Citadel Hill. Above him was the fortress, below the downtown, and beyond that the harbour. So this was what had become of Prince Edward's once-favoured city. Eric's head was stuffed with mostly useless details about Canadian history. The study of Canadian history had not made him happy. Most of what he remembered was trivial and not at all applicable to his own life. He wished he had studied masonry or car repair or music but here, before him, was the result of history and so it was worth some musing if only to pass the time or to enhance his inner time.

Most of the British princes of the eighteenth century were screw-ups and assholes, by Eric's estimation, although he had never used those exact words during his lectures. He should have, but he hadn't. The students would have admired him if he had called a spade a spade. Instead, he had called Edward "earnest" because of all his building plans and military aspirations, but the truth was Edward was a pompous bully, a most British character. He wasn't as lecherous as his brother, William, and he didn't drink quite so much. But that wasn't exactly high praise.

King George III wanted Edward away from England and had first sent him to Martinique and then St. Lucia before plunking him down in Nova Scotia to be commander in chief — a great job for a snob and a tyrant, qualities he had come by honestly.

Edward was fearful the French would attack Halifax and it wasn't mere paranoia. The French would attack the British outposts whenever and wherever they could so he ordered his lads to build a Martello tower — a nice, round tower like those found in Europe. And he ordered improvements to the fort at the top of the Citadel, above Eric's head. Edward, despite his loathing of the French, had as his mistress a French woman, Alphonse Therese Bernadine Julie de Mont Genet de Saint Laurent. Julie for short. She lived with him as a kind of common-law wife, and few pointed out the irony to his face.

Edward saw the arrival of shiploads of Black Jamaicans known as Maroons in his harbour and put them to work to dig the fort deeper into the top of Citadel Hill. Some of his friends took the most beautiful of the Maroon women as their concubines. Edward himself was not so much troubled by this lasciviousness as he was worried by the fact that Maroons worshipped a pagan god named Accompag and they buried their dead at ground level with rocks piled on their bodies. It made him think that he should ultimately order the Maroons off to some other distant place once they had finished their work for him.

On George's Island in the harbour, Edward had his workers build a fort in the shape of a star. He also fixed an enormous chain across the Northwest Arm so no enemy could sneak in there. He even ordered the implementation of a curious, but inventive, long-distance communication system — from hilltop to hilltop across the province. It involved flags, wicker balls, and drums.

Having recalled this entire roster of seemingly insignificant information about the past, Eric felt a wave of futility sweep over him. He and all the other scholars of history, he knew now, had been wasting their time. He made a mental note that someday he would write a different kind of book altogether, one called *The History of Kindness*. He would not document war or empire-building or royal lineage or technical progress of any sort. Instead, he would write the story of ordinary or great people down through the ages who did kind things.

Later that day, when he went to Molly's store and suddenly found himself at a loss for words, he told Molly of this half-baked plan. Molly said it was a wonderful idea. There was no such book anywhere that she had seen. And it was about time that someone wrote it.

CHAPTER TWENTY-TWO

THE VERY NEXT DAY, ERIC SHOWED up yet again supposedly looking for another book — research for his *History of Kindness*, and Molly steered him towards books about saints and other doers of good deeds. There were a lot of ignored books in that region of the store. Eric bought a biography of Sister Theresa and one about Albert Schweitzer. Then he popped the question.

"Could I buy you a coffee?"

"You could."

Molly liked Eric and she knew he was a tall, thin, lonely man who could use a friend. She expected he was complicated and hurt in some complicated way. Intellectuals, she knew, created elaborate themes to their suffering but she liked Eric nonetheless. He was not aggressive or rude and Leggo had already said that Molly should become his "ally." Eric was too young to be a time traveller but it was like he was from another time and place. Dart had said that Eric walked with "a very long shadow" and it wasn't just because he was tall but because he was being stalked by dark thoughts. Reg agreed. Maybe Molly could help "shorten his shadow."

The point was that Dumpster Teeth approved of Eric and they got all excited when they learned he was going to write a big fat book about the history of kindness. They had always been on the lookout for the "right man" for Molly, strange as that may sound. The Teeth were very old-fashioned about some things. Dumpster Teeth agreed if they ever made it big, they would set aside some money to take care of Molly. "She was there at the beginning when we needed her, man," Leggo had said. She was like mother and soul sister and angel and guru rolled into one. They would never forget that.

Eric and Molly ended up in a coffee shop by the harbour, overlooking the water. Eric was shy and Molly was kind of quiet and they watched a tugboat chundering by, tugging and towing nothing at all. Eric described where he lived above the Black Market and how he was getting used to the constant smell of patchouli perfume and vanilla incense. "And the skateboarders are like a tribe. I can't help but study their customs." He heard himself sounding horribly academic.

"I like that," Molly said. "This city is made up of tribes. There are skaters who always walk around with skateboards."

"And bloody knees."

"And there are the cell phone men and women."

"They're always one place physically but somewhere else in their minds. They always have to talk to some person who's not with them. Even if they're with another cell phone person, one phone will ring and then they both get on cell phones and talk to someone who's not there. Very unusual custom."

"Street people," Molly said, "another tribe. The city is cracking down on those who pick pop cans from the garbage to get money. The city calls it stealing."

"Those are the warlords. Keeping order by keeping the poor in their place."

"What tribe are we in?" Molly asked him.

"I'm not sure. I look in the mirror and I don't even know who I am, let alone what tribe I'm from. And you? You are one of a kind. I've never met anyone like you."

"I am an island."

"I think I understand." Like Dumpster Teeth, Eric understood just how vulnerable Molly was. She was truly of another time and place. Saint of dusty books.

"And there's a lot I don't understand. There's Todd, for example. I don't know what to do."

At first Eric thought Todd was another man. He was surprised at the upwelling of what must have been jealousy, although it had been a long time since he had felt such a thing.

"Todd is fourteen and he's very sick," Molly said. "I think his family has cut him adrift — not on purpose. They just can't deal with it. They think it's their fault or it's some kind of punishment or something. Now, like me, he's an island." In her mind, what she meant was that he was on an ice pan, far out at sea. It was a place of diminishing safety as the ice island would keep getting smaller and smaller.

A chill ran down Eric's spine, a drip of cold sweat, maybe from his neck, trailing down his backbone like cold liquid mercury.

"Do you remember fourteen?" Molly asked.

"Just barely. My head was in the books. I was a loner, but never alone. I believed in . . . " he stopped and looked out at the water, amazed at what he was thinking, at what had been in his head, at the words he was about to say.

"You believed in what?"

Eric avoided her eyes, her lovely eyes. He thought he should make something up — say he believed in God or he believed in Karl Marx or hockey even or Buddhism or tantric sex. "I believed that everything had a purpose. Including me," he said, finally, after the catalogue of false beliefs trailed off into infinity.

Molly smiled and sipped her coffee. "Thank you."

The old warehouse across from Molly's bookstore was being torn down, board by board, that afternoon. There was considerable noise and dust. In order to ignore the noise, it was necessary for her to keep the front door to her shop closed. Molly was surprised when the door opened and Joyce and Bartlett Kingsley walked in. The noise of the demolition followed them into the store and Bartlett hurriedly closed the door behind him.

"So good to see you," Molly said, even though she knew there was something wrong. She tried to establish eye contact with Joyce but the woman's eyes darted around the room. Molly felt a panic rising in her throat. "Todd?"

"No, no," Bartlett jumped in. "Todd's okay. I mean, Todd is the same. He's still in the hospital."

Molly blinked and tried to quiet herself.

"I need to just come out and say this," Joyce began, turning away from Molly and looking at the rows of old books. "I have to ask you to stop visiting my son."

The words came as a shock as Molly heard them one at a time. They didn't seem to fit together or completely make sense. Joyce's hands shook in front of her like she was choking some invisible thing. Bartlett drew his finger through his thinning hair, tried to say something himself, but gave up and went to stare out the window at the men tearing the boards off the roof of the old warehouse.

"Todd needs all the friends he can get," Molly said.

"Friends, yes, but not you."

"Why?"

"He thinks he's in love with you. He's only fourteen."

Molly had understood about Todd's feelings. She also knew how much he needed her to be there. But the frantic woman in front of her was something she could not understand. She knew how painful it was for Todd's parents to visit. She understood the guilt and self-loathing that went with being the parents of a dying boy, but she also knew that they visited only on weekends. Todd needed more than that.

"Of course, he's fourteen. I wasn't trying to lead him on."

"You have to understand, we don't really know who you are. We don't know why you would want to be there with him. It's hard enough for us . . . his parents."

It wasn't just fear Molly heard in her voice, but anger too, directed at her. In Joyce's mind, Molly had done an awful thing. She'd made the boy feel something he was not going to receive from anyone else — not his parents at this point, not some girl from school. Todd was still hanging on to a fourteen-year-old's belief in the possibility of anything. Even life after cancer, even love.

Joyce picked up one book from the table in front of her, then another. *Paradise Lost* by John Milton. *A Manual of Zen Buddhism* by D.T. Suzuki. Molly could see that Joyce didn't understand what such books would be about. And she understood that Joyce resented her friendship with her son. She mistrusted Molly. Molly felt something inside herself turn hard. Her instincts told her to protect herself, that something was happening here that could harm her but she did not know why it was happening.

"We've said what we came to say," Joyce finally stated, wiping her hands after having touched the books. Bartlett had not been able to say anything but remained with his back to the two women, studying the demolition like he was watching a television documentary. As they left, he turned and began to say something to Molly but couldn't locate any useful words whatsoever. He inhaled, swallowed his confused thoughts, and followed his wife out into the destructive afternoon.

Molly did not visit Todd on Monday, and when Todd phoned on Tuesday morning, his voice sounded weak. "I heard the weather forecast for today. It's warm and sunny. Today is the day I get to go outside."

"That's great, Todd. Are your parents taking you?"

"They went home to New Brunswick. I talked to Brad. He says he thinks I should do this. He talked to Dr. Jesperson for me. And he said okay. Actually, I was kinda surprised. He says he'll unhook the IV. They'll give me some pills to take while I'm unhooked."

"What about your parents?"

"My mother's a little nuts."

"I think I understand."

"She was too upset to say anything to the hospital — about you, I mean. But I spoke with my aunt Grace. She said she'll come by and take me out of the hospital. I told her that I wanted to spend some time, though, with just you."

"And what did she say?"

"She's cool with that. But it has to be today. I can't take any chances . . . about the weather, I mean. Today is the day."

"Why don't you let Brad take you out?"

"No. I want to see the city with you."

CHAPTER TWENTY-THREE

MOLLY MET UP WITH GRACE AND Todd not far from the hospital driveway on University Avenue. Grace hugged her and whispered in her ear, "I'm sorry about my crazy sister."

"It's okay," Molly said. "Why don't you come with us?"

Grace smiled. "No. You guys will be fine." Then she gave Todd a gentle hug. "Don't get lost. Call me on the way back."

"This is so great," Todd said, his eyes blinking in the bright sunlight. Molly began to gently push Todd's wheelchair along the sidewalk, cautious at first, trying to get a feel for the control of it.

"I'd like to go to the water. Can we go to the harbour?"

"It's a long way. Are you sure?"

"Yes. Please."

"I'm sorry you have to push me around like this."

"I don't mind at all."

As they moved down University Avenue, Todd looked up at the branches of the trees above. "I forgot how colourful the world is."

"The trees save the city from itself," Molly said and Todd understood. Molly was already worrying about Todd's strength. Todd had tried to convince her he was okay — as okay as he could be under the circumstances. He had some painkillers to take if needed.

As they passed another one of the medical buildings, Molly noticed an ambulance unloading a covered body and placing it on a gurney to roll inside. They were talking loudly about lunch. Molly pointed to the swallows up near the eves of the building.

"They fly like in *Star Wars*," Todd said.

"They do?"

"Like Luke Skywalker in the old *Star Wars* movie."

Molly had never seen *Star Wars* but she thought she understood what he meant.

They stopped and waited for the light to change and then moved on. Molly was beginning to like the feel of pushing Todd along the city sidewalk. She liked the fact that it was a warm late-summer day. It would be fall soon. She liked the slower pace of rolling along like this instead of walking at a fast clip. Sometimes people stared at them, but most did not.

To the passersby, Todd probably appeared pale and fragile. Molly believed some people passing him knew how badly off he really was. Most could possibly tell that he was a boy who was very, very ill. Todd looked around with a sense of wonder. "I want more than anything the ability to control time," he said suddenly.

"Why time?"

"I want the ability to make some things — this — last forever."

"Maybe you can do it. Give it a try."

"I will," Todd said. "I'm trying right now."

Molly held her breath intermittently as she walked. She thought that if she added her will to his she could keep his pain at bay for a while.

"I also want to be able to go back in time," Todd said. "Back through my own life and relive some things. I want to go back and do some things differently."

"We all feel that way."

"But it's different for me. You'll continue to go forward. I won't. I want to be able to get a full life from a short life."

Other people, his parents especially, told Todd not to talk like that. Some of the nurses he tried to talk to also kept telling him everything was going to be okay, that he was going to be "all right." His parents acted that way. They pretended. Dr. Jesperson did not. The doctor told Todd the cancer probably could not be stopped.

"Quality counts," Molly said. "Not quantity. Someone can live a long, but trivial, life. Others can live important lives and length doesn't matter. They can have a profound effect on others. Like you. You've had a profound effect on me."

"I have?"

"Yes. I don't know how to describe it. But I feel more alive when I am around you." Molly was telling the truth but once the words were out, she was fearful she had said something that would fuel Todd's fantasy that he was in love with her. Still, she did not take back her words but instead tried to move on to other things. "About time . . . someone once said that time is nature's way of preventing everything from happening at once."

Todd began to laugh. "Maybe everything — everything really *is* happening at once. Maybe this is it. There is only now."

And *now* was rolling them down Morris Street, getting them towards the harbour.

The water of Halifax Harbour rippled slightly from a gentle north wind. On the boardwalk, just south of the Maritime Museum, Molly pointed towards the harbour mouth. "That's McNab's Island over there."

"I read about that. Isn't it where the British Navy used to hang sailors who misbehaved? They'd leave the bodies swaying in the sea breeze so other sailors would get the point."

"That was long ago. Beyond McNab's and Lawlor's Island, out towards the ocean, is a low island with the lighthouse. That's where I grew up. You can't see it from here."

"I wish I had been there with you growing up on Devil's Island. I wish I could do that trick with time."

A muscular young man jogged by just then towing a kind of rickshaw with a man and a woman sitting in the carriage. He was breathing hard but seemed to like his workout as a human horse of sorts. Healthy as a Percheron and physically fit with those bulging arms and calves and that T-shirt soaked in sweat. Todd couldn't help but stare at him.

Along the wharf were commercial fishing boats and the tour boats that were moored here only in the summer. A whale-watching boat was berthed at the bottom of a sloping wooden ramp. Her captain was sitting in a lawn chair on the dock alongside, reading a book. Business looked slack. Molly had an idea.

She locked the wheel brake on Todd's chair and went to speak with the captain. He looked up when Molly blocked out the sun.

"How much would you charge for a ride to Devil's Island? Just out and back."

"A hundred dollars."

"I only have thirty. I'd have to pay you the rest later."

Then, still squinting into the sun, the captain noticed the boy in the wheel chair. "I can do that, I guess."

As soon as the boy was wheeled down the ramp, three men appeared as if out of nowhere to help load him on board. "We're going to the island," Molly told Todd.

The captain nodded, loosened the lines that tethered his boat, started the engine and gingerly pulled way from the dock. He reminded Molly of fishermen she had known as a child — the ones from the Passage who graced the wharves when she and her father would go ashore for supplies. This captain spoke very little but seemed pleased and content to be out for a ride in his boat. "Keep an eye out for whales, lad," he told Todd.

Molly could see that Todd was tired and she knew she was taking a new and bigger risk now that they were headed out towards the mouth of the harbour. What if something should go wrong? What if Todd needed medical attention? Molly knew she was being dangerously impractical, taking chances. But she had this deal going with time. She was negotiating for great alterations in the fabric of it. She was begging for a very large expanse of now and willing to give up any portion of next week or next year or whenever if she must.

Todd started making small talk with the captain about hockey. They both tossed the names of players and teams and Stanley Cups back and forth. Molly caught snippets of it in the wind. Molly felt the flood of sun on her pale face and breathed in the smell of the sea. The talk of a man and boy speaking with casual enthusiasm about hockey had the same musical lilt as a line from James Joyce. Trailing behind the boat was the wide V marking their passage.

They were passing Hangman's Beach on McNab's now. "Where's the hanging tree?" Todd wanted to know.

"No tree, really," the captain said. "The Navy built something called a gibbet. Nasty piece of work but it got the job done."

Molly kept focused on expanding the present as large as the universe would allow. Past Lawlor's Island, the lighthouse appeared on the Island of the Devil, now before them. As if on cue, a whale — a small one, a pilot whale — breached and then dove.

Molly would not take a chance on going ashore at the small cove on the north side of the island. She couldn't take the chance of moving Todd from the boat. "Circle the island as close as you can get, please," she asked the captain.

"Aye."

Molly stood beside Todd and pointed to the empty, storm-ravaged house where she had grown up. She envisioned herself as a girl standing at the door. She instructed Todd to see what

she retrieved from her memory. Through her words, she led
Todd on an imaginary walking tour of the island from the
back door, out to the raspberry patch, past the black and white
rabbits. They looked up at the hawks and at gulls perched on
the boulders by the shoreline.

Because the water was so deep on all sides, the captain was
able to bring his whale-watching boat in very close. He kept
an eye out for rocks, though, since he had never dared to come
this close to Devil's Island before.

It was a small island and they had completed circling it
two times when the captain looked at Molly who said, "Once
more" and it was on the third circumnavigation that Molly
was fairly certain that Todd had been granted his wish and
he *was* there with her on Devil's Island and they both were
young — twelve or thirteen maybe — and the swallows who
lived in the eaves of the shed were darting about like star
ships. And the wild rabbits were tame enough to pet and the
gulls spoke to you in a language that was recognizable. And
her mother was making lunch and her father was fixing the
door hinge to the lighthouse and Halifax was a million miles
away. And there was no such thing as the past or the future.
And there was not the remotest evidence that anything — not
even death — could exist in this version of here and now.

There were men standing about on the wharf in Halifax
when they returned, and they did not need to be asked to
help Todd ashore and help roll him up the gangplank to the
boardwalk. The muscular, sweating university student was
there as well with an empty rickshaw this time, and Molly
almost asked him to carry them back to the hospital but
stopped herself.

Instead, she found a cab, but then she was ready to wave
the taxi away because she thought she had no money, until
she discovered she still had the thirty dollars which she had

forgotten to pay the whale boat captain. In the end, he had never asked.

Molly asked the driver to wait as she went to a nearby pay phone and phoned Grace to meet her at the entrance to the hospital.

Then Molly realized that Todd was in pain as she and the Lebanese cab driver helped the boy into the back seat. Molly sat beside him and put her arm around him. And she lost her grip on time as it slipped back into its usual routine.

"Should you take those pills Dr. Jesperson gave you?" she asked.

"No," Todd said. "I'm okay."

Grace was there to meet them and looked concerned when she saw Todd. "How was it?" She asked tentatively.

"Amazing," Todd said. Molly could tell he was fighting back tears. And it was like a knife blade to her heart.

Chapter Twenty-four

THERE WERE TWO PHONE CALLS THAT evening, the first one from Grace thanking her for taking Todd on an adventure. There was a pause and then she continued. "Todd was in rather rough shape, though. Dr. Jesperson seemed quite concerned."

Molly agreed, and then she thanked Grace for calling.

"I know," Grace said, "but I don't think they'll allow this again. Molly, I know that you are good for him. He needs you more than any of us. Let's wait and see how he is tomorrow."

As she hung up, Molly began to worry about Todd. She was fairly certain something important — something good — had happened that day, that she had done the right thing. If Todd was going to have any life at all, then that life was to be lived to the fullest. Molly sat with a few old poetry books and tried to focus on the words, but she soon gave up. She felt exhausted.

As she sat at the small desk in her bedroom, she looked up once in a while to study the image of herself in the mirror across the room. A man or woman who lives alone has a dangerous relationship with a mirror. Some people who live alone keep only small mirrors. Some have those large, full-length mirrors in more than one room. Molly had an oval mirror above her dresser and she tried to use it as a reference point several times a week. She was no longer young but she thought her eyes still revealed the spirit of youth. The mirror also divulged a hint of uncertainty that always shocked Molly.

The second phone call came from Joyce Kingsley. When she had called her son, he was on a heavier dose of painkiller and had apparently told his mother a semi-coherent story of what had really happened that day. Dr. Jesperson had been there in the room at the time. Joyce was furious. "Leave him alone," she shouted at Molly over the phone. "You are not to visit him again. I am his mother."

"He needed my help," Molly began to explain but was cut off.

"This is the last time I'm going to say it. Leave him alone." Then Joyce slammed down the phone. Molly hung up and looked outside, across the street to the skeleton of the old wooden warehouse, all that was still standing. There were piles of debris from the demolition. Soon something new and soulless would be built there. Much of old Halifax was being torn down and replaced with buildings made of concrete and glass.

Molly gave up on the poetry books and tried to remove the echo of Joyce's insults and invectives from her mind. She thought she understood what it must feel like to be the mother of a boy who is dying and not to be able to do anything about it. That was the source of the rage. To be able to find an enemy — real or imagined — would give focus to the rage and the inner terror Joyce must be feeling. If Molly was the focus for those pent-up emotions, she could accept that.

Eric Walker was pleased with his shabby little room above the Black Market. He had purchased a four-pack of Guinness draft beer and sat by a lamp reading about Henry Larsen.

He learned that Henry Bjorn Larsen was born in Fredrikstad, Norway, near the Oslo Fjord in 1899. At fifteen he went to sea in a square-rigged sailing ship. Roald Amundsen inspired him to explore the Arctic and Larsen was inevitably drawn to the Canadian far north where he ate his first raw blubber on Hershel Island. Liking both the climate and the taste of raw blubber, he became a Canadian citizen, and one year later, in 1928, joined the RCMP, where he was assigned to the *St. Roch* for a voyage around the Western Arctic. Within a year, he was her captain. The *St. Roch* was a thirty-two-metre vessel made of Douglas fir with three sails and a 150-horsepower diesel engine. The rather round hull made the ship rock violently but she worked well through the ice. And there would be plenty of ice ahead for the little ship and her crew.

Larsen saw himself as a friend of the Inuit and a guardian of the North. The Inuit called him *Hanorie Umiarjuag* — Henry of the Big Ship. Henry was a short and stocky man who sang hymns outside on the deck of his boat when they were in the midst of terrifying storms. He had a passion for difficult things and a partiality to seafood, preferably uncooked. "Raw frozen fish," he told one of his correspondents, "gives one a warm feeling of well being."

Larsen listened to the stories of the people of the North; one of his favourites was about old Adam. Adam was caught in a blizzard, far from shelter, with his grandson alongside him. When they could walk no further in their attempt to get home, Adam had the boy lie down and the grandfather lay down alongside him, enveloping him with his arms. Adam died that night but his body sheltered the little boy enough so that he could be saved the next day. The Inuit and Larsen saw this as a most honourable thing to do. Larsen also grew to understand why, on so many occasions, elderly Inuit chose to wander off into the wilderness and die on their own so as not to be a burden to their families.

Canada was at war in 1940 when Larsen's boss in Vancouver gave him his new orders for the *St. Roch*. "Take her to Halifax, over the top." At that time, no one had ever completely travelled the Northwest Passage west to east. Larsen rose to the challenge and sailed north and then east, blasting his way through ice with dynamite when necessary until he eventually got his ship trapped in the ice near Tuktoyaktuk, where he stayed stuck fast until the last day of July 1941. Soon after that, his ship was seized again by the grip of ice and stalled near the North Magnetic Pole.

Henry had enlisted Inuit men and women for shipmates and they lived in tents above deck. And there were dogs too, always dogs, good dogs dependable enough to move your sleds across the ice or save your life if need be. When not wedged solid in the ice, there were still mountains of ice all around and growlers — smaller submerged icebergs — to watch out for, as well as endless problems with frozen rudders and propellers. But here was this man, Larsen, happy in a world of nearly-frozen everything, having the time of his life. His Inuit crew, who he considered his friends, made him soups from the heads of seals which would sometimes peer back at him from the great kettles with their large dark eyes and drooping moustaches.

And there were dark moments along the way — worst of all perhaps was having to perform the obligatory RCMP policing duties which, near the northern tip of Baffin Island, meant dealing with a man who had murdered his wife. Larsen had idealized the Inuit, believing them to be more sensible, sane and noble than the rest of the "civilized" world, yet here was a man who had murdered his wife and he shamelessly explained that it was because she was not a good cook. He had plunged a knife into her neck. It was an old artifact, something that looked like a museum piece with the initials M.F. etched on the blade.

Larsen was obliged to arrest the man and take him to Pond Inlet where it was determined he was guilty and he was to be incarcerated in a prison far to the south. The children of Pond Inlet gave Henry of the Big Ship small meteorites that they had been collecting and he cherished them, but the authorities insisted he also keep the murderer's knife. They did not want it anywhere in their community and insisted Henry should not throw it into the sea for fear it would taint the waters and make the animals go away. And if the hunting was no good, then they all might die. Larsen agreed and set off from Pond Inlet. It was near the end of September and there was just barely enough time left in the season to sail south.

Storms plagued him all the way to Bateau Harbour in Newfoundland and then the seas bellowed and roared some more around him as he sailed south to Halifax, having achieved what no man had before him. West to east across the Northwest Passage. The *St. Roch* wallowed in the waves and its crew was seasick like they had never been before.

Henry, cheerful and undaunted through most of the voyage, had darkened somewhat after dealing with the murder, and now he kept more to himself. When they arrived at the dock in Halifax, it had been a twenty-eight-month voyage since they left Vancouver. After that, the war caught up with the *St. Roch* and she was put on Atlantic submarine patrol.

Later, in July of 1944, Larsen was blessed again with a chance to go north, this time east to west — another first, to sail the Northwest Passage both ways.

CHAPTER TWENTY-FIVE

TODD IS ALREADY ASLEEP BUT THE drip with its dosage of painkiller takes him deeper. He still knows he is in a hospital bed but he is also lying on a beach with birds perched all over his body. Small, delicate seabirds. Petrels and shearwaters, the captain of the boat had called them. Todd remains in near darkness there in the IWK hospital but it seems that the daybreak is coming around unscheduled and his room has grown vividly and extravagantly bright with the morning sun. And then he feels a light sea breeze on his face and the birds rise up from him in a great explosion of fluttering wings.

As they fly away, they carry off all of his buried fears, his regret, his sadness. He is so light that he wonders if he can float — levitate like a magician. He feels as well a sudden freedom from all worry, fear, and guilt. Nothing has been harder on him than the guilt he feels about his illness.

One part of his mind begins to question whether this is real or imagined, dream or reality. Both and neither. What he feels and sees seems somehow more real than the day to day. Wherever it is that he has gone to, it is a place he is not anxious to leave. Todd inhales deeply and is carried farther up and away in the direction of the birds' flight. He blinks and then suddenly finds himself upright and dropped gently back onto solid ground — the moss-covered rocks of Devil's Island. Before him is the house, the lighthouse, the shed. Rabbits munching — black ones, white ones. Laundry blowing on a line in the sea breeze like billowing sails.

He begins to walk along the shoreline and feels the strength in his legs, the vitality in his lungs. He picks up a flat stone and skips it on the surface of the deep, clear water. Kelp fronds wave from the sea floor. A tug is passing by but he sees no one on deck. His feet find their way to a small pocket beach and he scoops up cold, wet sand, breathes in the smell of it, and then touches it to his cheek.

The petrels and shearwaters are above him now, buoyed on the south wind, hardly moving their wings. Todd shields his eyes from the sun, waves his hand through the air, thanks them for whatever it was they did to lift from him the burden of his troubles.

Todd decides to remove his shoes and looks down to discover that he is wearing hockey skates. He's suddenly wobbly now and it seems impossible to keep his balance as his skate blades sink into the wet sand. He laughs at the absurdity and is now fully convinced that this is a dream. If only it hadn't been for the hockey skates. Oh well, go with it. He looks off at the rippled surface of the water and decides he should be able to skate on it. He takes two knee-buckling steps forward, then pushes himself out onto the surface of the water, prepared to skate around the perimeter of the island.

Instead, he finds that he is left standing up to his ankles in the chilly Atlantic. He nearly topples into the water but steadies himself and takes a deep breath. The birds have flown off. Up above, there are small thin clouds floating by.

He tests his "dream theory" again by trying to levitate himself out of the water but it does no good. He wades ashore, sits and undoes the laces on his hockey skates. As he slowly unties the laces and takes off the skates one at a time, something falls into place. He feels certain, maybe for the first time in a long while, that his life makes sense. It has some kind of meaning he can't yet put words to.

Each breath now seems like an intentional gift from this sky, this sea, this day. He walks along the shoreline shelf of slate and then onto the moss and grass. He begins to walk towards the house in his bare feet. That's when she appears. The screen door creaks open, she steps out into the sun, and the door flaps closed. She is young. Her hair is blowing in the wind. She has to shield her eyes, having just come out into the brightness. On either side of her is a whirligig — the man chopping wood, a dog with legs running.

He keeps walking but she doesn't see him. Time for another test. He waves but does not speak. She still doesn't notice him but, instead, begins to pick wildflowers: red and white clover, daisies, Queen Anne's lace. So he calls her name. *Molly.*

She looks up at him and smiles.

Bartlett Kingsley thought it was a bad idea to drive to Halifax that night to check up on Todd. He'd had a couple of beers — nothing to get drunk on, although he wished sometimes he was a drinker so he could drink himself out of his own head. He was tired of being in what his wife called "his right mind." Todd's illness had changed her, he knew. Hardened her. It didn't seem to matter that the other kids were fine. Didn't seem to matter at all.

For sure, if Dr. Jesperson had asked him about an outing, he would have insisted he, himself, would be part of it. It would be a family thing, not just some Halifax woman taking their son for a stroll. But as far as he could tell, Todd had enjoyed a good day of it and it hadn't done him any real harm except for the fact that he was tired. There was no need to leave the house and drive all the way to Halifax.

But it came down to this — either he drove or she drove by herself and he didn't trust the car. There had been a battery problem. He could just see Joyce stalled and with a dead battery out on the Trans-Canada somewhere near those radio towers in the Tantramar Marsh at three o'clock in the morning. Besides, she was in an emotional state, worse than usual. Couldn't convince her to take something the doctor had prescribed for her nerves. He'd just have to see this thing through. His own pain he kept to himself, like it was an old, sorry photograph that he kept in his wallet, creased and bent up at the corners. He'd take it out and unfold it when no one was looking. He'd focus on just how bad it felt and get a good grip on it. His face would tighten up and his mouth would go dry. He'd let it go that far and then suck the snot back up his nose and fold up that hardship and put it back in his wallet and into his back pocket. And carry it around with him wherever he went.

Joyce spoke haltingly and angrily in the car. Bartlett insisted they stop at Tim Hortons and get some caffeine for the trip. He was also afraid that if the Mounties stopped him and detected the alcohol from the two beers, he might lose his license. He wondered if he explained the situation — he hadn't planned on driving — if it would make any difference. He thought it would. Cops were human after all. Then he felt guilty about using his son's illness as an excuse for himself and he wanted to say, damn it all to hell anyway, but he sipped his hot Tim Hortons coffee instead and studied the blackness along the Trans-Canada. He felt a hollowness growing inside him and wished he could speak about this to his wife, but he couldn't do that. So he'd have to ignore the feeling. He just knew that everything was out of his control. He tried to remember if it was comforting back when he believed in God. Did that help him feel any better? But he could not remember that far back.

Bartlett walked into the hospital room first, by himself, while Joyce argued with Brad in the hallway. Brad was working the early shift, the only counsellor on duty. Dr. Jesperson had gone home for the night. Bartlett thought it might be good for him to have at least a couple of minutes alone with his son, if the boy was asleep. If all looked well, he might just try to convince Joyce to drive back to New Brunswick without even waking him up. Bartlett was certain that the way she was all wired up right now, well, she would upset Todd in a big way and he wanted to spare his son that if he could.

Bartlett opened the door to Todd's room and walked in. He was startled to see that Todd was not alone. In bed with him was that woman, Molly, her arms around his son in an embrace. They were both asleep and looking peaceful. A great confusion swarmed into his mind. At first he simply couldn't comprehend what he was seeing, what it meant or didn't mean, but he closed the door gently behind him, his wife's voice shrill in the distance down the hall.

He knew of his son's attraction for Molly. And he had somewhat agreed with Joyce that there was something not quite right about the woman. But now here was something else. He believed that for some things that shock you in this life there were no easy or proper explanations. And now here was his ailing fourteen-year-old son in bed with a woman. The blood drained out of his face and he felt dizzy.

He decided he had to wake her and ask her to leave quickly and he'd try to make sense of this at some other time. But he was only two steps towards the bed when Brad and Joyce opened the door to the room.

The window was open slightly and Bartlett could smell the salt air of the harbour filtering into the room. He could hear the first birds of the morning — sparrows and a blue jay, some gulls in the distance. And in the split second before anyone had a chance to react or speak or even take a breath, he saw the peaceful look on his son's face and the way the morning sun painted the wall behind the bed the colour of gold.

Chapter Twenty-six

THE AUTOMATION OF THE LIGHTHOUSE ON Devil's Island was a bureaucratic decision made by men who had never set foot there. The technology was now in place and it was cheaper to automate than having to pay a lighthouse keeper's wages.

Molly had already moved to the mainland but made visits to her parents by rowing a borrowed dory to see them at least once each week. She didn't care if the weather was fine or if it was stormy. To be truthful, she liked stormy. She liked the feel of a lumpy sea, of water splashing, of working the waves this way and that. She adored the sensation of wrestling the waves and the chop, keeping a steady pace and a steady course through ragged waters and then sliding the dory into the smooth, protected little cove. She never let her parents know when she was coming. She just arrived. And they were always there. Nothing much had changed since her childhood. Everything was the same.

And then one day, her father had gone ashore for some tests on his kidneys. There had been blood in his urine and Lea said he should go see what that was all about. He rowed himself to Eastern Passage and one of the fishermen gave him a ride to Dartmouth Hospital. Hank sat in the waiting room performing basic magic tricks for some kids there. He made coins disappear and reappear in his ears. He made matchsticks move on a table surface, seemingly without touching them. In doing so, he made one crying little girl stop crying and smile.

Hank learned on his second visit to the hospital that he'd have to lose a kidney, there was no way around it. But he had two kidneys and he could go on living more or less normally with just one so Hank was thinking, what the heck. After the operation, he carefully transported the removed kidney back to the island in a jar of alcohol and put it on the open shelf in the kitchen where they kept the pickled beets and the pickled eggs and the sauerkraut they made themselves from the cabbages grown on the island. All things considered, Hank believed that he was not much worse for wear.

The head of the lighthouse division back at the Department of Transport heard about Hank's health condition and realized that this was an easy way to retire Hank for good and automate Devil's without much fuss. There had already been a lot of trouble with other lighthouse keepers who simply did not want to leave. Many of them were old and set in their ways — but old meant unreliable in the mind of a man who wanted to modernize everything. The lighthouse chief was convinced that a man with a lone kidney had no business keeping a lighthouse. He might die out there or have an emergency that would create an extra expense to get him ashore in a helicopter, or maybe he'd be too sick to tend the light and some big container ship would smash right into the rocks on Thrumcap Shoal without being able to get its bearing.

An official letter was sent to Hank and Lea and it was picked up at the post office in Eastern Passage by Lea.

And then one day, out of the blue, the boat just arrived. There were nearly a dozen strong men aboard to help pack and load and carry everything Hank and Lea owned over to the mainland. There was some great confusion and shouting and Hank said that a thing like this could not happen in Canada but that changed nothing.

Hank kept saying he wanted to talk to someone "to straighten everything out," so he got on the horn and talked to the Coast Guard boys. He told them to send someone in charge out in a helicopter right this goddamned minute.

But no chopper arrived. And Hank shouted and cursed and curled his hands into fists over and over. And finally Lea wept, at which time even Hank knew it was all over.

And it was a sad day for Devil's Island. Half the jars with the pickles and sauerkraut broke on the rough ride to shore due to careless packing. Hank's kidney jar busted too when one of those hefty, strong men tried to lift a cardboard box that got soggy on the trip to the mainland.

CHAPTER TWENTY-SEVEN

THE VIEW OUTSIDE THE NEW APARTMENT window was like poison to Lea and Hank. Hank was fairly certain the water was poison too. He'd only been drinking water from an island well for most of his life, an island in the midst of an entire ocean of salt water. But Hank's well water had been fresh and pure and clear, coming from bedrock deep down in the earth where nothing had been tainted by man.

Molly undertook the pleasant task of rowing out to the island twice a week with plastic jugs for water from Hank's beloved well. The men down at the wharf in Eastern Passage offered to take her out in their Cape Islanders but she preferred to row the borrowed dory. She needed the exercise and fresh air, she explained, and she liked rowing into the wind and against the tide. When she put her back into it, she could feel the satisfactory muscle burn in her upper arms.

Ever since Molly's parents were removed from the island, the level of the water in the well had come right up to the surface. She'd never seen this in the whole time she had been living there. It was a round well, dug by the hands of men over a hundred years ago. The water had always been clear and deep and beautiful.

Molly stared into her reflection in the water. There had been very little rain recently but the well was full and overflowing. Molly drank long gulps by cupping her hands and slurping down the water. In it she tasted childhood and every good thing. Looking into the dark clarity of the water she could see herself and she could see the night sky. She could see Orion and remembered her father making the constellation rise up into the night sky. She couldn't see the Milky Way.

When Molly returned to the mainland she told her parents, "Maybe we can find you a house to live in on another island."

"Nothing fancy or expensive," Hank said. "Some place not too far from shore but some place no one wants. Some place with an old barn or shack or something I can fix up in my spare time."

Molly asked, "What will you live on?"

Lea went into a long catalogue of edible wild things from seaweed to roots to plants plus other things she could grow in a garden even if she had just a "smidgen inch of soil."

"You know your mother can grow potatoes on a flat slab of granite if she wants to," Hank reminded Molly. And it was the truth. The trick was as simple as creating a pile of rotting seaweed.

"It doesn't have to be a big island," Hank said, feeling much better now and pulling quarters out from behind his ear. "And we'll pay you back," he said, tucking a quarter into Molly's hand, then somehow making it disappear without her feeling a thing.

With such great optimism over the potential move to an island, Lea and her husband found the Dartmouth apartment not nearly as bad, knowing it was just a layover on the way to an island, even if it was an island named Rat Rock. Unfortunately, Hank's health deteriorated and he had to have his gall bladder removed. The doctor, for some stubborn reason, would not let him take it home in a jar and that irked him. "What will they take next?" he asked his wife.

"As long as they don't take your self-respect and sense of humour, you'll be all right," his wife assured him.

Hank knew they couldn't move until his health improved so he and Lea started carving little wooden nameplates for the doors to all the rooms in their apartment. The kitchen was named "The Garden." The bedroom named "Bower of Bliss," the bathroom named "Bad Water Creek," the living room became "Happy Hearth and Home," and since there were no other rooms with doors, they started putting nameplates on walls until every wall had its own name — all bird names like Willett, Puffin, Shearwater, Dovekie, Merganser.

When Hank's second and last kidney stopped working, he blamed it on taking showers in the city water that had somehow been absorbed through his skin. He took on a bluish tinge, which made him think that maybe he was turning into a fish, but the doctor assured him it was his kidney. Hank hated being hooked up to a dialysis machine and kept asking everyone at the hospital how the hell he was supposed to stay hooked up to a machine if he was going to be living in his "new house" out on some island.

Molly and Lea were there at his bedside when Hank did his final disappearing act, despite the fact that Molly begged him not to leave. Molly went back to the Dartmouth apartment later that night and Lea cooked the two of them a big meal. A place was set for Hank, and Molly said nothing when her mother filled the plate with food and poured well water from the plastic jug into Hank's glass.

Lea refused to move in with Molly after the funeral and then, a week or so later, Lea decided she would stop eating. Just like that. There were doctors involved and much persuasive effort put into encouraging Lea's appetite but it was all to no avail. Molly would sit and read to her mother from cookbooks but her mother kept saying that the authors had it all wrong. Lea added, "Nothing tastes the same since your father passed on. It's like all the flavour of everything has disappeared. Have you noticed?"

Molly was very aware of how much had been lost. There were fewer stars at night, fewer birds above the harbour waters. Music on the radio sounded different. Molly forced her mother to come live with her and she cooked for her often. She tried everything but her mother would not give in. Her flesh now sagged on her bones and her skin colour, like her husband before her, was turning a dim blue. "Maybe I can turn myself into a fish like your father did."

Then came the intravenous tubes and even that did no good and, all too soon, Molly had two small urns of ashes sitting in the window of her bookshop where the sun warmed them on the bright days.

When the weather softened, Molly got a ride from an Eastern Passage fisherman in his big boat out past Devil's Island and the ashes were not tossed into the wind but settled gently onto the smooth, dark surface of the sea. Molly could tell no difference at all between the appearance of the ashes of her father and those of her mother and she watched as they drifted south and east. When she turned around to look at her childhood island home, she was amazed to see how low it sat upon the sea, as if the land wasn't even there at all, and the lighthouse and the house she had grown up in were floating on the surface of the water itself.

CHAPTER TWENTY-EIGHT

MOLLY SAT UP AND TRIED TO cover herself with the sheet. She didn't know how she got here, but she now saw that she was in the hospital bed with Todd, and she was naked. She had been awakened by the scream of Todd's mother, Joyce. Bartlett tried to get his wife to calm down but she was shouting at Molly now. "Who the hell do you think you are?" Molly looked afraid and confused. Hearing the commotion, a nurse arrived on the scene, a Black woman who sucked in her breath and said, "Sweet Lord Jesus."

At that moment, Brad walked into the room. A look of shock came over him and at first he seemed incapable of speech. Joyce was about to lunge at Molly but Bartlett grabbed her and held her back.

Brad took a deep breath. "Before anyone says anything they might regret," Brad announced, trying to gain some control over the situation, "we should think about the boy first."

Todd remained asleep, blissfully unaware of the mayhem in the room. The nurse found a blanket and handed it to Molly, who used it to cover herself. Then Molly began to cry.

Bartlett could barely hold his wife back. "Just take it easy, Joyce. We'll sort this out," he said.

"Someone call the police," she insisted. "I want someone to call the police."

"Let's just calm down first," Brad said.

A security guard arrived next. He and the nurse ushered Molly out of the room to a nearby office. Then they returned to pick up Molly's clothes.

Soon the police arrived — a man and a woman in uniform, both looking uncomfortable and even slightly embarrassed as they escorted Molly out of the hospital in what seemed like slow motion.

Mrs. Harriet Fitzhenry had not gone back to England as planned. She had read a tour guide about the *Titanic* victims buried in Halifax and had become obsessed with visiting each grave and then beginning to research the biography of each person buried there. She was a regular at the Fairview Cemetery and had donated money to it for the improvement and upkeep of the graves. She was staying at the Lord Nelson Hotel in a suite once occupied by the Queen on a visit to the city. She paid one of the office staff downstairs to type up her notes and she told him that the research was for a book she was writing, even though she didn't really believe she had it "in her" to write an entire book. Her son, her beloved dead son, Bertrand, now he had had several books in him. And they would have all come out had he not died. But that was a long time ago.

Harriet Fitzhenry had developed a long and thorough list of the people and things she blamed for the death of her son. She had held grudges long and hard against each of them for his death. First, there was her husband. He was pretty much at the top of the list for funding the boy's travels. But, of course, he could never have predicted the tragic outcome. Then Bertrand, himself, for deciding to go to Canada. But it did a mother no good to blame her dead son since she still loved him so much, alive or dead. Next, she blamed Canada and later focussed more specifically on Nova Scotia, and then Halifax. For a while, she blamed geology — Bertrand's passion that led to his unlucky death. The airplane industry was in line for punishment as were storms of any nature. She cursed the skies sometimes when it rained. And then finally, one day, she had been in Cornwall, at St. Ives, and she found herself lathering up a powerful hatred for the Atlantic Ocean, which had drowned her son. She was standing on a beach when she began to scream at the sea. She walked to the water, fell to her knees, and slapped her hands on the surface of the sea, shouting as only a grieving mother could.

And that had been enough of that. She had always loved the seacoast and the sweet, salty smell of water and sand, wet rocks, and seaweed. Ever since she had been a child. And she could not live with herself if she was going to go on hating this ocean or any ocean. So she tasted the salt of her tears — tears that she'd been holding back and holding back and holding back. And then she scooped up some water and drank from it and tasted the salt in it as well. But all that had been a rather long time ago.

On bad days, she pitied herself. A widow alone in a foreign city (even though Halifax didn't feel foreign) visiting cemeteries day after day, going to the archives and wearing white gloves and looking up old documents. What was it about the smell of old newspapers, the must of old ledger books? Why was it both stimulating and depressing? Was it because all of human history was both stimulating and depressing? Perhaps.

She was comfortable enough in the Queen's suite at the Lord Nelson, although the rooms, too, smelled of times gone by. It suggested something once grand, now faded. It had the detectable trace of something dwindling, half-forgotten, something that was once important but wasn't anymore.

Harriet Fitzhenry was an expert on cures for self-pity. Tea with clotted cream was one of them, but clotted cream was hard to come by in Canada. The staff of the Lord Nelson, however, was still working on it. Making anonymous donations to the do-gooders of the world was another way to cure self-pity. But over the years she had grown more adventurous with her cures. She started reading Victorian pornography, for example, but tired of that after a while and decided not to venture into more contemporary pornography, which seemed much less literary and, oh, so very tedious with its repetitive obsessions.

Even in Halifax, Harriet talked often on the telephone to a stockbrokerage firm in London, buying and selling stocks on whims. For example, one day she would ask her broker to buy six stocks that began with the letter M and six that began with the letter F. She told him to hold them for three weeks and then sell them all. Other times, she would tell her broker to buy German companies making ice cream or an Irish furniture manufacturer who was currently out of favour with investors. She held on to some stocks, sold some others. Lost money on gold mines in the Arctic where there was no gold, made money on oil drilling when it turned out there was oil. She could afford to win and lose and often baffled her brokers who were always trying to "educate" her about the market.

She racked up a profit from car parts in Argentina and lost it again to a food chain selling Mexican food in New England. The amazing thing was that she always seemed to end up breaking even.

Harriet's other novel cure for self-pity that she had invented here in Canada was to visit hardware stores. She loved to look at, study, and sometimes buy tools and building materials, plumbing parts, car accessories — anything you would find in a hardware store. She did not know why this cheered her up nor did she care to know why. It just did. So she frequented all the Home Hardware and Canadian Tire stores in Halifax and a few in Dartmouth.

But the crème de la crème was Ron's Army Navy Store on Agricola Street. She had first visited that location because it was the former site of the Mayflower Curling Rink. And the Mayflower Curling Rink had been where the bodies of the

Titanic victims had been laid out upon the ice before burial. The rescue ships had scooped the victims from the cold Atlantic and brought them to Halifax and needed some place to put them. The curling rink was the place to do it.

Sadly, the curling rink was long gone. On the same site had been built a family courthouse that was suitable enough to marry and divorce a goodly chunk of the Halifax population. And then the courts moved away from Agricola Street and the old courthouse building, an architectural hodgepodge of no great merit, became an army navy store.

Harriet was now a regular customer at Ron's. Sometimes she'd stand near the back of the store and enjoy the pungent smell of rope. Other times she'd buy ten-penny nails or small boxes of old copper fittings. Beneath her feet had once lain the prostrate corpses of the *Titanic* passengers, arranged in an orderly fashion, head to toe, on the sporting ice of the curling rink.

It was in Ron's that she bought a copy of the *Daily News* from the clerk. Outside, sitting on a bench in front of the store, she read the story about a woman found in a hospital bed naked. She had been sleeping with a fourteen-year-old boy. Certainly she had never heard of anything like that happening in the hospitals in England. Not in her day, at any rate. And what the woman was being accused of sounded very serious indeed. The only picture was a bland photograph of the outside of the hospital.

Harriet read the article and noted that the woman charged ran a used bookstore on the lower end of Winslow Street. When she looked up from the newspaper, the stores and the traffic were slightly out of focus.

Chapter Twenty-nine

Eric was walking down Spring Garden Road when he decided to spend at least part of the morning in the Halifax Library. Winston Churchill, cast in bronze, was frozen midstride before the main entrance. Churchill once said, "When you have to kill a man, it costs you nothing to be polite." Eric wondered why Churchill was posted here in particular or why the seagull liked sitting on his head. But then Eric was still wondering why he himself was here in Halifax. It had to be more than his interest in history, his so-called research into the life of Henry Larsen.

He sat himself in an old leather chair in the reading room where someone had left the morning paper. Eric had not been one to follow the news. News and history were two different species, he always believed. He had once had a notion of coming up with a strategy — a mental filtering system whereby anyone could sit down before a TV anchorperson, or with a newspaper, and immediately filter out what was mere "news" and what would be history. But in order to do that well, one would have to have a great command of previous history, stretching back at least to ancient Greece if not before. And one would also have to have some ability at prognostication — seeing into the future to know which stories of seemingly little significance now would eventually lead to great or calamitous effects.

On the front page of the paper was a photo of a car wreck and a hospital. A logical link. Car crashes and victims are trundled to the emergency ward. Eric's filters were not turned on. He found himself reading first about the head-on collision on a highway in the Annapolis Valley: two adults dead, one child, sitting in an "approved" child safety seat, survived with only minor neck injuries.

"Child grows up to invent a cure for human stupidity," Eric said silently to himself.

The story with the photo of the hospital was not about the accident victims, though. It was about a woman found in a hospital bed with a boy. She had been arrested. The boy was only fourteen. The boy (who was unnamed) was being treated for "a serious illness." His parents were pressing charges. The woman was named, however. She had no previous convictions.

Eric folded the paper and then rubbed his eyes. He remembered Henry Larsen's own words describing what he felt like upon arriving in Halifax, arriving back in the south, the so-called "civilized" world, after spending so much time up north. Everything had suddenly felt strange, Larsen confessed. "We almost had a feeling that we had arrived in a world where we really didn't belong."

Eric got up and walked back outside and stood by Winston Churchill for a long minute. He was thinking that this illogical, almost random, act of flying to Halifax and staying here had been a mistake. Molly had aroused the first real spark of something vital in him in a long while. The simple thing would be to walk away from it all. Fly away. The apartment was paid for until the end of the month, but what did that matter? He had no commitments. He could pack up his things in a matter of an hour or so, take a cab to the airport and fly to wherever he wanted to go.

At one time he'd had a craving to visit battlegrounds. The Americans had turned their Civil War battlegrounds into lovely, rolling, green state and national parks. He could picnic with the dead till his boots were filled and then head off to Europe, where nearly the entire continent was layered deep with battles, one after the next, bodies piling up for one political reason or another. He could have the time of his life.

Instead, he found his feet walking back to the corner of Winslow Street and heading south. He was thinking about something Molly had said to him about that island she had grown up on, how her father had told her that all around on the shoreline were the invisible bones of those humans and other mammals that had died at sea but she should not be afraid to step on them. Molly's father had told her that she had been assigned the task of protecting any living sea creatures she found that were injured. Together they had cared for a nearly starved harbour seal pup and a wounded sea otter. Molly had described to Eric the large, romantic eyes of the young seal, and the sharp teeth of the sea otter that had swum into the little island cove after it had been shot with a rifle by some teenage boys, joyriding in a Boston Whaler.

Terra Incognita was where Eric was headed. He was following his gut instinct into the unknown. Walking south on Winslow, past the Sebastopol lion, past the cemetery dead with their faded headstones, their high hopes of being saved by their "Lord in Heaven," and their relatives' chiseled optimism that they had moved on to live "in eternal life." Eric had already decided that the dead in all the world's battlefields could wait for his visit. They weren't going anywhere. Their invisible bones would still be there beneath the manicured grass lawns and clipped hedges. The dead could always wait. There was no hurry and if he never set foot on Gettysburg or Antietam or Bull Run, maybe he'd be none the worse for it.

History itself, half forgotten, hardly understood (like the name "Sebastopol" there on the concrete lion), surely deserved to take a back seat to the here and now. And what of the future? Eric had spent little of his academic career thinking anything

about the future until he had convinced himself there was no future worth pursuing. Halifax had changed all that.
No. Not quite right. Molly had changed all that.
No one was at the bookstore when he arrived. There were no lights on, but the door was not locked. He walked in and heard the small, old-fashioned bell ring above the door. He was hoping someone might be there to give him some more information about what had transpired. He knew enough not to trust newspapers to tell the truth — if there was a truth. But the store was empty and the books were not sharing any secrets. Centuries of words lined the shelves. Somewhere in the right volume, though, would be phrases and articulations for what he was feeling in his heart, his gut, and his head. Discovery and loss all at once. Having found and having had it taken away before he even knew what it was.

Harriet Fitzhenry found Eric sitting behind the sales counter reading. The bell rang as the elderly British woman walked in. "Are you a friend of Molly's?" Harriet asked.
"Yes," Eric said. "I think I am."
"Do you know anything about what has happened to her?"
"No, not really."
"Then I think we should find out," Harriet said and placed the newspaper story in front of him.
Eric had no idea who this woman was, although her demeanour somewhat reminded him of a female version of Winston Churchill. Eric opened his wallet and found the card for the taxi driver he had had met at the airport. He picked up the phone on the counter. Oscar Ryan said he would come right away.
On the drive to the police station, Eric sat in silence. Harriet asked Oscar to turn off the radio. Eric and Harriet both noticed at the same time that their driver had a tattoo of a fish on his

LESLEY CHOYCE

neck with the inscription, "Swallow your pride." Harriet blurted out, "Do you ever regret having that thing on your neck?"

"Nah," Oscar answered. "I have no regrets about anything. You move on and don't look back. I never look back," he said, looking back at them in the rear-view mirror.

"My husband," Harriet said to both men, "lived with all his regrets collected around him. He enjoyed his successes, and there were many, but he cherished his failures. That habit got in the way of him enjoying life and it rubbed off on me for a time until I got rid of it."

"How did you do that?"

"I stopped playing by everybody else's rules."

"And happily ever after, I guess," Oscar said.

"I didn't say that."

Eric walked with Harriet into the police station and was directed to Constable Rawlings, the police desk sergeant, a slender woman who seemed to immediately like Harriet. Harriet told her they were friends of Molly Willis.

"It has already been decided that she can be released if someone is willing to put up bail."

"That can be arranged," Harriet said.

"She has no previous convictions. This isn't the sort of crime we have seen before. At least people don't come forward. We're a little worried about the welfare of the accused, to be honest. We're not sure how people in the community will react to her."

"I understand," Eric said. "But certainly that doesn't mean she should stay incarcerated."

"No, it doesn't. She'll need to sit for psychological testing and remain available for further questioning."

"Certainly," Harriet answered.

"And your relation to the accused?" she asked.

"Family," Harriet responded.

"This will take a little while. I'll pull together the paper work. So be patient."

When she appeared, Molly's withdrawal from the world was quite evident. Eric sensed immediately that something had gone out of her and he was quite familiar with that look, he had seen it many times before in his own mirror.

Chapter Thirty

Where people go when they are still there in body but not in full mind was no great mystery to Eric. He guided Molly through the lobby of the police station as Harriet finished up with the paperwork. It felt like they had been in there for days.

Molly's bookstore now seemed like the saddest bookstore in Halifax, possibly in North America. Certainly there were sadder bookstores in Europe. Harriet told Eric she had visited some of them. One in Paris that made her cry and one in Vienna she could not even bring herself to enter. But for North America, Molly's used bookstore was sad enough to make it to number one. "At least I could put some of my money to good use," Harriet told Eric over a cup of Earl Grey. She meant the bail money. "My husband believed that money had a kind of essence — it wasn't alive, but it had a personality and a will. It liked you or it didn't. Yes, money loved the man but it turned on him sometimes like a rabid dog. I never had much interest in money and it had less interest in me. But we were always on speaking terms." She took a long, serious gulp of her tea. "I suppose we'll need a good lawyer," she announced.

"Yes, I think so," Eric said, noticing that she had used the word "we."

Molly was asleep upstairs and Eric wasn't sure what was required of him. He was pretty certain Molly needed professional psychological help. He'd been there. He knew. When he had been at his worst what he needed most was a map of some sort — topographical, psychological — something showing a clear trail back into the normal world. Unfortunately, no one had a map to give him. Only clues in the form of questions. Do you know where you are? Do you know what day it is? Do you know how you got here?

Eric found a cot in a closet in the store and set it up for Harriet, who had announced she was staying; she would not be going back to the Queen's suite at the Lord Nelson. Harriet slept in the self-help section of the bookstore beneath a row of old Dale Carnegie paperbacks and some books with titles like *I'm Okay, You're Okay* and *The Zen of Everything*. "An old woman on a cot," Harriet said out loud, as she put herself to bed beneath a single blanket.

Eric stood at the counter by a small pool of light from the desk lamp. He leafed through the mail that had come in that day. Publisher's catalogues with hopeful books, many of the new titles were promoted as being "powerful" or "ground-breaking" or "critically acclaimed." There were none being touted as "ordinary" or even "good."

There were bills on the desk and one postcard from a man in Russia. Junk mail too, enough junk mail so that he almost missed it. Beneath a Superstore flyer was an envelope with no stamp and no address. A scrawl only: "Molly."

"Remind me to send out for a toothbrush in the morning, will you, Eric?" Harriet said. "I never feel fully settled unless I have a toothbrush with me." And with that, she seemed to fall asleep, as if uttering the word "toothbrush" was like a switch that turned her off for the day. An old, kind woman asleep on a cot. She was wearing one of Molly's nightgowns. Dale Carnegie smiled down at her from above. Did the man ever not smile? Eric wondered.

Eric found himself opening the letter. It was from Todd. How it got here was a mystery but it was here. It had not been sealed. An invitation.

Dear Molly,
Whatever goes from here, I take my memory of you with
me. I take your island and I take our day together. I was
wrong about thinking I had missed out on so much.
You were kind to take a chance on me, although I feel
like I took advantage of you. I know you felt sorry for
me and since I became sick I learned how to use that.
    But I needed to get away from the hospital. I
needed to climb up out of where I was. Needed to
climb out of me, and you taught me how.
    The birds above your island — they told me I could
use their wings whenever I wanted. Do you think this is
something I imagined? When I need to sleep, I do just
that. I borrow their wings. When I need to make the
pain go away, I think about you.
    I don't dream much because of the drugs but last
night I dreamed I was a seagull. I flew over the city
until I found you and you turned into a bird too, a pure
white seabird. And then we were over the ocean, the
wind lifting us higher and higher above the sea.
Love,
Todd

Eric felt guilty for having intruded into something
so personal. What was he to make of this? Then he
shifted his thoughts to another direction. He was now
involved — whatever that would mean. It felt right and he
would not turn back. He studied his hands in the pool of light.
His pale hands, his long bony fingers, the ribbon of tendons
anchoring his fingers to his wrist. He turned his arms over
and studied the delta of arteries and veins.
    Harriet had begun to snore and it was a sound Eric
welcomed. He decided he would pick a book to read and then
fall asleep in a padded reading chair. But first he would deliver
the letter. He tiptoed up the creaky wooden stairs and looked

in on Molly in her bedroom. She too was sleeping. The light from the hallway spilled into the room and illuminated her face. Eric touched her hair once, felt the thrill of its delicacy in his fingers. He placed the letter on the night table so Molly would see it when she awoke. Then he turned and walked out of the room and down the stairs.

Once Eric sat down, he realized he was too tired to even read. He was alone with his own thoughts. Eric knew a few things about legal proceedings, and about hospitals and their psychological testing. He didn't trust much of it. He thought about his own divorce, for example. The pain of it all had been duly exacerbated by the law and lawyers. The scar tissue was still sensitive. And the very smell of the Ottawa hospital was still with him. His only ally then, it had seemed, was that Native guy, Ray. Eric kept meaning to give him a call. Check in. Something left unresolved. Raymond had called Eric, Grandfather.

Eric flashed further back to his time on Baffin Island. Why had he gone there, anyway? What had he been thinking? Maybe that, too, had been some form of mental illness. And maybe now he was attracted to people who were crazy.

The phone rang not much after nine the next morning. Eric had a sore neck from sleeping in a chair — something he had not done since his own university days. Someone had cut through some red tape and the officer at the Halifax Police Department said they would like to have Molly begin with a battery of psychological tests that very morning at the Abbie Lane Hospital. They would send a car for her.

"No, please," Eric said. "I'll see that she gets there."

Reluctantly, the officer agreed. "Eleven. You bring her upstairs to the fourth floor and check her in by eleven."

"Certainly." He hung up.

As Harriet prepared some tea and found milk and bagels in an old refrigerator in the back, Eric worried over what would happen to Molly. He stepped outside and discovered pigeons pecking away at birdseed that someone had scattered in front of the store. They waltzed about in crazy patterns. Eric felt himself calming down as he looked at the birds. He *would* take Molly for testing. In the hospital at least, Molly would be protected from prying reporters and possibly get some help. She seemed so confused. He would be patient. And he would be there for her if she needed him.

Harriet had put on her makeup and come outside to find him. She looked very businesslike, thoroughly no-nonsense, as was her nature. Handing Eric a cup of Earl Grey, she said, "Molly's up. She didn't say much. Still has that hollow look." And then, out of the blue, "Did you know she pulled my son from the sea?"

"No."

"It was a long time ago. But she told me about it. I can see it just like it was a movie running inside my head." Mrs. Fitzhenry told Eric about the storm, the plane crash. "A mother doesn't forget a thing like that." Harriet's hand shook slightly and she spilled some tea on the sidewalk, just missing the pigeons still pecking and weaving around their feet.

At ten o'clock a Black woman arrived, introduced herself as Elsie Downey. "I'm a regular customer," she said. "I understand there is some confusion over an issue involving Molly. I thought I could help out. I've been retired now for several years, you know."

"You are a friend of Molly's?" Harriet asked.

"Yes. She introduced me to many good books. I'll hold down the fort if need be."

"We need to take her for psychiatric testing this morning," Eric said.

Mrs. Downey looked up and across the street. "My niece was there at the hospital where the boy was. She explained to me about the confusion surrounding the incident." Eric could tell it was not a comfortable thing for her to talk about. "Perhaps there was a misunderstanding. The world is full of misunderstandings. When I was a school principal, I always tried to steer people away from jumping to conclusions, from assuming guilt on the basis of what something *looked* like. There is what *is* and there is what *appears to be*. The two are not always the same. I brought my own change for the register. Just in case there isn't enough here already for the customers. It's here in my purse."

Harriet smiled at the woman. "If you take care of the pennies, the big money will take care of itself," she said.

"I'll tidy up inside, as well, if things are slow," Mrs. Downey said.

Eric cleared his throat, "If anyone from the press shows up — TV people or newspaper reporters . . . "

"If any of them show up, they will receive a lecture from me about the decline of mass media. I will sit them down and give them a piece of my mind concerning proper usage of language as well. I promise you, they will not turn a deaf ear to what I have to say to them."

Chapter Thirty-one

THE WOMAN POLICE OFFICER, CONSTABLE RAWLINGS, was there at the psychiatric clinic of the hospital to greet them. She was trying to look important and threatening.

Along with Rawlings there was a rather nervous and severe administrator who introduced himself as Reginald Hyssop. "And you are?" he asked Eric.

But it was Harriet who answered. "We are Molly's family," she said with the greatest authority.

Hyssop seemed as if he was about to question them on that point but Harriet kept him fixed with her piercing eyes. "This is Dr. Soleri," he said, nodding to the man beside him. "Dr. Soleri will be in charge of this case. He's had considerable experience and is most competent."

Molly had been trying to achieve invisibility all morning. And it was working. No one seemed to look directly at her. Ever since waking, she had been attempting to translate what was left of herself into island fog. She believed that if she could make her body turn into salt air vapour, she could rise up and float out over the harbour. And if the sun came out and burned her away to clear, blue air, that would be okay too. She was aware of Eric and Harriet but confused over their identities. Harriet might have been her own mother but the clothes weren't right. Eric was, well, she wasn't sure who he was but she knew he was supposed to be there. There were a few things about him that disturbed her but she knew he was a kind man, if perhaps a damaged one. There was some specific thing about him that was important but when you are transforming yourself into salt air fog, your focus is not so good. All she knew was that Eric reminded her of a grown-up Holden Caulfield.

"She will be in our care for two days, during which time we will be administering some standard tests," Dr. Soleri said. He had large, dark eyes that made you think of a seal pup. Molly could tell that he too had experienced his share of pain and sorrow and kept it stored up in his shoulders and lower back, although his hands were like lively birds in front of him. Stormy petrels at sea or sandpipers zigzagging low over the water near shore. "I think the formal introductions are mostly over," he said, nodding to the administrator and the police officer. They both took their leave and Dr. Soleri waited for the door to close. Then he took a deep breath, walked from behind his desk, picked up Molly's hand, and touched her wrist. He appeared to be taking her pulse. After a minute of silence, he asked, "How are you feeling, Molly?"

She shook her head as if she didn't understand the language he was speaking.

"You have a strong heart. We are going to see what we can find out about you. That is my job, but my job is not just to test people to find out if they are normal. I have yet to meet a normal person."

He turned to Harriet and Eric, who were now a little baffled by the strangeness of this approach. "Have you ever met a person who is a hundred percent normal?" he asked them.

"My husband believed that most men were simply average if that is the same thing," Mrs. Fitzhenry answered. "But I never accepted that."

"Average and normal are cousins," Soleri said. "I went to school with them but they turned out to be not what they appeared."

"Dr. Soleri, can you help her — if she needs helping?" Eric interrupted.

The doctor let go of Molly's wrist and he touched her once gently on the shoulder, then returned to sit behind his desk and began to trace his own dark eyebrows with his index fingers as if grooming himself. "I have been assigned to assess her situation. As you know there are charges. Both the medical and the legal systems like to make us put things into boxes. Put something in this box or that. If possible, close the lid so it stays put. You put a label on the box and set it on a shelf. Just so. The trouble with people is they keep trying to climb out of those boxes. Nobody likes boxes unless you are a manufacturer of corrugated cardboard. Nonetheless, the tests can tell us certain things."

"And then?" Eric asked.

"I don't know. But give us a chance. I'm looking forward to working with Molly." Then he turned to her. "Molly, I understand you run a used bookstore. You are a great lover of literature."

Molly nodded. She was trying to remember what she had written in those letters to Holden Caulfield. She was also trying to remember what had become of her copy, her very first copy, of *The Catcher in the Rye*.

Both Harriet and Eric understood it was time for them to leave. They were reluctant to do so but, having met Dr. Soleri, with his gentle approach, they felt somewhat satisfied that Molly was in good hands.

Dr. Soleri sat quietly with Molly for a minute and then leaned forward. "I always like to get to know people by trying to find out some things about their childhood. I guess that's rather traditional of me but what was yours like?"

"We were island people," Molly said. And as she said this, everything about the island came back to her. She stopped speaking as she set foot on the sandy shore in the tiny cove on the north end of Devil's Island. Her feet found their way to the house. "At night my father knew how to make the stars come back. He knew where to place them — Big Dipper, Cassiopeia, Orion. Sometimes he could even rearrange them. And, if I asked, he could make them disappear as well."

Soleri told her that he too had lived on an island for a while, Anticosti, and that some part of him was also still an island person. "Some islands you never leave," he said.

"So soft this morning ours," Molly said, quoting from near the end of *Finnegan's Wake*.

Soleri did not understand the reference but he jotted the phrase down. For now, he thought, *sfumato*. It was the Italian word for smoke. His mother had been French Canadian but his father was Italian. He had often used the word to mean ambiguity. Sometimes there are no easy answers. No obvious right or wrong. Or worse yet, the right thing to do turns out to be wrong.

He allowed silence to do whatever medicine it could for a few minutes. His patient did not seem particularly upset or afraid, just distant. So very distant. "So soft this morning ours," he finally repeated.

"Do you ever feel that something very important has gone out of the world? Like Wordsworth said, 'The things which I have seen, I now can see no more.'"

Soleri felt that profound sadness that Molly carried with her. He was beginning to think that Molly was one of those fragile beings, too fragile for this world. Nothing really wrong with them, just too fragile, too sensitive. He did not like applying traditional technical terms to such a person other than this: *wounded angel*. Some were labeled schizophrenic, some clinically depressed. Many died young. It was a suicidal breed — these men and women, as if dropped into our world from another much gentler dimension. Easily abused the lot of them, easily damaged. Tough to cure — if even there was such a thing.

These were the luna moths, the child-adults. He wondered how many of them had come from islands. Soleri tried to stop himself from jumping to conclusions. *Sfumato. Curiosita.* Remain alert, open-minded, curious. A woman had been found in bed with a fourteen-year-old boy. She was being charged with a crime. He was not going to be allowed to speak to the boy. His assigned job was to analyze and assess. His true job was to use his entire brain, not just the part that put people into boxes with lids. "You love books, right?"

"Yes."

"All books?"

"Most. There are a few ugly books but most have redeeming value. I've found beautiful passages even in ugly books."

"Name an ugly book."

"*Mein Kampf.*"

"You read Hitler?"

"Have read. Past tense. I run a used bookstore. Someone dropped off Marx, Hitler, Freud and Jung. It was a funny combination but I read them all."

"Did you like Carl Jung?"

"Yes. Everything is a symbol. The birds are freedom. The horse running through the field is sex. A boat on a sea with no oars suggests you are at the whim of larger forces than yourself. But I think that is all your department."

"What about Hitler?"

"He wrote *Mein Kampf* in prison. If he had not been turned down as a young man from entering art academy, his life would probably have gone differently. He would have painted and taught art and he would have spent his evenings in the beer halls of Munich."

So Molly was not as "distant" as he had thought, as everyone had thought. She was on her island — of books, of ideas, of the past — but others were allowed to come ashore.

Next Molly began to recite a poem:

The Grizzly Bear is huge and wild
It has devoured the infant child
The infant child is not aware
It has been eaten by the bear.

Molly noticed Dr. Soleri's puzzled reaction. She smiled at him for the first time. "I'm sorry. It's just a silly verse — A.E. Housman wrote it. It isn't mine. My head is so full of things from books: poems, stories, lives. It all just rattles around and sometimes it comes out without me thinking about it."

Sfumato. Curiosita. "Who is the Grizzly bear?" He asked.

"I am, I suppose," she said. "I'm the bad one, is that correct?"

"Who, then, is the infant child?"

Molly studied on that for a second, placing her index finger to her lip. "I suppose that is me as well."

Chapter Thirty-Two

ON THE SECOND DAY OF MOLLY'S stay in the hospital, after a battery of clinical tests that had very erratic results, Dr. Soleri was beginning to wonder if Molly was somehow purposefully throwing a wrench into the works. But his instincts told him no. Multiple personalities? Too Hollywood. Stay focused on just what you see before you, he chided himself. *Sfumato.*

Molly seemed to reveal the most when he asked no questions at all. "My parents were forced to leave the island when they automated the lighthouse. They lived for a while in town but my father started going downhill right away. He died of kidney problems and he blamed it on the water — city water. My mother stopped eating after that. She didn't last a month without him. It was all very sad. There was nothing I could do."

"I'm so sorry," Dr. Soleri said and silence filled the room for many long minutes after that.

Soleri had been putting off the direct questions, the ones he was supposed to be asking. His time would be running out soon. Molly seemed to have become more focussed after mentioning the death of her parents. She seemed less distracted and confused. Soleri ventured forward. "Do you know what you've been charged with?"

"Yes," Molly said, looking down.

"Is that what really happened?"

Molly was thinking about Holden Caulfield again. Funny how he kept popping up in her brain lately, how he'd referred to his own mental problems as "that madman stuff."

Soleri saw that she was somewhere else. He didn't know about the letters to Holden Caulfield. He wouldn't know about Mrs. Fitzhenry's drowned son sleeping his final sleep with Molly watching him when she was just fourteen.

"Would you write something for me while you are here?"

"I would be happy to do that."

"Just write a story."

"About me?"

"Not necessarily."

"Will you then psychoanalyze it and tell me the house is the soul and the bird is freedom and the snake is evil?"

"No, I won't do that. I just want you to make up a story from your imagination. The imagination is a great domain. Everything is in there. I just want to see some of what is in your imagination."

"Whom will you show this to?"

"Only people you want me to show it to. If you write me a great story, I'll get you a literary agent."

Molly laughed. She knew he was joking but she also realized that she trusted him. She would write a story. She'd make something up.

Salina

Salina was a very beautiful, dark-eyed girl who lived alone with her father along a very remote and distant shore. It was a very cold place with much ice and few people. Her father eked out a living by catching fish but he was not very good at it and he wished for something better for his daughter.

Young men rowed their boats from very far away, often through ice fields, to meet Salina and try to lure her away with them. Sometimes they brought considerable food as gifts and her father was much impressed. He so badly wanted a better life for his daughter and began to believe that if she could leave him and go somewhere else, this would happen. He thought she should be free of him and go to a better place. In the night, he spoke to the spirits and they understood. The spirits even promised him that if he found a new home for his daughter — if she moved away — they would take care of him and so he was even more moved to find a new home for Salina.

Salina had long, dark hair and she would sit by a cove on windless days, untangling her hair with a comb made from the beak of an egret. She would do this for a long time and it would cause her to fall into a deep trance, singing to herself a song taught to her by the sea.

The young men came in their wooden boats of many sizes and shapes. Salina was not impressed by any of these men. Her father fumed over this because he wished to see his daughter off to a better life and he now wished to be alone with the spirits at night and see what they were willing to do for him. If only she would go with one of the young men.

One day, a young man arrived in a kayak, paddling from the horizon, straight into the little cove where Salina sat and combed her hair. Like Salina, the young man had long, dark hair and deep, dark eyes and he could have been mistaken for her brother but she knew she had no brother. The sea was filled with wondrous islands of blue ice that day. The sun shone on them and through them and created great beauty. The magic of the day and the beauty of the man dazzled her as he stepped ashore wearing fine furs.

Her father was convinced that this was the one who would finally take his daughter away to her new life and leave him alone with his spirits. The young kayaker gave gifts of furs and food to Salina's father and then described the wonderful island home where he lived — how warm and large it was, how plentiful the food. But when asked his name, he said he could not speak his name here in a foreign land, that it was forbidden to do so. Salina's father said he understood about such rules. Salina herself was more interested in the man than in his name and she believed she had fallen in love with the young man even though they had just met. Yes, she said, she would go with him to his home, wherever it was.

They paddled for days through blue-white pans of ice and small icebergs that shone with light from within, even at night. Finally, they came to a rocky island. It looked bleak and terrifying but this is where the young dark man paddled them ashore.

She stepped ashore first and was much disillusioned by what she saw. Worse yet, when he followed her onto land, he turned from a handsome man into a giant raven. "This is my home," he said. He pointed to a dead tree near the shoreline and beneath it was a pile of fish bones and animal bones and she knew that this was all there really was to the story about the wonderful warm and large home that was promised.

Salina was in total despair and tried to find something sharp to kill herself with rather than live with this raven. She looked about the shoreline for a sharp stone but they were all smooth and round. She considered picking up a large one and walking out under the water to drown herself but she could not even lift a single stone from the beach and, anyway, when she stepped into the water, she discovered it was so cold that it cut like knives into her feet and ankles.

Her unhappiness mounted as the days grew shorter and the wind howled around her. One day, when the wind was blowing against her back and towards her distant homeland, she cried so long and hard that her father heard her wailing.

Salina's father had already discovered that the promises of the spirits had been mostly false and he knew the right thing to do was to go save his poor daughter. So he paddled a boat long and hard against the wind and currents, threading his way through the ice fields until he arrived at the bleak island.

Salina hugged her father and then she followed him back into the boat. He pushed off and began the long paddle home, this time with the wind and current in his favour. He felt very sorrowful over how his daughter had lost the healthy colour of her cheeks and how gaunt she looked. He knew he had been a bad father.

Then, when they were far from shore, Salina looked back and saw the giant raven coming after them. He grew from a black dot on the horizon to a giant creature hovering overhead, larger now than the boat they were in. Each flap of the raven's wings made great waves rise in the water. Whirlpools formed on the right and left and her father could barely keep them from swamping. Finally, when he knew they were about to drown in the knife-sharp cold of the sea, Salina's father relented. "Please. Take her back with you. Just let us live." But the raven continued to churn up the sea into a violent storm.

Salina's father had grown frightened and he was already slightly mad from all of his time alone with the spirits. He was afraid that if he died now, the spirits would take him to the vast, freezing desert they had shown him, where he would live in starvation for eternity. Fearing more for his own life than his daughter's, he threw Salina into the cold, dark sea and he took his paddle and hit her hands with it when she tried to climb back into the boat.

Her fingers had frozen from the cold very quickly and, when hit with the paddle, they broke off and sank down into the sea where they turned into fish. Salina continued to try to use what was left of her hands to grab onto the boat but still her father beat at them with the paddle until they broke off and those, too, dropped into the stormy depths, where they became harbour seals and walruses.

Still Salina flailed her arms in desperation and anger at her father who had so abandoned her. Finally the blows of the paddle broke her arms and they fell from her body into the water beneath, where they became whales.

At that point, Salina looked up at the raven and implored him to save her. He swooped low and attempted to lift her with his beak but she had grown impossibly heavy. Despite his trickery, he did love this human girl with her long, beautiful hair and he tried again and again, diving into the water until he was fearful that he would be pulled down with her.

Giving up all hope, he lifted himself high up into the heavens until clouds obscured everything below him on the sea and he flew off towards the south, not knowing if he could ever find his way home again.

Salina did not drown but, instead, she sank down to the floor of the ocean where she became acquainted with the sea creatures she had created and others who greeted her with great affection. Here, she became a protector of them and harboured great disdain for the ways of humans in the world above because of the way her father had abandoned her. She would make up her own rules, from now on, for men who sought sustenance from the sea.

Her home was a place that would be visited by only the bravest of the men from above and always they would come begging her permission to catch fish and seals and whales. They were required to confess to all the evil things they had ever done and then they would be required to spend endless hours combing Salina's long hair that she herself could not tend to. If they could not untangle the hair, these visitors were punished and died. If they were kind to Salina, however, and begged forgiveness for their wrongdoing and promised to give thanks to all those living sea creatures killed for food, they were rewarded with the bounty of the sea and a happy life. But they were made to promise that there must be no waste and, to insure that, the souls of slaughtered sea creatures would hover above in the human world for three days after their death to report back to Salina if her rules were being followed.

If Salina was not satisfied that her creatures were being treated with respect, she sought revenge by creating storms of fierce, cold winds and giant waves, higher than the houses of men. Or she would order the fish and seals and whales to move on to some place else and leave the coastal people to starve. If it was her wish there was nothing anyone could do about it.

Salina grew very old in her home beneath the sea, but she did not die and, above her, in the boats and kayaks, she was often referred to simply as the Old Woman, although it was always in hushed tones and with the greatest of respect.

CHAPTER THIRTY-THREE

IT WAS DR. JESPERSON'S JOB TO tell Todd's parents that Todd was most likely not going to recover. It was purely and simply the cancer, nothing else. Despite the fact that this task had fallen to him many times before, he still acted nervous and unsettled. Any air of professionalism was overshadowed by the look on his face, the face of a man defeated by a disease he could not cure and who was about to lose a patient — a boy who would not grow up to be an adult.

Bartlett was the one to cry first. Joyce was holding back. If she had cried first, Bartlett may have been able to pretend to be strong. They both must have known how badly off Todd was for quite a while but had always been hanging onto the belief that something was going to come along and reverse the disease. Now they were being told that this would not be so.

"How much time?" Joyce asked.

"Given the deterioration, I believe it would not be much more than a week, possibly less."

Bartlett didn't know that his eyes would burn so badly once the tear ducts were freed up and the rivers of sadness began to flow. Joyce, on the other hand, looked like her face was frozen, the muscles tense in her cheeks. She was holding on until later. In the car. Bartlett knew she'd hold it in until they were in the car.

Bartlett sucked at the air as if he'd just climbed a mountain. "Is he going to be conscious again? We'd really like to talk to him. It's really important."

Joyce bowed her head. She didn't speak but she nodded her head up and down in agreement with her husband.

"Today," he told Joyce and Bartlett. "If you want to talk to him, we should do it today before his strength slips more."

Todd awoke to what he thought was bright sunlight but it was just the artificial lights overhead. At first, he wasn't even aware of any feeling in his arms and legs and wondered if they had amputated them, but soon came a tingling sensation. His bed was tilted up slightly. Dr. Jesperson was at his side fooling with the IV drip. His parents were right there in front of him. "We love you," his mother said as his eyelids fluttered and he tried to focus. His parents looked like they'd been through hell and he felt a pang of guilt. It was his fault.

His mouth was so dry. "Desert Mouth," he was fond of calling it. Jesperson gave him some water to sip, saw that the boy could hold the bottle himself and then disappeared from the room.

"I know," Todd said in a cracking voice. He sipped slowly from the water bottle.

"We'll get you through this," Bartlett said, but he knew the words were hollow. He had stopped crying now and would not cry around his son.

"If I say something stupid," Todd said haltingly, "it's 'cause I'm still pretty fuzzy in the brain. But it's clearing. How is everything at home?"

"Fine," Joyce said. "Everything is just fine."

"Is there anything we can do for you?" Bartlett asked.

"Could you hand me my hockey stick?"

Bartlett was surprised at this. It wasn't what he was expecting at all. But he turned and saw the stick was still there, propped up in the corner of the room. He walked over and picked it up, then set it alongside his son in bed and watched as Todd tried to grip onto it.

"I've had lots of time to think about what was important in my life. I figure I must be lucky 'cause I came up with a pretty big list. Hockey isn't way up on the list or anything. I just figured I could focus better if I held something in my hands. I like the feel of it. It helps bring me back.

"I dream about our house sometimes. I dream about me walking through it. I can see you, Dad, putting wood in the wood stove in the living room. And I see all of us there. And that feels pretty good."

"Do you want to go home?" Bartlett blurted out. It was the wrong thing to ask.

Todd tried to smile. His face was so pale; his lips were a shade of grey that looked unnatural. "No." He was thinking about his brother and sister and had long ago decided that he didn't want to be at home dying around them.

And then Todd started to speak about his trip to the island, and about Molly. He didn't know that anything had happened to her. He thought everything with Molly was still okay.

Molly had never quite been able to remember coming to the hospital or crawling into the bed with Todd. She still wasn't fully convinced she had actually done this. Dr. Soleri told her that the charges had been dropped. But she grew nervous when he told her that Todd's parents wanted to speak to her before she left the Abbie Lane. "They're downstairs," Soleri said. "I didn't know what to say to them. Would you like to meet with them?"

Molly knew she could avoid this if she wanted to. She could hear it in Soleri's voice. But she knew she had to do this if they wanted to see her. "Yes," she said. "I would."

Molly understood the pain and sadness in the faces of Todd's parents and was wondering why they were pretending to be so cheerful. For some reason or other, the man was carrying a hockey stick.

"Your friendship to our son meant a great deal to him," Bartlett told Molly.

"We reacted badly," Joyce said. "While I don't mean to say we approve or, well, even understand, we do know that Todd speaks very highly of you. He described in great detail the island you showed him. Why did you take him there?"

"It's where I grew up," Molly answered.

"It seemed very important to him," Bartlett said. "If you had asked us ahead of time, we could never have said yes . . . to any of this . . . but the way he described the place — everything about it. It must have been very important to him. How did you ever get him ashore there?"

"I didn't. He stayed in the boat."

"But he described it all in such detail," Joyce said, "as if he had walked around there himself."

"That would have been impossible. But I'm so glad it stayed with him." Molly knew that this was part of what she had intended to give Todd. She gave him the island. And now she knew that it had worked. Todd would always have the island to go to whenever he needed to.

Dr. Soleri was watching Molly's expression. Bartlett slid the old, taped-up hockey stick across the table to Molly. "Todd wants you have this," he said. And then he tried to smile as he shrugged.

"How is he doing?" Molly asked.

Bartlett and Joyce looked at each other, as if asking, *who is stronger? Which one of us can say the truth out loud?*

Dr. Soleri kept his full attention on Molly. Bartlett cleared his throat and could barely whisper the words. "He's dying."

Molly did not ask if she were free to go home. She seemed a bit more distant as she was led back to her room. An attendant took the hockey stick and said he would take good care of it for her, that it was just like the one his boy had. "A leftie, eh?"

Back in her room, Molly had decided that just because someone says a thing, it need not necessarily be true. Many things were possible. Books had taught her that — vast libraries of imagined experience had become vivid and real to her. And her father had taught her that a body could appear and disappear at will, even around his own family. And at night, a man or a child could look up at the stars and make some certain ones rise up from the horizon and move up into the heavens. There was a balance of things, of course, and nature was a system of necessity. If the tide moved in, it would eventually flow back out. If it rained, the water would eventually find its way to the sea. If something disappeared from your life, it would eventually be replaced with something else: better or worse or more or less the same.

Death, Molly believed, had some kind of accounting system. And Molly had a strong instinct that a trade was possible. As with so much else in her life, it was all a matter of focussing your will. What she felt for Todd had moved into a very important centre part of her being. The connection between the two of them was very strong. She had already given him the island. Now, if she were successful, she could give him something else. It would take tremendous will and commitment, though. As she closed her eyes, she saw the guide on the path in front of her, recognized the cold, stark beauty around her, felt the icy winds and took the first step forward on a path she had followed several times before.

CHAPTER THIRTY-FOUR

HARRIET FITZHENRY STOOD ON THE OLD Karlson Wharf on Halifax Harbour with the taxi driver, Oscar Ryan. Here was where the steam-driven ship *Mackay-Bennett* once unloaded the hundreds of bodies of the dead — those who had not survived the sinking of the *Titanic*. The *Mackay-Bennett* was known as the death ship, a morgue afloat with grim men doing a grim job. The crew had lifted the bodies from the sea any way they could and brought them to Halifax. They had shipped out of port with tons of ice and embalming fluid and returned with the freight of human tragedy. Theirs was not a rescue mission.

"The bodies were heavy but the souls were light," Harriet told Oscar.

"I never thought of it that way," Oscar said.

"No one has ever determined the exact physical location of the soul when it inhabits the body. Nor its weight. Men have proposed theories. But no one ever came up with a gland or an organ or even a sample tissue of the soul."

"Some would probably say the soul lives in the heart." Oscar was trying to keep up his end of the metaphysical discussion.

"The heart's a big muscle. Not a reservoir for something eternal."

"Or the brain maybe. Some place in the brain."

"Good a guess as any." Harriet looked south from where they stood on the old creosote wharf. There was a Sheraton hotel with a casino, the very idea of which soured her stomach. And two gleaming, white office towers that seemed so out of place for Halifax.

She walked with Oscar to the end of the abandoned wharf. Oscar was careful to steer her around the dangerous rotted boards and shards of old rusting cable. Harriet had insisted they ignore the No Trespassing signs. She now looked further south, straight out the harbour: George's Island and beyond. Devil's Island was not in view, hidden behind two islands and shrouded by yet another wall of fog that plugged the ocean end of Halifax Harbour.

"A man named Kenneth O. Hind, a minister of sorts from All Saints Cathedral, was on board the *MacKay-Bennett* to pray for the dead and counsel the crew on that ghastly voyage." Harriet had a wonderful theatrical way of saying the word "ghastly." "He probably told the crew that the disaster was the will of God. Do you believe that it was the will of God, Mr. Ryan?"

"I've heard that expression but it doesn't work for me."

"Me either. It's a cute little notion to stop a mind from thinking dark thoughts. There was a first-class passenger on a ship called the *Bemen* and it passed close to where the *Titanic* had gone down. Her name was Joanna Stunke. I do not make this up. That was really her name. I memorized her exact words. She said, 'We saw the body of one woman in a nightdress clasping a baby to her chest.' This was in those icy waters, Mr. Ryan, if you can imagine. 'Close by was the body of another woman with her arms tightly clasped around a shaggy dog.' Odd, but the image of the woman holding onto her dog haunts me more than the woman with the baby."

"Both make me shiver," Oscar admitted.

"It was hard work on the *Mackay-Bennett*. Hard, grim work. One hundred nineteen victims were buried at sea, weighted down with iron weights loaded here on this wharf.

I forget why those victims didn't deserve a land burial. Could have been that they were from steerage — the poor who had no relatives that could have afforded funerals. Three hundred and twenty-eight bodies were recovered. John Snow had a funeral home in Halifax and he was privileged to get the bulk of the work. Right place at the right time, one supposes. Probably had some pull with the right people. A man who knew his way around a corpse and a casket.

"Millionaires died as well as those hopeful, impoverished immigrants from below deck. George Winder from Philadelphia. The sea took the wind right out of his sails. Major Archibald Butt who had worked for President Taft. Down with the ship. John Jacob Astor, of course, richest man in the world. But his money couldn't keep him afloat. He had a young little wife, though, who survived. Imagine that. Astor's body would have been unloaded right here on this wharf, a rich man's corpse pale as all the rest. Ben Guggenheim, another millionaire, didn't survive either.

"Altogether, there were 1,523 dead. Harriet took a deep breath of the salty and odoriferous harbour air. Raw sewage still spewed into the harbour and it gave a kind of tang to the damp air. "One can almost smell the death that still lingers here if one tries." Harriet slipped into the third person on occasion. Her mother had told her always to speak of herself in public as "one" but she had moved on with the tide of modernism and mostly abandoned that usage. Only on solemn moments like this did she live up to her mother's grammatical expectations.

"So there, Mr. Ryan, I've had my fun for the day. Now it's back to attend to the living." Harriet still felt a strong tie to Molly, even though she knew so little about her. She could not ignore the fact that Molly and her family had provided the last refuge for her son even though she was absolutely certain that her son's soul had slipped out of his body seconds before he drowned. When she had received the awful news, she had tried to console herself that it was "God's will" and that very idea had eventually turned her into an atheist of sorts. "Religion is the devil's handiwork," she told Oscar as he led her over a particularly rough section of the old wharf.

When Eric and Harriet arrived, Dr. Soleri admitted there were many things that still concerned him about Molly. "I've jumped to several conclusions about a story I asked her to write for me but I still don't know what it means. It's like a dream. It could be that it's like something a literate person would make up to satisfy a guy like me. It's so full of symbolism and ripe for interpretation. Maybe she's just stringing me along.

"I am convinced she has undergone some kind of emotional crisis," he continued. "It's now compounded by the fact that the boy is very ill and probably dying. The charges have been dropped but maybe the grief is just beginning."

"What are you saying, doctor?" Harriet asked.

"I'm saying that some people are just too fragile . . . ," he said but he didn't finish the sentence. "But it would do her no good to stay here any longer. She can go home."

All Molly seemed to want to do was sleep.

"The beginning of health is sleep," Harriet said. "A clever form of anaesthesia, too."

While she slept through much of the day, Eric minded the store and continued to read from various books, falling into an almost meditative state. He knew that his once-frozen heart had thawed. He felt tied to Molly. As did the others — Harriet, the Dumpster Teeth boys, who came around bringing homemade vegetarian grub: hummus, pita bread, tabbouleh, and goat cheese salads. Elsie Downey showed up often to help keep shop, working for free, and giving impromptu readings from Black poets: Langston Hughes, Countee Cullen, David Woods, Maxine Tynes, George Elliott Clarke, whoever she happened to be reading at the time.

Later that night while Molly was asleep and Harriet was asleep as well in the room fixed up for her to stay in, Eric sat up alone in the quiet store. A man alone with his thoughts. He drifted back to his arctic odyssey. The feeling of absolute hopelessness and failure that had driven him there.

Eric reread the story Molly had written for Dr. Soleri. He had asked to see the story and Soleri had said no, at first. Patient confidentiality and all that. But then Soleri apparently had changed his mind and given Eric a photocopy of what Molly had written. This was the third time he read it and it both fascinated and disturbed him. He just wasn't sure what to make of it.

Then he phoned Ottawa. The switchboard attendant at the Ottawa hospital was not helpful at first. He wanted to speak to Ray. No, he couldn't remember the last name. He was Inuit, from the North. A janitor who likes to talk to patients.

"I'll put you through to his boss."

Eric explained to Ray's boss about coming to consciousness in the hospital room and the janitor being there to talk to him. He wanted to thank him for his kindness. Ray's boss said okay and looked up the number.

Ray answered. The TV was on loud. A hockey game. "You say you are who?" he asked.

"It's me, your grandfather," Eric answered.

"Grandfather, let me turn this down. Montreal is losing anyway. I can't stand it when they lose."

Eric made small talk and then asked if Ray would listen to him read a story.

"When my grandfather tells a story, I listen."

Eric read the whole thing over the phone and when he stopped there was silence on the other end.

"What do you think it means?"

"It's about Sedna."

"Should I know who Sedna is? I thought my friend Molly just made it up."

"Does she think she made it up?"

"Yes."

"Then my people should sue for plagiarism or something," Ray said, but he wasn't serious. It was that offhand sense of humour he had.

"She doesn't want to publish it."

"Oh. Okay then."

"She was in a hospital. The doctor asked her to write something, a story. This is what she wrote."

"Was the guy a shrink?"

"Yes."

"Yeah. They'll do stuff like that to you. Well, she had to get this from somewhere. It's an old Inuit legend with a whole lot of different versions. The daughter, the bird and that business with chopping off the arms. You know who told me that story for the first time?"

"Let me guess. Your grandfather."

"No. My grandmother. My grandfather had a grudge against Sedna, because he was not lucky at hunting the seals. He was okay with the fish but not the seals. My grandmother said it was because Sedna didn't care for my grandfather. My grandfather sometimes said he didn't even believe in Sedna but my grandmother sure as hell did.

"Sedna was some kind of undersea spirit. She was very powerful. The shamans were always sucking up to her. She watched over the fish and the seals and whales. Just like in your friend's story. And if you killed too many seals or didn't give the fish bones back to the sea — if you fucked with Mother Nature in general and were not kind — then Sedna would have your ass. Although that's not the way they used to say it. Like I say, my grandfather and Sedna did not get along. So my grandmother secretly dropped little gifts in the sea for her just so the family could eat. Sedna could be very vindictive if she wanted to be. She was always a bit cranky after that bad business in the boat with her father."

Eric was thinking that Molly had probably read this in one of her many books. "What happened to the raven in the story?"

"Oh, he's still there on that island. He loved her all right and felt bad for the grief he got her into."

"Did your grandfather ever get on good terms with Sedna?"

"He couldn't. The older he got, the more he kept saying he didn't believe in her at all. But my granny always kept dropping those little gifts into the sea. She figured that someday her husband might drown and you know who was going to be there at the bottom of the ocean to meet him?"

"Yes."

"My grandmother said the first thing he should do if and when he met her — even if he didn't believe in her — the first thing was to keep his mouth shut about that. And the second thing was to brush her hair. That was the way the shamans tried to soothe Sedna when she got really pissed at men. So my grandmother always insisted that my father carry with him a little comb carved from whalebone. Just in case."

"And he carried it even though he didn't believe in Sedna?"

"My grandmother said she would not have sex with him unless he did this one small thing for her. And my grandfather loved sex. They were always a very frisky couple. And where we lived we didn't have a lot of entertainment. Even when my grandparents came to visit, they'd go at it. Sometimes I'd wake up in the night and hear them in the next room. When I was little I didn't know what they were doing and, in the morning, if my father was going out on the ice with my grandfather, my grandmother would ask, 'Do you have the comb with you?' and he would pull it out of his pocket and show it to her and they both would smile."

"What were the gifts your grandmother gave to Sedna to keep her happy?"

"Oh, many things. She sometimes had to go out on the ice herself until she found open water and drop in a meteorite or two she'd sneak from my grandfather's collection. But she was good at finding her own valuable rocks, too. She dropped in great cubes of iron pyrite she found on the beach. She told me she also dropped in real nuggets of gold and I thought she was lying to me until, one day, I went with her to the edge of the ice and she took one that was the size of a walnut out of her bag. She let me hold it and then told me to give it to Sedna. So I did. 'Now I won't have to worry about your grandfather, for a while,' she said, and we went home to fry some seal meat."

CHAPTER THIRTY-FIVE

MOLLY TOOK A LUNGFUL OF SWEET bookstore air and began to feel herself reawakening to life. She inhaled Shakespeare and Li Po and everything on the J.D. Salinger shelf. It was like breathing in the perfume of wild flowers on a seacoast — the perfume of low-lying cranberry flowers in spring, wild iris, musky marsh mallow and fireweed, sweet clover and even the scent of wild bayberry. This is what filled her lungs. The flowery smell of old books.

She knew she was not being very good company to those who were trying to help her. First, she thanked Elsie Downey for staying on and working.

"Any time you need me, you call," Elsie said. "I've got all the time in the world and some of it might as well be yours." Elsie had a nice way of putting it. As if you could literally give your own time to someone else.

Eric had brought Molly home and now he stood awkwardly there in the coppery afternoon sunlight, not knowing what else to do with himself but thumb through some old *National Geographic* magazines, looking at pictures of deserts: Gobi, Sahara, Kalahari, Mojave. His mind was filling up with dry sand.

Mrs. Fitzhenry was sitting in the chair by the front window reading a biography of John Jacob Aster and scowling. She looked up from her book and turned to Eric. "The more wealth a man has, the more his flaws stand out, I think."

Eric nodded in agreement as if he too had always believed this.

Molly puttered around behind the counter and noticed that everything was orderly and in great shape. Elsie had seen to that. There was cash in the cash register and the bills were all arranged by denomination as was the small change. She still felt very tired and she believed that, in the hospital, she'd become addicted to sleep. Ten hours, twelve hours, sometimes more. Dr. Soleri said extended sleep was fine, not to worry about it, but he had said that about everything, including her odd story. She now knew that the story was part hers and part borrowed but she did not know where she'd taken it from. Maybe it would come to her later. She found an old hardback copy of *Leaves of Grass* and decided to go to bed with Walt Whitman. She had not forgotten about Todd. But she was not prepared to work on that tonight. That would be a long journey requiring a good deal of preparation. "The earth, that is sufficient," Whitman wrote. "I do not want the constellations any nearer."

Better yet, "All truths wait in all things." A visit to Whitman's mind was always worthwhile.

Like Walt Whitman, Molly had learned early on to gaze upon a thing and become that thing.

"There was a child went forth every day;
And the first object he looked upon, that object he became."

An absence of transcendental poets and Buddhist monks on Devil's Island during the tenure of Molly's childhood did not hinder her from apprenticing herself to nature and seeking whatever wisdom could be gained from such teachers as wind, rock, sky, bird, grey seal, starfish, crab, and imagination itself. A child like Molly quickly learns the skills of becoming and, with plenty of time on her hands to cultivate these habits, she becomes a master of the craft.

A washed up starfish, say, missing an arm and deposited on the shore at high tide, was a good beginning. Become the creature as it is dying, losing its life to the stinging rays of the sun. With a human companion, it is possible to make one's way back into the sea and life is renewed. What once appeared to be dead now shows signs of life, small, filigreed tendrils moving once more in the cold, clear water of the tiny island harbour.

From there it was only a matter of disciplined practice at resurrecting birds and mice and, finally, a rabbit. The line in those days between what was real and what was imagined was so indistinct that it hardly even mattered. What Molly believed to be true was true. Teachers did not dispute these things, since she had none, nor fellow playmates, for there were no other children on the island. Her mother was not about to intrude upon her daughter's self-education and her father was, in fact, a fan of it. Molly heard him once telling an Eastern Passage fisherman that he had seen her bring a dead herring gull on the beach back to life. And the fisherman, missing the point of miracles altogether, responded by saying, "We got a lot of gulls around here. Your kid starts bringing the dead ones back to life and we're gonna be overrun."

The raven was found on an icy morning in late February, not fully dead, but starved, half frozen, frozen salt water on its flight feathers. If it were not for the movement of the eye, Hank would have assumed it was dead. He thought of it as a ghost of a raven, a cold, dead bird whose spirit had flown off to someplace kinder and warmer than Devil's Island on that winter day. He thought of finishing it off so that whatever spirit was left inside the bird could fly off and catch up with the rest of his ancestors.

But then Molly opened the back door, and stood there in her nightgown in the freezing air. She insisted on taking the bird up to her room and there was no way stopping her once she got a thing like that into her head.

Hank and Lea sat downstairs that morning by the wood stove listening to scratchy marine weather reports about freezing sea spray and cold fronts. Hank figured they might go through a full cord of firewood in one month. Maybe have to get one of the boys ashore to haul out another load. Lea hummed old sea shanties during the marine weather reports and a couple of Gaelic tunes that her grandmother had taught her. Frozen sea spray and scratchy radio went well with an old Scottish lament. To Hank, the words were a hodgepodge of sounds. Even Lea didn't know what they meant and figured she was singing them all wrong, but it felt good on a frozen morning to be singing something old with your beautiful young daughter upstairs trying to heal a mostly dead black bird.

Molly read Robert Louis Stevenson's *Treasure Island* to the raven, having assumed that no one had ever read *Treasure Island* to him before. Molly was fairly certain that he liked the part about the pirates. Then she grew quiet and closed her eyes, listened to the radio below and her mother singing. That helped her to work the chill out of her legs and melt the ice from her wings.

The raven was fighting her efforts at revival. In fact, the dying bird was taking her to a place she did not want to go. The skies were so dark and the wind more enemy than ally. But if she could just fly high and far enough, she would be out of the storm. Molly was determined not to give up.

And when they were out of the storm, she looked down on a vast frozen land beneath her. There were severe snow-covered mountains and lower hills, and an entirely frozen sea beyond. In the middle of the frozen expanse was an island that they were flying towards.

The raven was not used to being in a closed space and when it awoke in the morning, at first light, it crashed into the glass of the window and scudded to the floor. It tried a second time but Molly captured the frantic bird and whispered to it until it grew quiet. Her father force-fed the raven some cracked corn and barley. When the snow stopped and the sky cleared they let the raven go and it flew straight over the harbour northward. And that was the end of that.

Why her father was so stubborn about rowing ashore during the approach of a tropical storm that October was never clear to Molly. The truth was that Hank had forgotten about the wedding anniversary and had no present for Lea. He was the worst of husbands when it came to remembering birthdays and anniversaries.

Well, it was the day before the anniversary and Hank believed the storm would veer out to sea. He prepared hurriedly and told no one where he was going. So he rowed to the Passage and went looking for a gift for Lea. He found a book on whirligigs at Fisher's Bookstore in Dartmouth and he thought he was home free.

The great storm, however, was out there waiting for him to shove off. A torrent of rain poured down upon him not ten minutes into his return leg home. It ruined the unprotected book and drenched the captain in a matter of minutes. It came on with such volume that Hank was up to his ankles in rainwater. His vision was fully obscured but he judged that all he had to do was keep the boat into the wind and he'd find home.

When the storm hit the island, Lea went looking for her husband but he wasn't around. "Your father's disappeared again," she told Molly but neither thought much of it at first.

"He's probably in the lighthouse," Molly said.

"Let's just stay put until the worst of it blows over."

Molly was twelve. She'd had a wonderful summer and it was coming to an end. Her skin was tanned and her arms and legs were strong from outdoor work. It was four o'clock in the afternoon when she heard the sound of her father drowning. The sound might have come from far away or from inside her head, but she recognized what it was, her father trying to scream as water filled his mouth. It was unmistakable. She took a deep breath and felt the salt water filling up her lungs.

The tropical storm had swamped Hank's dory and he had held onto the gunwales as long as his arms would allow. But a man can take only so much punishment from the sea until it wears him down. Hank had a stubborn voice in his head that told him a lesser man would be discouraged by this but not him. He could handle the adversity and all would be well. Trying to stay afloat in the water, assaulted over and over by waves, he knew he was being pulled away from Devil's Island and could end up anywhere in the harbour. All he had to do was hang onto his optimism and ignore the reality of the situation as much as a human mind could.

But finally he gave it up and within him swelled a massive sadness and regret: he would never see his wife and daughter again. He would not have his triumph of giving Lea his hard-won anniversary present and he would not share his bed with his loving wife ever again. That thought suddenly made him struggle harder to stay alive. But it was just then that a ten-foot wave bore down on him and drove him under.

Beneath the stormy surface of the harbour there was no sound as he sank downward, his now-useless arms at his sides. Just before the blackness took over, he started seeing things. At first, he imagined himself not in water but walking in a blinding snowstorm. Out of nowhere came the figure of a man, an old man perhaps, trudging against the cold wind. Then that image faded as quickly as it had appeared. The snow vanished and so did the old man. In its place, he had a crystal-clear vision of his daughter, Molly, back when she was eight years old. She was sitting on a great granite boulder by the shore, reading a book. She looked up at him as he approached and she smiled.

LESLEY CHOYCE

In the midst of the storm, there had been reports of fishing boats ripped from their moorings and floating freely in the harbour. It was getting near dark when a Coast Guard rescue boat headed out into the turbulent waters to see what it could see. Sure enough, there were fishing boats and a couple of cabin cruisers adrift. When the captain approached the MacDonald Bridge and trained his big lights upon the concrete supports, he thought he saw a body draped on a ledge. A closer look revealed a man, unconscious or possibly dead, lying there above the waterline and so the captain told his rescue men to suit up, they were going to retrieve whatever was left of the poor sod.

What was left of Molly's father was a humiliated and humbled man who couldn't begin to comprehend how he could possibly be alive. "I'd been and gone," was the way he described it to the Coast Guard captain. "I'd swallowed most of the harbour. I'm surprised there is any water left."

Hank truly didn't have a clue as to how he had ended up on one of the concrete platforms at the base of the bridge. And when he arrived home by Coast Guard vessel the next day, he once again was without a present for his wife on their anniversary. "Well, you're present enough," Lea told him and that night they did not sleep with their backs to each other.

The morning after the storm, Molly's stomach had hurt. She looked at her floor and discovered that she had vomited several times in the night, although she had no memory of it. The rug on the floor was soaked through and through with a clear fluid, as if she had drunk a great volume of water and heaved it up over and over through the night. She felt exhausted and confused but when she heard her father's voice downstairs, she ran down and hugged him, suddenly remembering her dreams of drowning and what it had been like to die as she looked up at the surface of the harbour from far below.

Hank was unusually affectionate to his wife and attentive to his daughter for a long time after his swim in the stormy harbour. Hank was, however, leery of going back in any boat for nearly two weeks until the fear subsided. Then he began to build a new dory. And every time he shaved a plank or cut with precision the wood for the boat, he did so with the utmost care, making complimentary and encouraging comments to the wood as he worked.

Chapter Thirty-six

MOLLY'S THOUGHTS WERE FILLED WITH TODD. In the morning she phoned the hospital but the phone felt cold in her hand, and the voice of Dr. Jesperson on the other end was cold as well, the voice of a professional. His language was contained by walls and fences. "I think he's too ill today to speak with you," Jesperson said. "His parents are with him. Perhaps in a day or so you can talk to him." Molly closed her eyes and envisioned Todd lying there. His face was calm, he was not conscious. She gently set the phone down, and conceived of an imaginary connection, a thin but tenacious thread leading from herself to the boy in the bed.

When Molly was six years old, her mother had convinced her that mothers were capable of making the sun rise up out of the sea. Awakening on a winter morning when it was still dark, Molly had been inconsolable because the sun was not there. She believed that the sun had departed from the earth and feared it was her fault because of the dead pilot whale. Molly had already ordained herself the protector of all sea creatures, which was a very large job for a six-year-old. The beached whale had been struck by a large freighter coming into Halifax Harbour and washed up on the south side of the island. At first, Molly had believed it to be, from a distance, a large boulder that had been dropped from the sky. Alone on a cold morning, she had surveyed the whale and its wound. She had put her hand on the wound and chased away her fears in order to bring the whale back to life.

When she failed to do that, she grew sullen. At home, she did not explain why she was so sad but her father performed some magic tricks with forks to try to cheer her up. He could make one fork sing and another he was able to bend without touching it. They were very old forks, of course. Then he brought out the old ornate knife left behind by Captain Larsen who had visited the island before she was born. The story had been told many times.

Leah took out an old cloth and some silverware polish and polished it until it gleamed. The blade was dull and Hank took out his whetstone and sharpened the blade. He set it on the table and discovered that it was so well balanced that he could spin it round and round. But each and every time, no matter how much or how little effort was put into the spin, when it stopped it was pointing north.

And so it sat, often on a shelf in the kitchen. It was used to cut bread sometimes, or meat, or to marvel at — Hank testing it again and again to see if the knife could be tricked into a spin that would not result in northerly results. Lea discovered that even if it were left resting on the table, pointing south or east, later it would be discovered to be pointing north.

For six-year-old Molly, the knife with its single ambition was at first a wonder but eventually just a part of day-to-day life.

On the morning that Molly believed the sun would never come up, the knife sat mid-table, pointing north, and Lea stood at the kitchen window facing southeast. It was December and close to the shortest day of the year. Molly had not understood why the mornings were all dark now and not like summer at all. All she *knew* — and she was certain of it in that way that six-year-olds are certain of things imagined — was that the sun would not come up today or any other day ever thereafter.

And she believed it was her fault because she had failed to save the biggest of the sea creatures in the waters around her island.

She had tears in her eyes when her mother asked her to sit down at the kitchen table and face the window. Outside it was pitch black and some stars still shone down on the frozen shores, sprinkling fragments of light on frosted sea rocks.

Hank was sleeping in, "like a bear hibernating," Lea said. This morning the magic would have to be a mother's work. So Lea held her right hand, palm forward, against the glass pane, causing it to mist up and then turn to a thin leaf of frost in the shape of the hand. But Molly was not impressed.

"I want the sun back," she said.

"Be patient."

Molly squirmed and spun the knife in the centre of the table.

"Shh," her mother said. "You must be quiet. And keep looking out the window. I want you to see how your mother can make the sun come up in the sky. Not all mothers can do this, but I can."

Molly did not believe her mother. She knew the sun problem was her fault and she should be punished. She stopped the spinning knife and pressed her finger onto the very tip of it until it pricked the skin and produced a bubble of blood. Molly thought it looked beautiful and wondered how it could be that she felt no pain. Then she sucked the blood from her finger and discovered for the first time in her childhood how sweet and salty it tasted. Her blood was red, yes, but it was made up of water from the sea.

Lea was humming one of her old Gaelic songs — wordless, all vowels and soft consonants. And she made the sky shift from black to grey. Molly stood on the chair now to get a better look. She stared out at the dark ocean to the south and east of her home. She was forced to admit that the colours were changing but it wasn't good enough. There was no sun.

"Where is the sun?" she asked. "I want to see the sun."

"Be patient," was all Lea said.

And then it happened. The winter sun burst up over the ruler-flat horizon of the sea. It was a thin, radiant line at first and soon a giant half-circle and, finally, it lifted itself up out of the sea and the world was bright again. Lea let her hand drop to her side and watched as the sun melted the frost of her handprint from the glass. Molly was impressed and amazed. She knew her mother was capable of miracles but she was also afraid, as her mother turned her back to the window, that the sun might sink as quickly as it arrived back into the sea again.

"Don't stop, please."

"It's okay," Lea told her daughter. "The sun will stay up there until late this afternoon."

"Can you do it again? Right now?"

"That's enough for one day. Tomorrow maybe." And Lea got on with boiling some water for tea. She did not notice that the knife from the Arctic had begun to spin slowly of its own accord. Molly noticed this and thought she must have absent-mindedly started it spinning. She watched it and, as the sun grew higher in the sky, a great golden beam of light reflected from the shining blade and danced around like a summer bird that might have flown accidentally into the room. It fluttered around the room, animating everything until the knife came to a stop, pointing north.

Reports of Lea's triumph reached Hank later that morning when he gave up on his hibernation. He was much impressed but insisted that he too had some tricks up his sleeve and proceeded to entertain his daughter with the familiar bending of forks and making them sing but none of that seemed to interest Molly, so he disappeared for a while and he did that very well and convincingly. When he reappeared — as usual, from behind a door when someone was not expecting it — he insisted that tonight he would make the moon come up. Women could raise suns but only men could raise a moon.

The first night, clouds interfered with his moon raising and he was more than a little disgruntled, but clear weather prevailed the following night and Hank did a fine job of pulling the moon up from its resting place. And the moon had a face whereas the sun was faceless. And that was something worth noting.

By summer, there was still a sense of rivalry between mother and father as to who could perform what miracle. Hank would listen to the marine-band weather and try to predict exactly when the wind would come up or the rain would start and he'd take his young daughter down to the shoreline and talk to the sky in a conversational tone, asking it to produce wind or rain or the occasional rainbow. Sometimes it worked. Sometimes it didn't. But Molly loved to hear the conversations her father had with the sky. Sometimes when nothing happened, he'd admit his failure. "I don't have the energy for this today, Molly," he'd say. "You try."

And sometimes Molly succeeded. Her mother had already taught her to put the sun to bed and her father had taught her to produce a good full arch of a rainbow, and the occasional squall at sea — one that formed far away but raced straight towards them until it was upon them, drenching them to the bone.

But later on, as Molly grew interested in more subtle things, she became increasingly fascinated with the stars of the night sky. She had names for many of the constellations: Ursa Major and Minor, Big and Little Dipper. Cassiopeia and Orion. Of course, they appeared at night, thanks to the handiwork of her father. "I can even do it in my sleep if need be," he said. "Or if I'm inside eating a late supper. I can even do it with my eyes closed."

Molly wanted to fully believe her father as always but she was now at an age where doubt was creeping into her mind. Maybe those things just happened. Maybe there was no magic at all. Hank and Lea both felt sad that Molly was beginning to doubt their supernatural abilities. Molly had discovered that she herself could bring up the sun, put it to bed, or call forth the moon. First she did it by trying as hard as her parents did, but then she put less effort into it and it still sometimes worked. She tried not at all and even then it still worked.

"Do something different with the stars," she told her father one night, testing him. "Rearrange them."

"That would be tough," Hank said, "but not impossible. I'll have to do it slowly, over a period of months."

"No. Do it all at once."

"I can't do that."

"Then do something else. Do one thing. Do something to Orion."

"I could probably make him disappear."

"No. Not that." Molly was afraid if Orion disappeared he might not come back. "Make Orion move. Make him walk across the sky."

"I'd be afraid he'd trample the others."

"Then make him come up from the sea like the sun or the moon."

Hank thought about this for a long while and finally, while sitting down and spinning the knife on the table, he said he would give it a try.

And try he did, failing three nights in row.

But on the fourth night he made Molly focus on the horizon line long and hard. When two stars appeared, he claimed those were the shoulder stars but Molly did not believe that either. When the three belt stars arose, he claimed victory but she still was not convinced. Soon came the other two bright stars below and there was Orion but still Molly was not satisfied.

"Now make him move up into the sky where he belongs. Slowly so he doesn't hurt anything."

Hank had no choice but to do that as well until old Orion was back in his usual place. It was nearly midnight. "I'm exhausted," her father said and his daughter gave him a big hug and he carried her in to bed.

Chapter Thirty-seven

ERIC HAD READ ALMOST ALL THERE was to know about Larsen — in the captain's own autobiography and those other more pedantic books. He knew that Larsen, for all his love of the North, feared it and its people would be devastated by changes that were inevitable, even though he, himself, through his travels, had helped to map and open up the North for exploitation.

Of course, there was much Eric could not know about Larsen since he had been such a private man. Henry Larsen had a profound fear of the dark side of human nature. An RCMP officer, he preferred ice and dogs aboard ship — even cleaning up after them — to having to deal with people. The Inuit, he knew for a fact, were as capable of misbehaviour and crime as were any ethnic group of humans upon the great, round face of the earth. And this was a disappointment to him.

As he was dying on October 29, 1964, Larsen had visions of mountains of ice. A tad over twenty years after completing his navigational feat, the world was in trouble again. Larsen was certain they were headed into an all-out nuclear war — the darkest hour of the darkness of men. He began to sing a hymn in Norwegian as his breath began to fail.

Eric went alone to the hospital to find out how Todd was doing. In the hallway leading to Todd's room, Dr. Jesperson stopped him and explained that it was necessary for Eric, Molly, and any of Molly's "associates" to stay away and not get further involved. If Todd was indeed dying, Jesperson said, there would only be bad news to offer and better to keep a "buffer zone," as he called it, between that news and Molly herself.

Harriet Fitzhenry arranged the chartering of the boat to take Molly to her island but said she could not go along. "I'm bad luck on boats," she said. "I'd have nothing to offer you but seasickness. I don't like boats and they don't like me. The sea always wants my breakfast. Besides, I have my work to do. I've got a tour of the cemeteries lined up. Quite a few of the *Titanic* crowd are up at Fairview and some at Mount Olivet and Camp Hill. Good place to meet a gentleman ghost or two."

And so it was that, on one fine morning, Eric and Molly sat aboard Captain Mike's charter boat as it pulled away from the Halifax wharf and headed out to sea. They had both brought along backpacks with food, warm clothes, and rain gear, just in case. Molly began to tell Eric what it used to be like in June on the island when the gulls lay their eggs — big brown things with dark speckles. "You had to be careful where you stepped. And the gulls would fly overhead like a circus, swooping down low so you might think they would grab your hair or pluck out your eyes.

"When the babies hatched, they grew quickly into big, brown, fluffy things that did not look like their parents at all. Since they couldn't fly and had no fear of people, I used to sit with them and pretend we were having tea. I had a tea set, which my mother had given me. I had so many friends with feathers. But when they grew up, they were afraid of me. And they flew away after that. I don't know where they went."

Over the roar of the engine, Captain Mike shouted out his own observations about seagulls. "Gull shit on a good car will tear into it and eat the paint right off. It's the acid in their stomachs. A herring gull can eat a hubcap and shit spark plugs."

Eric was of the opinion that Molly was still in some significant psychological trouble. He hadn't known her long enough to be sure if this was her natural state — or if there was some real problem here. Was she a danger to herself? His own reference points as to what were normal in a person were of no particular use. He knew that he appeared more or less normal to people but that was not the case. He reminded himself sometimes in sobering moments of happiness (or at least relaxation) that he had gone north to die because it seemed like a simple, clean, cold thing to do. And he still wondered why it had not happened as planned.

Eric pointed to Hangman's Beach on McNab's Island as they passed it. Some locals had erected a modern effigy of a hanged man on the rocky spit of land. "The gulls would have your eyes," Captain Mike said. "Once your neck rotted through, you'd fall onto the stones and the crabs would snack on whatever was left. The British Navy may not have had much going for it in the way of compassion but they had their discipline down pat."

"My father would take me there," Molly said, "to McNab's and we would pick blackberries and raspberries by the bucket. I counted thirty-four herons once in the marsh there. When we accidentally startled them, they took off and flew around and around over top of us. It was like being inside a tornado of grey wings and I thought it was going to lift us into the sky."

Molly looked up as if she was ready to levitate and it would not have surprised Eric if she could do just that. Looking at her with her hair blowing in the soft sea wind and the calmness in her face, he couldn't stop himself from reaching out and touching her cheek. His heart began to beat wildly as she put her own hand on top of his.

Eric let his hand slip down to Molly's shoulder and then it slid down her arm to take her hand. It was the boldest move he had made with a woman since . . . since forever. Molly looked off toward the farther island now rising up out of the sea before them, the lighthouse clearly visible, the old house still standing starkly, both in bold relief to the blue, blue sky behind them. "I want to stay on the island tonight," Molly announced.

"I'll keep you company," Eric said.

Eric knew that whatever was going to happen out here was beyond his control. But he would not leave her there alone. He knew that she needed this, whatever *this* was. He felt like he was still waking up from a long sleep, a lifetime of it. And now he found himself squinting in the bright sun.

He thought about the harbour itself — a great point of intersection for so many thousands of lives. The forcefully recruited English sailors aboard a brutal warship captained by sadists — all of them watching the carcass of a deserter swinging in the breeze. Themselves off to fight the French for an untenable empire. And later, those incoming European immigrants, running from their lives of despair and headed towards hope somewhere on an empty prairie.

Ships coming and going at war. The convoys with their men safe in Bedford Basin, then spilling out into the Atlantic where German U-boats waited to destroy them. Larsen, avoiding war himself for the most part, by threading his way through icy passages from Vancouver to Halifax and back.

As Molly watched the island grow larger before them, she continued to hold Eric's hand and began to reminisce again. "Most of the island is bedrock. Some sand, some patches of grass and bush on thin soil but it's mostly just a rock set in the sea. Where the rock is exposed there are lines through it — creases, cracks, and gullies. I'll show you when we get there. I studied the patterns because I was a girl living on an island, I guess, and had all the time in the world. I thought of them as paths and I would follow them."

"Your paths sound like the ley lines in England. Magnetic or energy paths that pilgrims used to follow from one sacred site to another."

"In my own childish way, it was exactly like that. It was probably all in my head. I was very ambitious about entertaining myself once the gulls were fully grown and flown away.

"I discovered one of the paths that led from one shore to the other. Southeast to northwest to be exact. It was very visible on the southeast — a great chiseled crease in the bedrock by the sea. Towards the middle of the island, the bedrock wasn't evident at all because there were shrubs and grasses growing but still there was an animal path, made by the rabbits and mice, perfectly in the same line. But it arrived on the northwest shore as a great cleft in the rock with a tiny pocket of sand by the water. I could walk from one side of the island to the other on this path with my eyes completely closed. I could feel the path in my head. I never tripped and never wavered from it. Why I would do this I don't know but when I did, I would arrive at the tiny beach and nestle down between the walls of rock on either side. And I would always feel safe and happy.

"The path bisected the island almost perfectly in half but when I walked from one end to another, I felt like I was responsible for connecting everything on my right side with everything on my left. Everything. As if I were repairing whatever was wrong with the world, whatever was divided."

"Steady, you lads and ladies," Mike interrupted as the deep-sea waves began to roll under the boat and he veered off course a bit to steer straight into an incoming hummock of water.

As Eric gripped the side of the boat with one hand, he reached out and put his arm around Molly to steady her and felt her warmth against him.

CHAPTER THIRTY-EIGHT

THE LITTLE COVE ON THE NORTH side of the island was waiting for them. Its tiny protected bay was like a still pond, sheltered as it was by the big, round granite rocks and the great mass of the island itself.

Mike cut the engine and they floated in until his keel kissed Devil's Island sand. Molly and Eric were rolling up their pants and holding their shoes up to the sky as they slipped over the side and their feet dipped into the water. They were giggling like small children. Mike handed them the backpacks. "So long," he told them as they waded ashore. "When should I come back for you?"

But of course they didn't answer. They turned around and waved to him and walked up out of the water like royalty arriving on the shores of their new kingdom. They heard Mike start up the engine and the captain headed back to Halifax with the wind behind him, the sea waves rolling beneath.

Ashore, Molly and Eric sat down on the sand where the rising and falling of the tide had left threads of eelgrass that looked liked cursive writing. Long lines of it went from one end of the beach to the other in successive rows as if on the sandy page of a very unusual handwritten book.

Feet dry, shoes back on their feet, packs with food and supplies on their backs, Molly led Eric around the perimeter of the island through tangles of wild roses, some with rose hips the size of small apples. Finches and sparrows skittered about, swallows too, and gulls, plenty of gulls flying above the shoreline. Eric was not used to walking on the loose stones and he wobbled as he walked, which Molly found most amusing. Molly held her hand out and touched things as she went, as if greeting them and bestowing a blessing. Rose hip, sea oat, beach pea. A smooth stone blessed for its roundness and dependable weight. The shoreline itself was a linear museum of flotsam: plastic pop bottles still capped, the leg of an old doll, polyethylene rope, some broken sunglasses, and a warped plastic comb.

When they arrived at the windward side of the island, Molly showed Eric the fissure — the crease in the bedrock that led from one side of the island to the other. And then she closed her eyes and led him back across the centre of the island. At either end of the journey, Molly placed her hands palm downward on the surface of the water: open sea to open harbour. Eric had tried walking part of the way with his eyes closed to see if he could feel anything — magnetic or otherwise — but kept tripping. The ground was uneven and sometimes there were loose stones that wobbled as he landed on them.

Then, to the lighthouse, where Molly touched its sides. They walked across what was once the "yard," the low, wind-mown grass between light and home. No rabbits, no baby seagulls. Only a scatter of dried seaweed and a few old, bleached boards.

Everything, including the house, looked weathered, but clean, as if the sea wind had scrubbed and scoured to prepare for Molly's homecoming. The house itself was perfectly intact, windows unbroken, roof all of one piece. Molly turned the rusted metal door handle.

Eric understood that Molly was here for some reason that transcended nostalgia. He wanted to know exactly what it was but he waited for clues rather than asking.

They were standing on the smooth floorboards of the kitchen and he felt as if the light sifting in through the windows was lifting him from his feet. It was a weightless room. Molly poured some water from her backpack into the hand pump at the sink, priming it, then working the handle, repeated the process several times until water flowed from it. The sound of the squeaking hand pump reminded Eric of folk music he'd once heard played on a wind instrument from Japan.

Molly tasted it. "No salt," she said. "Only memories." She cleaned and filled a blue and white stippled porcelain-coated metal pot and set the water on the table, cupped some in her hands and held it up to Eric's lips. He drank, slaking a thirst that had been in him for longer than he could remember. Then he kissed her cupped hands.

"If you find us some driftwood, we can cook a meal." She pointed to the old cook stove.

While Eric foraged for wood, plentiful enough on the shores despite the fact there were no trees here on the island, Molly walked in and out of the old rooms of the house with their door plaques naming each.

Picking up scraps of wood from the shoreline, Eric couldn't help but think that this simple "occupation" was a hundred percent, no, a thousand percent — if a percentage figure could even be attached to it — a *thousand* percent better than the legwork or research for a scholarly paper. History was not dead after all, just washed up on the shores of a Nova Scotia island. Eric shuttled some wood back into the kitchen and then returned to some rocky outcrops at the waterline where he had noticed colonies of black mussels clinging to the rocks. He harvested twenty or so of the largest ones and then gathered some seaweed from the water — sea lettuce, rockweed and dulse — to take back to Molly. On the way back he became intoxicated by the smell of bayberry, and by way of olfactory research, figured out which shrub it came from and gathered some branches.

By the time he arrived back at the house, he was convinced man had been much happier as a hunter-gatherer. It beat the bejesus out of university department meetings. Eric wondered how *Homo sapiens* had learned to rob themselves of such basic satisfactions.

Over a candlelight dinner, eaten from mismatched old plates, Eric spoke for the first time about happy moments from his own childhood. "But today," he concluded, "is a day I will never forget."

Molly was strangely polite but distant. She was trying to be in two places at once, even though she understood how important this shared experience was to Eric.

The other place she needed to be was in the hospital room with Todd. And as the sky darkened and the night arranged its lights above them, corralling the light of distant energy from suns a billion miles away, Molly lost the stomach-fluttering weightlessness of the afternoon kitchen and found the weight of responsibility settle upon her.

Eric apologized after a while for "chattering like a chipmunk," and tried to ask Molly more questions about her childhood, but she didn't answer. He worried that maybe the trip here was not such a great idea for someone recently released from psychiatric care. And now the responsibility was upon his shoulders. He sobered himself; although he had drunk no alcohol, he admitted to himself that he had felt somewhat drunk with happiness, a bit self-indulgent perhaps, but it had been such a long, long time since life was like a handshake instead of a kidney punch.

"Let's go out," Molly said. And they put on two old fisherman's jackets from a closet, musty but useable. The night was clear and cool.

"No moon."

"That would be my father's job," Molly said but did not explain.

"Your parents created a wonderful childhood for you."

"The best."

"They taught you too, right? You never went to school?"

"Yes."

"What did they teach you?"

"Everything," Molly said. "They taught me all I needed to know."

Eric gave permission to the silence to join them since it had been bullied away by him so often that afternoon and evening. Molly's breathing was somewhat strange, perhaps from the chill. He took off his own coat and put it around her.

"Should we go in? I'll build up the fire."

"No. Let's just stay here for now."

But Molly was not there. She was instead standing beside Todd's bed and had taken possession of the pain the drugs could not touch. She matched her own breathing to Todd's and waited for him to give a sign that he was aware of her presence. It did not take the form of words or images. It was a simple awareness. Todd, she believed, would know she was on the island and he would be happy for her. His awareness meant to Molly that Todd was with her on the island now. This was how it was done. Now *Todd* was in two places at once. This was the opposite of learning to disappear. And it was one of those home-school lessons learned from her parents, although they had not taught her directly. She had figured it out by using the tools they had given her. It *had* been a good education, one of the best possible.

The Milky Way was a cloudy band over their heads. Eric was still waiting for her to say something.

"Do you know which one is the North Star?" she finally asked.

"There."

"Good."

"Big Dipper?"

Eric traced it with his finger.

"Cassiopeia?"

He wiggled a W.

"Hmm. The Seven Sisters."

"It's a bit fuzzy but that batch over there, I think."

• 242 •

"Centaurus?"

Eric didn't know what Centaurus looked like but he knew his mythology. While Molly had been learning from the best teachers in the world, he had been subjected to the likes of Mrs. Phyllis Gilfoy who forced her students to memorize Greek mythology from Aphrodite to Zeus. "Centaurus started out as a god named Chiron, I think," Eric said. "Half man, half horse. He taught men and gods alike in matters of philosophy, music and what else? Oh yeah, setting bones. If you were busted up, he could fix you, but when he himself took a painful poisonous arrow in the leg, he couldn't do a damn thing about it. And the problem with being immortal is that the pain would stay with you for eternity. Somehow, this wound made him even better at helping people but he really wanted to die. Prometheus, a mortal who had his own problems, agreed to trade places with him, and so he had a way out. Zeus had been paying attention to all this and decided to give Chiron back a form of immortality so he turned him into your constellation. But I still couldn't tell you which one it is."

"There," Molly said, "and, by the way, thanks for the history lesson."

Eric now felt slightly embarrassed he had said so much.

A shooting star arced to earth then but it happened so quickly and was in such a crowded field of other stars that neither was certain it had happened at all.

"One more," Molly said. "An easy one."

"Okay."

"Orion."

Eric scanned the crowded ceiling of night and could not find it. He looked but it just wasn't there. "I give."

"Watch this," Molly said.

And her father rose from his sleep on that cold, clear night so many years ago, and he watched from the upstairs window as his daughter awakened the hunter.

CHAPTER THIRTY-NINE

TODD WAS BACK ON THE ISLAND. Even though he had not ever really set foot ashore, he was there walking around the familiar territory in broad daylight, one of many return journeys. There were gulls and a few half-tame, half-wild rabbits. And the smell of bayberry. It was good to be away from the hospital, away from his sickness and away from himself. He was fairly certain Molly was around here somewhere but was still somewhat surprised when he walked down to the little pocket beach and saw her walking along the shoreline. He walked up to her but didn't say a word. Molly stopped and smiled at him. Then she pointed one finger to the sky above and when Todd looked up he saw a vortex of blue herons swirling above them.

Eric was not uncomfortable sleeping alone on the hard bed. He didn't really mind the smell of the old, musty blankets. In fact, the smell reminded him of something good from his childhood — playing in an old shed or, if not playing, sitting in there, on an old wooden milk crate, reading. There had not been many friends in his childhood except for those books that he used to read. On the island, Eric was still fairly certain that the sum total of his own life did not make any sense. It did not add up to anything. Yet he knew that he was going through some kind of inexplicable transformation. He believed that this readjustment, whatever it was, could take years but he didn't care. Things mattered now. He cared.

Before Baffin Island, things sometimes seemed to make sense but nothing mattered. Now, not a lot of things made clear sense, but everything seemed to matter.

Eric promised himself he would simply keep his romantic interest in Molly in the background. He cared for her deeply and he wanted badly to sleep with her. To make love to her. But he would move slowly. He intended to look in on her several times during the night — he would do this just to assure himself she was okay. The Orion thing — all fascinating and wonderful, but weird. What would Dr. Soleri make of her actions today, her fading in and out on him? What would Soleri make of Eric's own belief in her ability to make stars move at her command?

When Eric awoke at dawn, the thin grey light of morning made his unfamiliar room seem entirely colourless — as if the whole world had gone black and white. With his first waking breath, he said her name out loud and then his feet found the floor and he hurried to her.

Molly lay on her back on the bed where she had once slept as a little girl. Closing his eyes, he lay his head down over her mouth and, holding his own breath, listened to her breathing. It was the sound the wind makes when gently stirring the tops of tall spruce trees. Eric covered her with another blanket. Then he cupped a hand on each side of her face and leaned above her again, daring to brush his lips against her cheek.

Here on an island at the mouth of Halifax Harbour, cut off from the mainland, Eric felt entirely isolated from the rest of the world. His love for Molly was now something so strong that it overpowered him with its weight. But something was wrong here and he didn't know where to begin to help. He wasn't sure if he should wake her or let her sleep.

He looked through the window, out at the sun coming up, and at the sea not far from the house. And then he looked back at Molly and recognized her for the first time.

The snowstorm had surprised him on his reckless hike on Baffin Island. Eric had wandered north. He had no map, only a compass. He had with him, however, an unhealthy supply of pharmaceuticals from his medicine cabinet back at home. He had only sampled a handful — nothing dangerous, just enough to take the edge off his usually overly-alert mind. What he wanted to do was lose himself in the barren wilderness. To throw his fate to the unseen forces and let them decide. His intention was to be reckless and poorly prepared, as if giving those unseen forces a temptation they could not resist.

The temperature had dropped dramatically and Eric was poorly prepared for that as well. If he died, he did not want it to look like something he had planned. If he lived, well, he would think about what his next "test" would be. But it was somehow important to him that it appeared to anyone who cared — and there would be precious few of them — that his fate was simply a matter of carelessness.

With the snow came wind. The dense flakes blew horizontally across the landscape. Eric walked onward in what he thought might be a straight line. There was hard packed snow beneath him now and soon he was unsure if he was over land or sea. It mattered little. He turned his back to the wind briefly and sampled another pill from his supplies, careful not to overload his system too soon. Then he threw the remainder of them off into the snow and trudged on into the wind that would help deplete his energy more quickly.

He felt cold but not pain. And he fell often, each time surprised that a primitive part of his brain reacted instantly, bringing him back up onto his feet to lean again into the onslaught and push on against it with no other bearings whatsoever. His plan was simply to keep on going until exhausted.

And then someone appeared in front of him. It was a slender, dark figure — at first, he thought it might be some kind of animal, although it became clear it was a person walking toward him, almost right to him, and then suddenly turning and slowly walking away. He fought the urge to go in the opposite direction but, instead, stood motionless. When he did not move at all, the figure turned and came back towards him. As he started to walk toward it, it turned again and he could not help but follow with great difficulty, moving ahead to whatever destiny awaited him.

By the time he arrived at the doorstep of a shocked Inuit family living in a battered wood frame house on the edge of town, he was half-frozen, totally disoriented and exhausted. He banged once hard on the door with his fist, and then turned to look at who or what it was that had led him here. Just before his guide vanished into the storm again, she turned around and he saw her face, the face of a woman he had never met before.

And then he awoke in a hospital bed in Ottawa with the janitor addressing him as grandfather.

CHAPTER FORTY

DURING THOSE CRITICAL, AND MOST CERTAINLY, final days, Todd was not conscious except for brief moments when his eyes would open and he could speak a few syllables that seemed to take so much out of him. Joyce and Bartlett stayed by his side, wanting to be there when it happened yet urging their son to save his strength, telling him there was no need to speak.

And then the breath left him and did not come back. Todd's parents were as prepared for this as they could be. At their bidding, the doctors and nurses stayed outside the room and Bartlett was the one who switched off the monitors himself.

Joyce's sorrow transformed itself into small channels of tears trailing down her face. Bartlett was determined to remain strong until he was alone. He would do this for his wife. There was a silence in the room unlike anything they had known. A mother and a father hovered over their son, heads bowed.

Todd had been fading and, at one point, had drifted far, far away for several days. While unconscious, he'd found a way to take the pain and turn it into landscape. Maybe it was partly the drugs in him but, inside his thoughts, he taught himself to take one thing and reshape it into something else. At first he could turn sea into sky, ice into fire, rocks into birds, sorrow into a green forest, longing into a mountain river and, eventually, he learned how to turn pain into something beautiful — an entire, beautiful island. This is where he went when he had to get out of the room and out of his cancer-ravaged body.

It was on the island that he realized he was about to leave himself for good. It was night and he was walking through an old house. He was not afraid. The floorboards creaked and it was chilly. He kept opening doors but found only empty rooms. And then he opened one door and saw a man asleep in a narrow bed. He didn't know who the man was and shut the door gently as he left. Then he found a girl asleep in a bedroom and he felt guilty that he was spying on her. But he didn't walk away. Her hair was spread out on the pillow and was also covering part of her face. The light was dim — just starlight through the window glass. Todd brushed the hair gently to the side and quickly realized again that this was Molly. Not the older Molly he knew but a much younger Molly — a girl his own age.

He sat down on the side of the bed and suddenly felt very, very tired. Right then he could not, or did not want to, transform his weariness into anything else — not into a cloud or into a bird or into a lake. The word "death" no longer frightened him and he was well-prepared for this ultimate release from cancer and from pain. He was satisfied that this was the beginning of a much more powerful transformation. He lay down beside Molly and put his arms around her.

Author photo by Daniel Abriel

LESLEY CHOYCE is the author of seventy books for adults and young adults. He has taught at Dalhousie University for the past twenty-five years and is the publisher of Pottersfield Press. He's worked as a rehab counselor, a freight hauler, a corn farmer, a janitor, a journalist, a lead guitarist, a newspaper boy, and a well-digger. He also hosts a nationally-syndicated TV talk show on BookTelevision. Along with the Surf Poets, he has released two poetry/ music albums, *Long Lost Planet*, and *Sea Level*.